Men-y Phases

K.C Lawrence

To all of those who have been part of my journey,
past and present, many thanks.

No fear, just love, KCL x

Although this book has been presented as a novel, some of what you are about to read is real. They are personal experiences that I, or people close to me, have lived. While I have taken great liberties to embellish and exaggerate the story line, at the heart of each of the men-y involvements, there is truth. I am grateful for the lessons that these lovers, and life, have given me, and by sharing them, hope to help others to understand the complexities that love can bring.

Chapter 1

October 2021

As Mia stood in front of her soon to be husband, she couldn't help but smile. She looked out to the turquoise blue ocean, that was twinkling in the sunlight on this beautiful, warm day. She was acutely grateful for their beach, their home, their life. She tried to stay grounded but couldn't help but feel giddy with joy.

Their photographer had just phoned, stating she was running a little late, giving the bride and groom time to enjoy another glass of wine as they waited. Mia could vaguely hear the small talk being undertaken between their modest group of guests and their wedding celebrant, but she really wasn't listening. She was lost in the way she felt, not quite believing, she was finally here... standing in front of the love of her life, about to marry him.

She looked down at her hand being tightly held by him. Her eyes moved from his grip, up to his strong, tanned forearm. She momentarily flashed back to the beginning of their relationship, sitting at a restaurant, and watching him lift a glass of red wine to his full set of lips. Those muscly forearms, those full lips and his kind, beautiful soul. She had known from that day she had wanted to be with him. And here they were, about to become Mr and Mrs.

Getting married had never been a priority. They had spoken often and openly about not needing an official commitment, just happy being in a solid, loving partnership, that had only become better over time.

But the life they had created needed to be celebrated, and the decision to finally formalise their union, was the perfect way.

Finally, the photographer arrived, and the celebrant indicated it was time to commence the ceremony.

The plan was a simple exchanging of vows, with no fuss. Mia understood her partner was an unconventional romantic. He wasn't comfortable with grand gestures of romance, but more importantly to Mia, he provided a solid love that made her feel like she was the most important thing in his world. Their wedding ceremony would represent their relationship, not too frilly, however, full of love. But it seemed he had a little surprise.

As their pre-determined vows tumbled out of Mia's mouth, she was conscious not to speak too quickly. She paused to catch her breath after uttering... 'unending love and devotion'. Then she sweetly spoke about wanting to 'share her thoughts, hopes, and dreams', before finishing with 'looking forward to spending the rest of our lives together'.

He repeated the vows with assurance and conviction, looking at Mia in a way that connected them on a deep, divine level. There was a small silence at the end of his proclamation, before he reached into the top pocket of his white linen shirt and produced a small card from which he read...

If you ever fall in love...
Fall in love with someone who wants to know your favourite
colour and just how you like your coffee.
Fall in love with someone who loves the way you laugh and would
do absolutely anything to hear it.
Fall in love with someone who puts their head on your chest just
to hear your heartbeat.
Fall in love with someone who kisses you in public and is proud
to show you off to anyone they know.
Fall in love with someone who would never ever want to hurt you.
Fall in love with someone who falls in love with your flaws and
thinks that you are perfect just the way you are.
Fall in love with someone who thinks that you are the one they
would love to wake up to each day.

Maxine Rose

Mia was flawed, as such a public declaration of his feelings was extremely out of character. It seemed he had left his grand gesture of love to when his timing couldn't have been more perfect – their wedding day.

'I've fallen in love with my someone,' he beamed, as he put the card back into his pocket. Mia gazed at him with so much love; she thought her heart would explode. She still couldn't believe this was her reality. It had taken her half a lifetime, and many versions of herself to find him, but she'd never been happier.

Then, a slight breeze started to play with her hair, distracting her from the perfection of the moment. It felt like a ghost reminding her of the detours she had taken in her past, wanting to ensure she fully appreciated this long-awaited instant.

'This is where I belong, where I have always belonged,' she thought, as she looked into her new husband's eyes hoping they would anchor her to the present. But the mind's trap door had been opened, and like Alice falling down the rabbit hole, she fell back to where her journey with love began.

*****

Karl

Chapter 2

January 1986

Mia looked up at the new guy as he strutted into her senior year maths class, ten minutes late. This would have made any normal person feel awkward and self-conscious, but she immediately noticed his air of assuredness and instantly found him interesting.

Noticing her also, he placed his school bag in the aisle and threw himself into the seat beside her. Mia's eyes moved back to the teacher, who continued to address the class during this distracting arrival.

It wasn't long before the stranger leaned into Mia and whispered, 'Looks like I haven't missed much.'

She was a little startled at his familiarity, with his lips nearly touching her ear, and quickly judged him on this gesture. She tilted her head slightly toward him, and sassily whispered, 'I don't think you'd miss much any time.' She was chuffed at her quick reply and could feel him grin without needing to look at him.

Mia had always considered herself too young to be a candidate for anything serious with the opposite sex, either physically, or emotionally. However, recently hormones had started to race and although she had remained reserved from experimenting too much, she had started to understand her own female potency.

Her hair was short and brunette – cut very on point for the '80's. Her complexion was clear of the blemishes that seemed to be plaguing most of her peers, and for her age, she had a body that had already developed in perfect proportion, toned and curvaceous.

When it came to her interactions with her male piers, she kept things light-hearted with a dash of flirtatiousness. Her smart mouth made people laugh, and with her relaxed disposition, she was popular to be around.

She was also good at perceiving people's characters, always engaged and interested in anything they chose to reveal about themselves. But she was wary to disclose too much about herself. She was a champion at remaining warm enough to be appealing but projected a periphery that only the determined would think about trying to penetrate.

When the bell sounded, indicating time to move to the next class, Mia turned to look at this fresh face. He too turned his body square on to hers. 'I'm Karl.'

She couldn't help but be drawn into his ice blue eyes. They were a startling colour, but she was quick to perceive a slight hurt in them that contradicted his initial, impervious impression.

'Mia,' she uttered, trying very hard to stay nonchalant.

'We best get moving. I'll see you around Miss Mia.' Karl smirked, knowing that he had piqued her interest.

She tried not to watch him as he walked away but helplessly gave into his magnetism, scanning the back of his body. His hair was ash blond and cut into short, flicked layers. His shoulders weren't muscly but broad enough to give him a solid frame, and his school pants were filled out, outlining a strong, lower body shape. Even with his back to her, his sexual appeal aroused something in her that she had never felt before.

She was sure he wanted to be understood as cool, charming, and sexy. Her earlier sassy comment had been correctly executed. As she walked to her next class, she wondered why she was so drawn to him. *I've always liked puzzles,* she thought, innocently dismissing the feeling of enticement. But she knew she would be looking for him next maths class.

Two days later, Mia had butterflies dancing in her stomach as she hurried to see Karl again. Since she had met him, a longing curiosity had been building in her. But now that she was minutes away from seeing him, her insecurities started to play.

'What if he doesn't remember my name? What if he doesn't sit next to me?'

'Hang on! Why is he under my skin? Get a grip.'

Her whole life she had been told she overanalysed and overthought. She would dissect situations, throwing up potential scenarios, making sure she was prepared for anything. But these machinations could also lead her to feel unnecessary fear and insecurity.

Usually there was an offset commentary that would also trigger, eventually giving her perspective, pulling her back to reality.

As she entered the classroom, she noticed Karl was already seated.

'Play it cool.'

Karl looked up and met her glance. 'Hey Mia,' he said, as he patted the seat next to his, signalling for her to come and sit.

She was relieved. He did remember her name and he seemed to be looking for her as much as she him. Her butterflies fluttered a little more as she smiled back at him, a little unnerved at how happy she was to see him, and at how cocky he was.

'How are you settling in?', Mia asked, addressing the fact that he was the new kid.

'Great thanks,' Karl replied. And for the first time, she noticed a slight English accent. He continued, 'This is my third high school in four years. I'm used to new beginnings.'

Once again, the teacher interrupted their conversation with the day's tutorial, and their conversation was cut short.

Karl seemed to fidget all lesson and by the end of the class, Mia was consumed on how to get their conversation back to where they left it... 'new beginnings'. She turned to find him watching her. He grinned and muttered quietly, 'Where do you sit at lunchtime? I'll find you so we can chat without being interrupted by Mr Tedious.'

She smirked at this personal quirk of his, putting titles on people, Miss Mia, now Mr Tedious.

'I sit under B block, at the art class end,' she answered, thankful for Karl's initiative. 'See you then.'

She quickly packed up, wanting him to watch as she exited. She had learnt through her interest in dancing, how to make her body look its best; her chest was out, her back was elongated, and her rear was taut and firm. She turned around as she reached the classroom door, to catch Karl's keen eyes all over her.

Just over an hour later, she sat down after picking up her lunch from the tuckshop. She looked up and noticed Karl, still a fair distance, but walking her way. She felt excitement build.

Then she noticed the female school captain, Cassandra, intercept his path. They weren't near enough for Mia to hear their conversation, but she knew enough about body language to detect female pheromones were being secreted.

Cassandra was a picture of perfection, long blond hair, blue eyes, highly intelligent, athletic, and classically beautiful. She always looked impeccably groomed and emotionally unflappable. And it was now obvious; she had an interest in the new guy.

Mia turned her back on the scene as a small niggle of uneasiness stirred, but by the time she felt Karl's gentle tap on her shoulder, it had gone.

'Looks like it's proper chat time, you know, one lasting more than half a dozen words,' Mia said, in a slight autocratic manner. This was her way of hiding her keenness.

'What have you got for lunch?' Karl asked, not immediately addressing what she had said.

'Toasted cheese and tomato,' Mia replied.

'I've got a vanilla slice. How about we halve everything and make it a two-course meal?', he suggested, with unrefusable appeal.

'So, I'm sure you have a few questions, Miss Mia. Fire away.'

'How presumptuous,' Mia thought, but quickly conceded, he was right.

'Ok, let's start with an obvious one. What star sign do you think our maths teacher is?', Mia teased.

At first, Karl was perplexed looking at Mia's deadpan face. Then they burst out laughing together, breaking the anticipation that had gripped them since they first met.

'Funny,' Karl acknowledged.

'Okay,' Mia calmed, looking directly at him. 'Last name?'

'Thompson, the proper way, with a "H". T-H-O-M-P-S-O-N,' Karl spelt it out. He obviously didn't like it being spelt wrong.

And with that, his background came spewing out. Mia listened to key facts, born in England; English father; Australian mother; moved to Australia when he was young; mother remarried; younger half-sister; lives Southside of Brisbane; over an hour bus ride to school; mother finds it hard to settle. Then there was a long pause. Karl looked down for a minute, then reconnected with Mia's eyes. 'I haven't seen my real father since I was five.'

'There it is. The over-confidence is used to hide the hurt.'

She knew too well how this game was played. The self-assurance, hiding hurts and distrusts, aloofly holding everyone to the outside, and never allowing emotions to be exposed.

'We are similar creatures.'

They started to spend every lunch time together. It wasn't long before Karl learnt Mia's father was no longer in her life. He'd left the house when she was four, and she felt life was better after that. She was different to Karl in that way; she didn't miss her dad. Not like he missed his.

Mia quickly shifted the conversation to the more positive subject of her mum, Elizabeth. She lovingly spoke of her mum's easy-going nature, saying all her friends loved coming over on the weekends because of their home's relaxed vibe. Elizabeth was English and had come to Australia when she was fifteen. This was of particular interest to Karl.

'Maybe one day I can meet her. Your drama free home sounds like paradise,' Karl commented. Mia could see there was still something he wasn't telling her, but she was fast learning, Karl only revealed what he wanted and in his time.

And that was what she wanted, his time. With every instance together, they started to perfect a flirtatious banter that was the right mix of funny and harmless suggestion. It was fun and exciting, and Mia started to feel things she hadn't before.

On the surface, they seemed to be great friends that spent a lot of time together. But as they danced around each other, she could feel his simmering fascination begin to swell also and wondered if he would ever be tempted to pull her over the friendship line.

Chapter 3

Karl was sitting at the bus stop waiting to go home for the weekend. He was so far away in his thoughts that he hadn't seen Mia approach. Her proximity startled him when he finally looked up and found her standing in front of him, gently calling his name.

'You looked a million miles away Mr Karl.' Mia had subconsciously adopted Karl's "title" trait.

'Another world,' Karl replied.

'Well while you were off travelling, you missed your bus,' she quipped, trying to lighten his mood.

He smiled at her in appreciation of her efforts. 'Well then, I think I should come to your place for the weekend. It's about time I met your mum.' His mood instantly shifted back to his normal cheekiness with the thought.

She was stunned, but sensed this wasn't just a whimsical request, it was something he needed. She kept this perception to herself as she turned on her heels and jibed playfully over her shoulder, 'You'll be on the couch in the rumpus room. Don't think for a minute you're sharing my bed.'

With that, he jumped to his feet, quickly catching up to her. 'Wouldn't dare dream of it,' he muttered, with a hint of mischief.

Mia was nervous turning up with Karl without any notice, but there was no need. Elizabeth never failed to make everyone feel welcome and at ease in their home. She greeted him like she had known him forever, and Karl seemed to feel comfortable straightaway.

Over the following months, staying on the weekends turned into his normal ritual. Every Friday, he'd go home with Mia and stay until Monday morning, where they would wander back to school together. He even started leaving sets of clothes in her room.

Her mum grew fond of him quickly. The three of them always had things to discuss, with nightly conversations starting as he helped prepare dinner, that would continue around the table. Karl always engaged with a genuine curiosity to hear Elizabeth's point of view on anything raised, and his dry sense of humour always made her laugh. It made Mia happy to watch her two favourite people interact with so much ease.

By the second month of their weekend arrangement, the lure between Mia and Karl was undeniable, and one night, he snuck into her bed after Elizabeth was asleep. He pressed his body up against her back, just holding her, before falling back to sleep. He disappeared by dawn.

At first, Mia froze with shyness because of her inexperience with intimacy, and she pretended not to notice he was there. But as the weeks went on, and this routine became habit, her hunger for him intensified. She changed from awkwardness to assuredness, melting into his body as he arrived, letting him hold her while she imagined them becoming more intimate. His restraint was like an aphrodisiac.

And soon enough, her desire for him spiked. One weekend, after a Friday and Saturday night of controlled politeness, as Karl slipped into her sheets on the Sunday night, she instantly turned towards him, so their mouths were nearly touching, and their breaths were shallow, full of anticipation.

One of Karl's hands went to the middle of Mia's back, pulling her to his hungry body. Their lips finally met, causing an exhilaration that only a first kiss can. This moment had been months in the making. A teasing, slow seduction made up of playful, mischievous wit, loaded with charm and magnetism.

They slowly undressed and explored each other. Karl took his time so she didn't feel rushed, and she could taste how blissful sexual teasing could be. For her first sensual sensation, and with his experience, he gave her a lot of pleasure.

She also learnt ways to please him, and he appeared to be delighted enough with just foreplay. But after some time of being caught up in the ecstasy, he climbed on top of her, pinning her to the bed, wanting her to forego her innocence completely.

'I'm not ready,' Mia said mindfully.

Karl didn't move, hesitant to concede, with his expression begging for her to reconsider. She could feel him throb, as his lust made him desperately want their union to proceed, but her words had unexpectedly immobilised it.

He finally rolled off her. 'Okay.'

She went to touch him, hoping to soften the harshness of the arrest.

'No Mia, let's just leave it there.' He held her for a short time, in an uncomfortable silence. Then finally left.

Mia lay awake. Anticipation, stimulation and now confusion was a cocktail for no sleep. Was this run-away behaviour normal? They had never done awkward before. She tossed and turned for the rest of the night, until she heard her mum in the kitchen.

As she sat herself at the kitchen table, Elizabeth remarked, 'Didn't you sleep well Mia? You look tired.'

'Just woke up early Mum and couldn't get back to sleep.'

With that, Karl emerged from the rumpus room. Without looking at him, Elizabeth asked, 'Sleep well Karl?', in a tone that left Mia thinking her mum knew what was going on.

'Like a baby thanks,' he replied. 'Good morning, Miss Mia,' he said, as he resumed his cool, collected pretence, with no hint of any evidence regarding their eventful night.

Mia looked directly at him and knew that what they had shared was now buried somewhere within him. With his aloof demeanour, she also knew there was a good chance it would never be acknowledged and there was no guarantee it would happen again.

Chapter 4

The following few days, Mia felt off balance. Due to the unusually quiet walk to school on the Monday morning after, she had been left feeling she had done something wrong. Was he trying to make her feel guilty? Their relationship had always been effortless, but now there was an elephant in the room, and she wasn't sure how to discuss it.

In the week that followed, she accepted that Karl had retreated to friends' mode, and she decided to mirror him. She badly wanted to clear the air but meekly went back to being the girl that first peaked his fascination with her witty banter, that needed nothing from him. Their classroom and lunch break routine resumed but it was slightly strained. Something had changed.

That week, she also noticed on one occasion, Karl lingered just a little longer with Cassandra. Mia watched, as she played with her hair and tipped her head to one side. The classic flirtation gestures that Karl now seemed to be engaged with as he beamed a smile back to her.

Mia looked away imagining a loaded exchange between herself and Karl, '*Can you please explain to me what the hell is going on? Did last Sunday night mean anything? Why have you shut me out?*'

But as he approached, she tamely reset to what he was comfortable with, leaving her provoking queries and requests concealed. Her instinct told her there was a threat looming, but she continued to avoid addressing it.

By the Thursday of that week, as they were leaving their maths class, she turned to him and asked casually, 'So weekend at mine still on?'

'Can't see why not,' he replied.

Because of his behaviour throughout the week, she wasn't sure what to expect, but at least he was still coming.

Friday morning arrived, and she was excited and apprehensive all at once. Her thoughts drifted to him being back in her home and she allowed herself a minute to imagine him glide in beside her, to recommence where they had left off last Sunday night.

'Stop that! Don't get ahead of yourself.'

But as their class started, there was no sign of Karl. Mia reasoned with herself that there may have been a problem with his bus, and he was just running late.

Lunchtime came and went, still no sign of him. She even looked up to where Cassandra sat, hoping he had stopped for a quick chat. But she too was looking for him.

* * *

'No Karl?', Elizabeth enquired when Mia arrived home alone.

'No Mum. He didn't come to school today. I'm a bit worried.'

'I'm sure he's fine. Maybe he's unwell,' Elizabeth offered.

But Mia was in knots. She tried her hardest to be happy over the two days, but she was distracted. Late on the Sunday afternoon, whilst sitting together, Elizabeth said, 'I can see you care about Karl a lot.'

'Yes Mum, I do.'

'He's a good friend Mia but be careful to keep your expectations of him realistic. I think you're going to be left wanting more from him than he can give. That's not good for you. I don't want to see you hurt.'

Mia wasn't ready to hear this. She didn't want to resign herself to Karl just being a friend. But she had to admit, that's exactly how she had felt all week, wanting to be closer to him emotionally. After feeling so close to him on Sunday night, the aloofness that had returned by Monday morning had left her feeling needy.

In her immaturity she still hoped he would be different, and she may be the one to make the difference.

Monday, Tuesday, Wednesday, Thursday morning came, still no Karl. A whole week. Mia realised that she didn't know much about his home life. She didn't have his address or home phone number.   She only knew he lived on the southside of the city, with his mum and half-sister.

Then he arrived. Friday morning maths class had started, and Mia was sat in her normal position. He walked in with his head turned away from her. He sat down next to her and said, 'Don't look at me. Face the front until after class.' Mia was shocked by his authoritarian tone.

As the bell rang, she spun around to find Karl still shielding his face from her. 'Look at me,' she said, trying to restrain the concerned she was feeling. He slowly turned to look at her.

'What the hell happened?', Mia exploded with worry, as she saw his right eye was the colour of midnight.

'You should see the other guy,' Karl remarked with a sly sneer.

Without thinking or remembering where they were, she instinctively went to throw her arms around him. Karl flinched and pulled backwards, and she realised the wall around him was even thicker now.

They both got up to move out of the classroom and once outside, Mia again asked, 'What happened?'

'I really can't talk about it yet. Can we just do normal?', he pleaded.

'Normal? I haven't felt normal since before desire became a factor between us.'

After a small pause, she said, 'Okay, well Mum missed you so much last weekend she's threatened if you're not with me this afternoon, I don't get fed.' She wasn't sure where it came from but was relieved to see his face soften a little.

'Well, we can't have that,' he finally mumbled.

* * *

On their arrival, Karl seemed anxious about Elizabeth's reaction. He was relieved to be invited back to this temporary haven but wasn't up to explaining.

The look on Elizabeth's face said much more than any words. After a quick assessment, she decided not to ask. Her experience and intuition stopped her. In the most maternal way, she just tended to Karl's eye and any pain relief he required.

Although Mia had wanted him to come to her through the night, she knew he wouldn't. She was quickly grasping, that what had been their ritual, was now unlikely to continue.

The following morning, Karl slept in, finally emerging just before lunch. It was obvious he was still in pain, which Elizabeth continued to nurse in a way that seemed foreign to him. They all lay by the pool for the day, with little conversation, encouraging Karl to relax.

By dinner time, he seemed more comfortable. The healing of being in a tranquil environment can't be underestimated. They were all in the kitchen preparing dinner when Elizabeth suggested they all have a small glass of brandy. Karl tensed immediately. Using her quick observation skills, Elizabeth started the discussion she believed he needed to have. 'Is your eye a result of too much alcohol Karl?'

Without hesitation, he clarified, 'Not me drinking, but yes.'

She let his words linger in the air, to see if he was going to expand on them. He deliberated for a minute on whether to expose himself any further, finally adding, 'My stepfather likes it way too much.'

That was all he could say, but it was enough to give Mia, and Elizabeth, a better understanding of him. Mia flashed back to some of her own childhood memories, a father that liked to drink too much and not feeling safe.

Elizabeth changed the subject and decided the brandy could be left until another time.

On the Sunday morning, he'd woken early and found himself alone with Elizabeth in the kitchen. It started as the usual small talk over a cuppa, but she found a way to bring it back to how he was feeling. At first, he took the benign track by commenting that the pain in his eye was going. But Elizabeth had a way of looking at someone if she felt the response to her query was inadequate. Karl was now facing such a gaze.

'I was ten when he arrived. I didn't like him from the start. He always smelt like smoke and alcohol. I still can't understand what Mum saw in him. Before I knew it, he'd moved in. They got married. I was made to change my last name to his and my baby sister was born.'

It was like a water spring had been unplugged and Karl continued delivering his answer at a dynamic rate.

'That's when the alcohol indulgence became unhealthy, and the hitting started. First Mum, then me. I used to take it. But this last year, something's changed. I've started to fight back.' He paused for a minute.

'The other night he arrived home drunk and in a foul mood. I knew it was going to escalate quickly so while Mum was trying to defuse him, I got my half-sister to her bedroom, down the other end of the house. She's only five.'

Karl closed his eyes remembering the fear on his little sister's face that night. He'd tried to distract her from the drama that was going on by urging her to imagine flying through a rainbow.

'Once I got her settled, I told her to stay in her room. I knew I had to get to Mum. As I closed her door, I heard Mum yell, and I found her cowering in a corner with a red mark on her face.'

Still with his eyes closed, Karl recalled the feeling of adrenaline racing though him as he faced the human, he incomparably loathed. His stepfather stared at him, daring him to come closer.

'He got me a beauty', Karl pointed to his eye. 'But this rage inside of me took over. I grabbed him by the collar with both hands, lifted him into the air and pinned him against the wall. I put one hand around his throat, and I told him that it would be the last time anything like this was to happen, or I'd kill him.'

Karl's eyes opened, as his body shuddered reliving the words he had spoken. It was a part of himself he didn't recognise, as it was so far removed from his normal, cool demeanour.

Elizabeth reached for his hand, and he let her take it in a rare sign of needing comfort. She decided to ask one last question, 'Where's your father Karl?'

'I'm not sure. Mum and I left England before I started school, and I don't think he knows where I am. And I'm not sure where to start looking for him.'

She wanted to soothe the wound that Karl had laid bare and ease the heavy burden he was carrying. But his disclosure had also invoked her protective instinct for her daughter.

'Mia's father liked a drink and wasn't nice at times. Never to the extent you or your mother have experienced, but enough to taint Mia's childhood, and for me to end the marriage. After he left, she was reluctant to visit him. I encouraged her to see him when she was younger, but now that she's older, I support her decision not to have him in her life.'

Karl looked cautiously at Elizabeth. He could feel the shift in her and started to doubt if confiding in her had been a good idea.

As if she had read his thoughts, she continued, 'You'll always be welcome here. I care for you very much. But so does my daughter, more than I think you realise. From what you've just told me, I can imagine it's hard for you to know who to trust, or who to care for. Please don't hurt her.'

He was stunned at her frankness. He was digesting her words when Mia bounced in enquiring, 'What did I miss?', not reading the room and assuming it had just been normal chit-chat.

'I was about to have a shower,' Karl excused himself.

Elizabeth commenced the usual breakfast routine, believing Mia didn't need to know any part of the exchange that had just occurred. She decided she'd go out for the day, hoping by giving them space, Karl would tell her.

But they spent the day mostly in silence by the pool, with Mia still not mentioning any of her internal mayhem, and Karl retreating even further, not wanting any responsibility for Mia's feelings. Their connection was fraying, only adding to the hurt that was already churning.

* * *

The following morning, whilst walking to school, Mia felt the first of Karl's harsh moves that would disassemble their friendship. After she asked if he was okay, his response was short and clipped, 'Yep good.'

'You don't seem it,' she continued.

'Just drop it.' Deafening silence resulted for the rest of the way.

They got to school and were about to go to their separate classes when Mia asked playfully, 'Let's share our lunches today. I'll get the toasty, and you get the vanilla slice. We can meet at our usual restaurant under B block.'

'Can't today,' Karl replied elusively. 'Might catch you tomorrow.'

Mia's stomach rolled as he disappeared. This reaction was next level coldness.

At lunch, she tried to keep herself from looking up to where Cassandra sat but eventually the curiosity got to her, and she saw he was there. It felt like a kick to the stomach that she didn't see coming. He had positioned himself to avoid looking in Mia's direction, but she could see enough to know he was in full entanglement of a lustful spell being cast. Fears of him slipping away consumed her, as she quietly questioned, *'Why is he doing this?'*

Karl's behaviour continued all week. When he saw Mia, he'd say 'Hi' but would keep moving. He sat with Cassandra every lunch, and by himself in their shared maths class.

Mia waited for him Friday afternoon at the bus stop. At the start of the week, she excused his actions on needing space and tried to convince herself he'd snap out of it. But now, she was furious and couldn't overlook what seemed like punishment. She needed an explanation.

He stood in front of her like he had been expecting the confrontation. With all her anger and hurt, she spat, 'What the hell Karl? I've been going over and over in my head, every moment of last weekend, which seems to be when this massive shift in our relationship happened. Every conversation, every action and I can't pinpoint anything I've done to justify you cutting me off.'

Karl looked right at her and prattled off the words like he had been rehearsing them. 'This isn't about last weekend. It's about how needy you're getting. You knew when we met, I'm all about fun. No attachments. That's just me and I have no plans to change. This is done. You'll thank me one day. End of discussion.' He ensured the ending was clean, with no niceties.

Mia couldn't speak. Her fury gave way to the realisation that it was over. Hearing the words come out of his mouth made her world stop. No more flirtatious banter. No more sharing lunches. No more laughing with the person that made her laugh the most. No more sleep overs. Just, no more everything.

After she arrived home, Elizabeth listened to her distraught daughter's account, not offering her opinion on it being over. 'And Mum, he said to me... "I have no plans to change". I never asked him to change. I'm not sure where that came from.'

But Elizabeth knew. She recalled the Sunday morning conversation she had with Karl and knew her words had brought this to a head. But the relief she was feeling far outweighed the doubts she had about her candidness. She comforted Mia, hoping the hurt wouldn't last for long and that one day, she would understand Karl had done the right thing.

Chapter 5

'Hey Mia,' a familiar voice called after her as she made her way to the next class. It was one of Karl's friends, Patrick. He was eagerly chasing after her.

Since the start of the year, Karl had managed to strike up friendships with some of his male peers, but Patrick was the one that seemed the tightest with him.

'Are you going to Cassandra's party on Friday night?'

Mia felt annoyance at the mention of her name. 'Don't think so.'

'Come on. Half of the school will be there for you to hide amongst, if you don't want to see them together.' Karl had been flaunting his new infatuation with the blonde host. 'You never know, it might be the first step in getting over him.'

Mia wasn't ready to "get over" Karl. It had been a month since they last spoke, and she was still coming to terms with being separated from him. Any physical desire she had for him had now taken a back seat compared to her pining for his company. She just missed him and the way she had felt when their friendship seemed unbreakable.

'I'll think about it,' Mia replied, with no intention of going. She'd stay at home, indulging herself in her melancholy.

But as she walked to her last class that Friday afternoon, she turned the corner and copped an eyeful of Karl's new affiliation. Swirling in a cesspool of lust, Cassandra was giggling as he whispered something in her ear. The image made Mia feel sick.

She tried to pass without them seeing her, but just when she thought she was in the clear, she heard Cassandra call, 'Hey Mia, I hope you're coming tonight. A good party might stop you looking so miserable.'

Mia spun around to face them. Cassandra looked very pleased with herself, but Karl lowered his head, not able to look at her. She regained her composure the best she could. 'That's very nice of you Cassandra. You know, I wouldn't miss it. Would you like me to bring anything, like some class for you?'

Mia noticed Karl half smile in appreciation of her sassiness, but she was gone before Cassandra could come up with a retort.

'Damn it, now I have to go.' But she sensed the sadness being replaced with a fire that she hadn't felt in a while. She convinced herself she would go, whatever she was going to face.

* * *

As she headed up the driveway of Cassandra's house, Mia could hardly hear herself think. The music was at eardrum piercing volume. She noticed people everywhere, in various stages of drunkenness, and recalled what Patrick had said about half the school being there, and decided his prediction was right.

She made her way into the hub of the shindig, an unofficial dance floor, with schoolmates dancing like possessed zombies as only music of the time could inspire.

Patrick soon found her, and they had a conversation in gestures because of the noise. At the end of it, he went to get her a glass of wine, and she turned her attention to others in the room, not wanting to affix herself to him.

After an hour or so, she finally spotted Karl and Cassandra. They slipped past the improvised dance floor to refill their drinks. Notably, Cassandra looked to be drunk. The alcohol disabling any of her remaining inhibitions, as she continually touched him seductively.

Suddenly, Patrick jumped in front of Mia, blocking the view she had got herself entrapped in. He pulled her to dance with him, turning her so she could no longer see them. But she soon spun the other way and caught Karl and Cassandra disappearing upstairs.

She continued to dance with Patrick for a couple of songs, but then decided she needed to find Karl and confirm the imageries in her head.

She motioned to Patrick she was off to the bathroom, but without him seeing, slipped upstairs, following Karl's trail to a closed bedroom door. She hesitated as she stood in front of it. She could hear Cassandra's slurred voice and odd giggle.

'It may not be Karl with her.'

'Of course it's him. Get it done.'

The pragmatic far outweighed the innocent now.

She turned the door handle without detection, walking into a dark room. She felt for the light switch as her eyes started to adjust. There was minimal moonlight glimmering through an open window, and she could now see Cassandra's silhouette, writhing on the body underneath her. Her back arched and her head fallen backwards.

Mia heard the climax of male pleasure as she turned the light on, bracing herself for the unpleasantness she anticipated she would see. Karl's blue eyes seemed expressionless as he looked at Mia. Cassandra was so drunk, she was unaware someone had interrupted them.

Mia ran down the stairs and out of the house. She didn't know where she was going, she just needed to get out of there.

Patrick had seen her exit, knowing the only thing that could have upset her so much was Karl. He raced after her, pleading, 'Stop Mia. Stop.'

And she finally did, a block away. He came to the front of her, studying the streamlines of tears on her face, and pulled her to his chest as the symphony of emotions exploded.

She only quietened when there was nothing left. He motioned for her to come and sit on the sidewalk. They sat in silence until he thought she was ready to hear what he had to say.

'This is classic Karl,' he started. 'He can't let anyone too close because he doesn't know how to trust. As soon as he thinks someone is starting to care for him, or worse, he's starting to care for them, he sabotages it. The way you guys rolled in the beginning suited him. He convinced himself it was just a spunky friendship. But once he realised there were real feelings involved, he pulled away, picked fights, pretended you could be replaced. Tonight was all about making you think you aren't that important to him. I can only imagine what he set up for you.'

Patrick's words slowed the swirling of thoughts and emotions inside Mia, but she wasn't sure if she should believe them.

'Why do you think you know him so well?'

'Because he spoke to me about you. I've no doubt he cares about you, but it makes him feel uncomfortable, even stressed. So, he's moved to destruct mode. He needs to feel in control.'

Patrick continued, sensing Mia needed more to put her shattered mind and heart back together, 'I'm sure you'll agree, he's damaged, and he's not prepared to grow up yet. There will come a time when he'll want more than an easy piece of arse falling over in front of him, but it's not now.'

Mia smiled at the reference.

'He's not for you Mia, not this version anyway,' Patrick said, caringly. He hoped his words may negate any of her self-doubt. He knew, although her virginity was still intact, some of her innocence was lost. And in his mind, Patrick decided that Karl was a fool.

After he got her a taxi and sent her home, he headed back to the party. It was no longer heaving, and the music was much softer. Karl was standing at the front door.

'Going home?', Patrick asked.

'Yes buddy, I'm done here. To be honest I'd have preferred to have been playing cards and eating pizza with you than endure the lack lustre performance I've just experienced. The expectation didn't match the reality with that one.' Karl gave a small nod in Cassandra direction. She was looking lifeless, propped up against the bathroom door.

'Anyway, I've made it clear it was a one-time thing. Got out of there and came looking for you. Where did you disappear to?'

Patrick looked at Karl knowing he was only pretending to feel like a winner. He couldn't help but strip away some of the playact. 'I was just having a chat with Mia. She's so cool. I understand why you were friends with her; well, until this Cassandra obsession.' Patrick knew his words would cut through some of Karl's armour.

'Mia's okay then?', Karl winced as her name fell out of his mouth.

'Awesome,' countered Patrick, staring at Karl with a smirk. Patrick continued, 'See you Monday,' as he moved passed him, thinking for the second time in less than an hour, 'You fool.'

* * *

For months after that night, Mia believed her and Karl would never be friends again. He avoided making eye contact with her, including when they were in a class together. The events at the party had hurt, but his continuous, elusive behaviour was worse. His rejection of her, even as a friend, caused her to shut down to the idea of letting anyone too close to her again.

Patrick did try though, and she allowed herself to enjoy his company, even saying yes to going with him to their senior formal. But she put up a solid resistance to letting it go beyond friendship.

* * *

As the year was coming to an end, she did notice Karl slowly thawing out. A slightly warmer Karl started with very stiff greetings of "Hello Mia" when he passed her desk in their classes; to eventually joining Patrick if he decided to sit with her at lunch time. But Karl still didn't have a lot to say.

She also noticed that he seemed to ignore Cassandra if she tried to gain his attention as he passed her at lunchtime. She had obviously just been a piece in his sabotage game.

Mia had to admit to feeling relief after both these developments. Even with his heartless behaviour, she still wished they could go back to when they first met.

So, on the last day of school, the thought of never seeing him again, daunted her. As everyone started to say goodbye, she struggled between wanting to mention staying in touch and allowing herself to be vulnerable to his response.

They eventually came face to face, and she still wasn't sure how to handle it. Without saying a word, she stared at him, soundlessly asking if he too was struggling with the potential finality.

His rigid expression tempered, validating he was, but still unable to vocalise it.

Mia felt satisfied and decided to leave it all unsaid.

What had happened between them was silently accepted, as they finally parted with a softly spoken Karl saying, 'Good-bye Miss Mia.'

Chapter 6

Get my Driver's licence
Get a job
Stop thinking about Karl

Getting her driver's licence gave Mia a feeling of freedom and independence, which soon led her to fantasising of travel. She decided formal tertiary education was not for her; and commenced working as an administration officer for a bank in the heart of the city. She was determined to save money and start exploring the world.

To compliment her day job, and because of her dance experience, she also started instructing aerobic classes a few nights a week at a local dance studio. It was fun, kept her fit, and was a contrasting environment to the staid finance world.

Mia let the year flow. When she wasn't at work, she was enjoying a full social life, partying with her new dance studio friends, or gatecrashing university socials with her old school mates.

She had heard that Karl was doing well but she hadn't seen him. They had been like ships in the night at any post-school gatherings.

Another development was Elizabeth had met someone special. After several months and several dates, it was obvious that her mum was very happy. His work required him to travel, so Mia hadn't spent much time with him, but she had instantly liked him on their first meeting.

December 1987

Mia arrived at the inner-city restaurant for her work Christmas party, along with all her fellow bank colleagues. There were eight team members, with six bringing partners. Like Mia, her manager, Brian, was there companionless. The function room, that he had booked, was very intimate. The lighting was low, and their table was the only one in the small, secluded room.

Brian insisted Mia sit next to him, stating they were the only two "single ones". She thought nothing of it as he had always been warm and pleasant. Sometimes, he had touched her on the shoulder or around her waist, but in her naivety, she put it down to his friendly nature.

'Besides, he speaks about his wife so lovingly,' she rationalised, every time a peek of discomfort crept in.

As the night went on, and a lot of alcohol was consumed, the conversations rolled openly. The group had a good workplace rapport, and with the intoxication levels rising, the camaraderie became even more relaxed.

After the main course had been cleared and the group was waiting on dessert, Brian turned to Mia and slurred, 'What is a pretty thing like you doing without boyfriend?'

'Too smart I guess,' Mia deflected with her usual quick humour, not realising the danger.

'No, I mean it Mia, you are quite something,' he continued, as his hand slipped onto her knee, and he ogled at her chest.

Mia was flustered. All her quick wittedness suddenly dried up and she couldn't speak.

'Get a hold of yourself. Surely someone else at the table is seeing what's happening here.'

She looked around to find the others in their own conversations, with obvious signs that their judgements were impeded.

Brian's hand slowly moved under Mia's skirt between her thighs. She crossed her legs instantly to stop its advancement from going any higher. She looked at him seriously, but her voice slightly quivered, 'What are you doing?'

'Do you know what you could have? An experienced guy like me could make your first time unforgettable. It would be your first time, right Mia? You've got this virginal air that drives me crazy. God, what I would love to do to you.'

Mia nearly vomited. Although she felt like she didn't have the strength to stand, she managed to rise from the table, saying a quick good-bye to everyone and not waiting to see if any of them found her behaviour strange.

She headed for the bathroom in shock. She needed to regain her composure and work out the way home. She splashed her face with some water, not caring that her make up would run and she'd look a mess.

It took her ages to have the courage to leave the ladies room and walk out the front door. As she moved down the front stairs, she heard Brian trying to call out but having trouble articulating her simple name. She turned around to face him as he came towards her, wavering from side to side. 'I hope you're not going to cause me any trouble.' He reached for the side of her face to touch her affectionately, but she managed to turn before he could, and cross the road faster than light travels, into the safety of a taxi.

When she got home, she showered, trying to wash off the disgusting feeling that was lingering on her. As she lay in bed, she thrashed about, thinking how was she going to get through to the Christmas break? It was only the first Friday of December. She drowned in fear and anger, thinking about seeing him again.

She used the weekend to try and process what happened, deciding not to speak to anyone.

On the Monday, she made herself go to work as usual. She hid her distress as everyone commented on how great the night had been, and that she should have stayed longer. Someone mentioned Brian's drunk state, but it was obvious, no one had observed the tasteless encounter between them.

Brian finally emerged from his office, skulking around, remarking how wonderful the night had been. He eventually stood in front of Mia's desk asking about her weekend, like nothing had happened.

As he retreated to his office, shutting the door, Mia felt confused.

'Could he really have no recollection? Was he really that drunk? Am I over-reacting? Maybe he made a once off mistake?'

Mia's head was muddled. Her equilibrium was so off, and she wasn't sure what the truth was.

The week continued uneventfully. Any interactions she had with him were totally professional. So, by the end of the week, she had started to convince herself it was better to forget all about it.

But as she was washing her coffee mug in the kitchen Friday evening, ready to leave for the weekend, she felt him come in, closing the door behind him. Immediately she was unnerved and turned to face him. She started to ramble about what she was planning to do over the weekend.

Without a word, he trapped her against the sink, and she froze with fear. He grabbed a clump of hair on the back of her head and thrusted his tongue into her mouth. She tried to push him off, but he pinned her down with the weight of his body.

This confirmed his actions at the dinner had been intentional and rapacious. Now, he was sober, and knew she was protesting to her fullest. In that moment, Mia knew he had been indulging himself all week about what he had wanted to do to her, waiting for his moment to pounce.

This deduction incited an anger within, that gave her a potent strength, and she finally forced him off. He stumbled backwards and while he was off balance, she shoved him again, making him completely lose his footing. She could see he was going down, one misstep, two missteps... falling into the communal rubbish bin, backside first.

She stared at him with fierceness in her eyes, daring him to get out. He couldn't; he was stuck. She commanded her fury and in a steady voice declared, 'You're a disgusting pig. My resignation will be faxed through over the weekend. Do not pursue me or I will tell everyone what you are and what you've done.'

She shook as she walked past him still wedged in the bin. She grabbed her bag and left the office.

* * *

At home, she finally confided in her mum. Elizabeth was mortified and supported her decision to resign. They both knew it was futile to report the incident. It was 1987.

'I understand men think about sex a lot, but did I do something to encourage this?', Mia asked.

'No, and Brian isn't a man, he's a predator. He sexualised you in a way that is primitive and detestable. There's a big difference between that and how most men think about sex,' Elizabeth reasoned with her daughter. 'A lot of men will want you. You're beautiful and your confidence is very attractive. But it should be your desire you surrender to, not theirs. Just please make sure that when you do give yourself, it's to someone that means something to you.'

She hoped her words would be enough.

Chapter 7

It was the Saturday morning before Christmas and Mia was still recovering from what had happened a couple of weeks prior. She was in her bedroom when she heard the home phone ring. Elizabeth came into her room and with a sense of urgency said, 'Mia, Karl's on the phone. He sounds upset.'

'I haven't seen him for twelve months. Why's he ringing?'

'Hey Karl, what's up?', Mia was trying to disguise her surprise.

Karl was mute.

'Karl, are you there?'

'Yes.'

It was obvious he was crying. 'What's wrong?', her tone changed instantly to that of the girl that wanted to comfort him.

There was a break in his weeping. 'They've found his shoes and wallet, but there is no sign of him.'

'Who?'

Still trying to compose himself, he finally said, 'Patrick.'

* * *

Within ten minutes, she was driving to the coast.

She'd stayed in touch with Patrick after school, and they'd often meet for coffee. He had just completed his first year of studying psychology, the perfect choice for him Mia thought. He was intellectually and emotionally mature, and he enjoyed unravelling people's complexities.

As she drove, she recalled the last time she'd spoken to him, only a few weeks back. He said Karl and a couple of the other boys from school were joining him for a week down the coast to celebrate their first year out of school. She knew this meant a week of drinking, chatting up girls and late-night poker games. Patrick had been excited.

'What had gone wrong?', Mia thought, as she pulled up at the address Karl had given her. She moved to the front door but before she could knock, Karl opened it. He looked wrecked. He stood to one side without saying anything, gesturing for her to come in.

Ironically, they found themselves in the same position as the last time they had been together; standing in front of each other, finding words hard. He was there alone, and she started to understand that by asking her to come, he had admitted he needed her.

Suddenly there was a knock at the door. When he opened it, Karl found a uniformed police officer filling the entrance. Mia was right behind him as the police officer launched into a series of facts. A body had washed up ten kilometres down the beach from where Patrick's shoes and wallet had been found. Patrick's parents had been contacted to come and formally identify him, but it was the opinion of the investigating officers, that it was Patrick. It appeared he had drowned. Nothing suspicious.

Mia thought Karl was going to fall backwards. The force of the information caused him to tremble. She steadied him, placing her hand on the small of his back. He thanked the officer and shut the door abruptly, cutting off any further information. Karl didn't want to hear anymore. He pushed pass Mia and started to pace like a caged beast. He still didn't speak. He just moved around the room with agitation and discomfort. Mia stood, tears rolling down her face as the aftermath of the news sunk in. Their beautiful friend Patrick, gone.

Karl reached a point where he couldn't keep the lid on the building explosion within him, letting out a sound like a wounded animal.

She wasn't sure what to do with his pain, and her distress also spiralled out of control. She fell to the floor, curling up into a ball.

Regaining some control, his impulse was to go to her. He knelt beside her, smothering her like a blanket with his entire body and holding her with all his strength. Emotion erupted from them both, uniting them in grief.

The noises of their enduring agony eventually stopped, and a period of silence prevailed as they breathed in unison.

Karl finally got to his feet, asking 'Would you like a drink? I have wine.' This was his way of trying to get a hint of normality back into the situation.

She quietly nodded as she stood.

As they sat on the couch, she noticed it was getting dark. She wondered how long they had been on the floor but wasn't really interested in the time.

After a couple of mouthfuls Karl uttered, 'He just went for a swim. Thursday morning. When he didn't come back, we just thought he'd met a girl. But when he didn't turn up for check out yesterday, I knew something was wrong. He's too responsible. The other boys were still going on the theory he was having the time of his life somewhere and decided to go home. But I went to the local police station. They didn't seem concerned at first and suggested I hang around for another day, in case Patrick showed. So, I organised to hire the unit for another couple of nights. When he still hadn't appeared this morning, I went back down to the police station early, and they sent a team to search the beach. They found his shoes and wallet in the sand dunes. I knew it wasn't good.'

Karl gathered his thoughts. 'That's when I rang you. I can't explain why. Maybe it's because I know how much Patrick means to you too.'

He paused for a minute.

'Or maybe it's because I needed you, here, with me,' he paused again. It appeared to have taken this tragedy for his walls to come down and to confess what she meant to him.

He continued, 'I'm sorry for the way I handled us. I was messed up. I didn't feel in control with what was happening at home, or how much I wanted you. It freaked me out. But it was never about not caring about you.'

His eyes were teary. He instantly looked different to her. He was vulnerable; accessible.

Mia started to sift through the complex maze of feelings she had for Karl. She had spent a long time trying not to think of him, so it became easier not having him in her life. And yet, as he sat in front of her, full of anguish and admitting his need for her, she helplessly returned to wanting to fix his hurt. Her heart felt his familiarity that she had once loved.

'Another wine?', he asked.

'Better not if I'm driving.' Mia didn't want to assume she was staying the night.

'Stay. Please. I know I'm being selfish but please,' the words came out beseechingly.

Mia was conscious their grief was shaping these unexpected contemplations, and that any reunion would be fleeting. But she still had undeniable feelings for him, and knew he would always mean something to her. He was the first boy to tempt her to love. And with his present, unguarded demeanour, she couldn't help but allow her desire for him to take possession.

He moved to her side and cradled her face in his hands, pulling her gently towards him for a tender kiss. His touch on her skin made her feel electrified, and she lost herself in the exhilaration. Strangely, the heartache they were sharing unlocked the want that had been prematurely silenced, and it was now off the leash.

Karl took the lead without indecision. He led her to his holiday bed where they fell, spending hours treating each other to the pleasure they had previously denied themselves. Mia unreservedly surrendered her body to him, and her fear was replaced with relief and satisfaction. As they nourished each other, he reflected to her a myriad of looks; fondness, sadness, contemplation. He was no longer expressionless.

After reaching the climax of their union, they slept in each other's arms. Mia woke at various stages of the early morning, coming to terms with the indulgence she had allowed herself to spoil in, but also acknowledging it was only a temporary distraction from what was now front of mind, Patrick was dead.

As the sun peaked through the window, she opened her eyes to find Karl was already awake. She wasn't sure how he would handle "them" in the cold light of morning, but she could see the wall was still down. He turned, sweetly kissing her, and sincerely declared, 'I will never forget this.' His eyes were soft and assuring. He got out of the bed and proceeded to the kitchen.

She knew what they had shared was inimitable, but she wasn't going to spoil it by thinking it was something it wasn't capable of being. She got dressed knowing it was time to get going before sentimentality convinced her she wanted more.

She instinctively knew there was no need to discuss anything. He followed her to the door as she headed to leave and nostalgically embraced her one last time. She wriggled out of his clasp when she felt the tears start to well in her eyes, and then quietly mouthed, 'Goodbye Mr Karl.'

Mia let herself cry on the drive home. She knew that what had happened between them would never be repeated. But she had finally felt him, without the façade, and she was now confident she did mean something to him.

She then flashed back to when a wise Patrick pointed out, *'He's not for you, Mia.'*

She spoke out loud in the hope he could somehow hear her, 'Not even this improved version, hey Patrick? You knew us so well. I'll miss you so much.'

Mia then understood, the tears she was crying weren't for Karl, they were for Patrick.

catch and Release

Chapter 8

1988 – Mia's New Year's resolutions

Stop thinking about Karl
Get a new job
Travel

Mia next saw Karl at Patrick's funeral. She had considered he may retract after their intimate night, but there were no signs of this past behaviour. He came to her after the service, where they embraced emotionally. Their friendship was solid.

'I don't regret it. Being with him felt great. But friends it is.'

* * *

She was still taking a handful of classes at the dance studio but wanted to find something that was going to make her good money, fast. She was very keen to start travelling.

After her class one night, one of the owners of the studio approached her. Tiffany was sharp and always looking for ways to promote the business and make more money.

'Mia, I've been contacted by a nightclub owner in town. He wants a couple of dancers to work for a few hours on Friday and Saturday nights. We'd be suspended in cages above the dance floor. It's some sort of gimmick he wants to try, to heighten the crowd a bit. The money is awesome; all cash in hand. And we can advertise the dance studio as well. Just you and me. Interested?'

Mia was interested. This just might be how she could get her travel money together.

'We've been asked to go in this Thursday, to officially meet the owner and see if we fit with what he's looking for. Would you like me to pick you up?' Tiffany subtly pushed Mia into committing, knowing that she had kindled her interest.

'Okay', Mia reacted with slight hesitation.

* * *

A few days later, they arrived at the club about noon. Tiffany knocked on the back door, which was soon opened by a man who looked like he belonged in the Italian mafia. He was average height, thick dark hair, and a mass of gold chains around his neck. Mia was on guard as soon as she saw him. 'Come in ladies,' the words oozing out with as much oil attached to them as he had in his hair. 'Welcome to my playhouse.'

The area was dimly lit, but Mia could see that it had a massive crowd capacity. She noticed the bar was opposite to where they had come in and assumed it was close to the front entrance. The stench of stale beer wafted through the air, reinforcing Mia's preliminary aversion to the place.

As the three of them walked forward, she felt the flooring change from carpet to a harder surface. They were now standing on the dance floor, where their host turned and presented himself like a rock star. 'My name is Tony. And you are?'

'Tiffany.'

He changed his angle.

'Mia.'

'Well, I'm delighted with what I see in front of me. Hopefully this arrangement will work out for all of us. Can I get you beauties a drink?'

'No thanks Tony. We'd like to get on with things. Maybe you could explain what you want us to do,' Tiffany pressed, seemingly still comfortable with the situation.

'Well, see these two cages above us? You'd climb up that rope ladder into them. As you hover above the crowd, I envisage, how do I say this, provocative dance moves, suggestive writhing. Sex exuding out of the pair of you. I want every male in here turned on. In fact, every female too,' he chortled. Let me be clear, this isn't a strip club but, the costumes I've designed cover just enough.'

'Could we see them,' Tiffany asked, without skipping a beat.

'Of course. I want to see you in them. I need to be sure you are right for the job. I'll go get them. They're on the bar.'

As Tony walked away, Mia took her opportunity, 'What the hell have you got us into Tiffany?' She wasn't sure if she was furious or terrified.

'Stay cool,' Tiffany countered.

Then Tony was back, with a pair of skimpy, sequinned, stringed bikinis, and different sized strappy, platform heels to try on.

'You can use the bathrooms to change, or ... just undress here. I could then see the whole package.' Mia's skin crawled.

'We're going with option one thanks. Back in five.' Tiffany grabbed Mia's hand and ushered her to the bathroom, where they changed quickly without any conversation.

As they walked toward him, Tony's lustful gaze couldn't be denied. He scrutinised the small, jewelled patches that just covered Mia's nipples, and the part of her he was fantasising about invading. He looked over Tiffany as well, but didn't take his eyes off Mia for long.

'Turn around for me,' he demanded as they stood in front of him. He was eager to see Mia's firm, youthful rump completely exposed as the beaded string cut up its middle and tied either side of the small of her back. 'Very pleasing,' he mumbled, while his grubby mind journeyed somewhere sick and depraved.

'Tony,' another male called as he was coming passed the bar.

'Ah Enzo. Just in time. Come and see our new gems. These two are auditioning to be our cage dancers,' Tony said. He then proudly presented the new arrival. 'This is my brother, girls. He owns part of the club and runs other, more specialised parts of our family business.'

'Bella,' Enzo purred, thinking the Italian praise may impress. Tiffany and Mia remained quiet.

After a minute of the men speaking in Italian and giggling like children, Enzo chimed, 'I know you have come to show us you're dancing skills, but you may also be interested in another part of our business. We provide personalised river cruises for hard working businessmen, who may need a couple of hours of relaxation during their workday. We include a top-class lunch and drinks, all served by beautiful women, dressed much like you are now. We pay these girls very well.

Enzo let his words linger in the air, then resumed, 'On the odd occasion these gentlemen want more than food and alcohol to relax, but we leave it to the girls to decide if they want to provide such luxury.' He put his arm around Tony and continued, 'We are all about empowering our girls, leaving the details of these transactions to them.'

Another pause, and then he finished his sales pitch with, 'Let's just say these willing participants get ahead much faster. If either of you are interested, here's my card. Give me a call and we can talk some more.'

Mia's brain exploded. These guys were running a secret prostitute ring right on the river. She felt way in over her head.

Tiffany spoke, 'We'll think about it and get back to you. Now we really must be going.'

'But I need to see your moves. Get in the cages,' Tony ordered, as he pulled out a vial of cocaine.

Tiffany remained impressively calm, 'I'm sorry Tony, but that will have to wait. Unfortunately, one of our instructors called in sick this morning and I need to get back to my business. Being a successful businessman, you understand that right?'

This played well into Tony's ego. He couldn't argue with her logic and Mia felt Tony's grip loosen on his expectations.

'We'll get back to you in the next couple of days.' Tiffany said.

The girls changed, handing back the costumes, as Tony and Enzo sniffed the white powder that had been cut on a table beside the dance floor. The two men now seemed detached as they accepted their playthings were leaving.

* * *

In the car on the way home, Tiffany said, 'I'm sorry. I had no idea the extent of what they're involved in. But I'm still considering the cage dancing. Would it be something you would still consider? Think of the money.'

Yes, she wanted money, but Mia felt like a mouse that had just escaped a mouse trap. She believed being associated with these types of men was a slippery slope that would have consequences. Their repulsive misogyny reminded her of the bank incident.

But she was still gathering her thoughts and decided to lie for now. 'I'll give it some thought.'

* * *

Reg, Elizabeth's boyfriend, was over for dinner that night. He'd been spending a lot more time at their place and Mia was very fond of him. There was polite conversation during dinner, but Mia was struggling and Elizabeth noticed.

When she asked her about her day, Mia tried to stay brave but teared up as she relayed what had happened. Elizabeth nearly choked on her food as she listened to her and saw how clearly traumatised her daughter was.

Reg stayed quiet. He knew it was Elizabeth's opinion that Mia needed right now. But he was hoping to guide her when the time was right.

As Mia said goodnight to him on the way to bed, he decided to comment, 'Mia, life is all about choices. Good choices lead to good things. Surround yourself with things that make you happy.'

Mia lay on her bed, hoping sleep would come soon. *'Why do men only want sex from me? Am I somehow suggesting that's all I'm capable of giving?'*

She shuddered, thinking about the desperate girls that would have been lured onto that boat. Those who believed that's all they had to offer. *'At least I know I have more, right?'*

In the lounge, Elizabeth explained to Reg that this was not the first time Mia had been exposed to such ugliness. She spoke about the bank manager and how Mia had handled that.

'She's escaped, twice now, very intimidating circumstances. The damage seems minimal, but I'm worried about the conversations in her head. I wonder how her self-esteem is really doing.'

'Let me help you with this Elizabeth. I have an idea.'

Chapter 9

Mia woke full of anxiety. She didn't want to get out of bed or leave her bedroom ever again. She really didn't want to deal with Tiffany or the dance studio. So, she lay there for a few hours, trying to see a way out.

By mid-morning, Elizabeth decided to check on her. She found Mia paralysed with worry. She embraced her daughter with a reassurance that made Mia feel instant relief.

'Mum, I don't want to go back to the dance studio. I need to find something that makes me feel I have more to offer than being physically attractive. And I don't think I can have another conversation with Tiffany. She's so persuasive. I should never have agreed to go with her yesterday without knowing more of what we were getting into.'

'It's okay, Mia. I'll go with you when you speak to Tiffany. And then you won't ever have to go back there. Do you feel up to some breakfast? Reg would like to talk to you about something.'

* * *

Reg put aside the newspaper he had been reading as Mia and Elizabeth settled down to breakfast. He waited patiently until Mia looked up and smiled at him. He needed to deliver his notion sensitively, as Mia seemed a little emotionally fragile.

'Mia, I have a suggestion that I'd like you to consider. After speaking with your mum, we think it's something that would be good for your self-esteem, and we all need help with that from time to time,' Reg kindly added, hoping to normalise the way she was feeling.

'I have a friend who runs the top deportment school in town. There's a course that goes for a week, and the days are long. But you'll learn things that will help you feel more confident.'

'Like what?' Mia was both angst-ridden and enlivened.

'A range of things about etiquette and refinement. How to conduct yourself with self-assurance, and skilful communication. They'll cover personal grooming, image and style. You'll graduate well versed in all aspects of decorum. Everything you'll need to know if you meet a Prince,' Reg grinned.

He paused, letting the information resonate for a minute. In a slightly more serious tone, he said, 'All of this will help you feel more certain, allowing your inner beauty to shine. It will entice interesting people with decent levels of culture and class. Mia, the people you attract will always mirror how you feel inside.'

'It's a great idea,' Elizabeth confirmed, as Mia looked at her.

Breakfast proceeded in silence as Reg went back to reading his paper. When Elizabeth started to clear the table, Mia looked up and said, 'I'd like to do it, but I can't afford it.'

'Reg has offered to pay,' Elizabeth was quick to react.

Mia was shocked. 'That's very generous. Thank you.'

'This is important for you Mia,' Reg responded, not looking up from his paper. He wanted to appear nonchalant about her decision, but he was thrilled to be helping her. He was in love with Elizabeth and wanted his relationship with Mia to be an extension of that.

* * *

That afternoon, Mia and Elizabeth drove to the dance studio. Elizabeth stood within earshot, like a lioness guarding her cub, as Mia informed Tiffany that she wouldn't be back. Elizabeth's presence safeguarded the conversation, and Tiffany had no choice but to accept Mia's resignation without a fight.

Within a fortnight, Mia was nervously opening a door under the sign 'The Finishing Touch – Deportment and Etiquette'. She was greeted by an elegant, middle-aged woman who made her feel very welcome. Mia pinned her name tag to her blouse and sat down on an open seat. By the time the first class started, she counted a dozen girls, all eager to soak up what was on offer.

She thrived, and by the end of the week, she wasn't the same person. At the small graduating ceremony, the girls were to perform a mini catwalk show in front of invited family members and guests. They picked their outfits from a sizeable collection provided by local designers. Mia chose a musk pink pantsuit, with long sleeves and padded shoulders. She accessorised it with chunky, gold jewellery and strappy high heel sandals. With properly applied makeup, and her hair cut even shorter and dyed blond, she felt completely transformed and liked what she saw in the mirror.

She strutted the new version of herself in front of the room of onlookers, looking a million dollars. She was so different to the broken bird she had been two weeks earlier.

'You look amazing Mia. I'm so proud of you,' Elizabeth threw her arms around her after it was all over.

'I feel amazing. Thank you so much, Reg.' Mia hugged him as well, grateful for the opportunity he had given her. His response was stuck, as he choked up with pride.

'Some of the girls are going up to the Hilton for a few celebration drinks. Do you mind if I go?'

'Not at all. You deserve it,' Elizabeth answered.

* * *

As half of the graduating class sat at the exclusive cocktail bar, four young men watched from across the room. They were in business suits, obviously enjoying a few drinks after work.

50

The group eventually approached the girls, offering to buy them drinks. It wasn't long before one of them asked Mia her name.

'Mia.'

'I'm Michael,' he held out his hand to shake hers. He continued to get to know her a little better with smart conversation and good humour. About an hour after, he said, 'It's been a pleasure to meet you, but unfortunately, it's time for me to go. Enjoy the rest of your night.'

'Thank you. You, too.'

Mia found it refreshing to have enjoyed a man's company without him asking for her phone number, wanting to see her again, or worse, touching her without being invited to.

'Reg was right. I will attract people that mirror how I feel inside. I'm on the right track.'

* * *

The next few months saw Mia frequenting upmarket spots with some of the same girls; establishments with classy clientele that allowed them to practice their new social skills with confidence. She started to date multiple men but always kept the association insubstantial. She wanted to keep life fun, reeling in her suitors with proficient flirtation, only to let them down gently before things got too cosy. She was still protecting her heart, and became an expert at "catch and release".

One Friday night, as she sat at The Hilton's bar waiting for her friends, she started a conversation with the bartender. He was there most nights, so they were past the point of being strangers but weren't entirely acquainted either. Their exchanges had consisted of Mia's drink orders and a lot of shy smiling.

'I feel rude continuing to ask you to make me drinks without knowing your name,' she said charmingly.

'Danny,' he grinned back at her with mischief all over his face.

'Mia', she smiled appealingly. 'You're here a lot, Danny. Do you like it?'

'The customers are enjoyable,' he playfully replied.

Mia's smile broadened as she studied his face for the first time. He had almond brown eyes with a lot of thick brown hair framing his face. She found him attractive.

Their conversation was soon interrupted by Mia's friends arriving. As Mia stepped away with the girls to look for a table, Danny said, 'I finish at ten. Any chance of a coffee or drink?'

'Maybe. Let's see how the night goes,' Mia quipped, already knowing they would be having coffee when he finished.

* * *

As they sat across from each other in the new, chic coffee house, Mia was curious to learn more, 'How long have you been bartending?'

'About eighteen months. I'm studying to be a nurse and needed a job that would fit in around that. The pay is pretty good. Not all venues pay their staff as well as The Hilton does. Of course, the more shifts I do, the better the pay looks. What do you do?'

'I'm in between jobs, but I'm looking for something that will allow me to make money, fast. I'm keen to travel overseas. My mum has relatives in England, and I want to use that as a base to explore Europe.'

'The hospitality thing would be good for that. The course that qualifies you is super easy and not that expensive. You won't have any problems finding yourself a job after you finish. It could also be handy overseas, if you wanted to do some work whilst you travelled.'

After a couple of hours of getting to know each other, Danny walked Mia to find a taxi. He confessed, 'I've really enjoyed chatting. Will I see you soon?'

'Yes, soon,' once again playing it cool but already knowing she would be at his bar next Friday night. There was an attraction between them, but Mia was so focused on getting overseas, she didn't want to entertain any involvement.

* * *

Over the weekend, Mia picked her time to speak with Elizabeth and Reg about her potential new plan. She was worried a hospitality vocation was not what Reg had in mind when he financial contributed to her future. But he seemed happy when she explained the goal was to travel overseas.

'You couldn't get a better life education,' he remarked, in his old-school way.

Elizabeth was mostly excited. She was thrilled at the idea of Mia getting to know her family that she had left as a teenager to come to Australia.

But she also realised that there would be lengths of time that she wouldn't have contact with her daughter. Being without Mia would be hard to get used to, but she knew this adventure would be great for her. So, she swallowed her uneasiness and pretended to be completely on board.

Chapter 10

Before too long, Mia had completed her hospitality course, and Danny had kindly lined up an interview with the bar manager at the Hilton. She soon found herself on the other side of the bar, serving drinks rather than consuming them. She took every shift offered, spending more time at work than at home, and was very popular with the regular patrons, as she always remembered their usual drink orders.

She and Danny often worked together. She looked forward to seeing him, as their flirtation made work more like play. When the bar was busy, they moved well together but on the odd occasion, when they brushed against each other, she started to feel an electricity between them, and a temptation to submit to the enticement.

One Friday night, Michael, whom Mia had met the night she finished her deportment course, was back with his friends. He recognised Mia and didn't hesitate to sit up at the bar, chatting with her when she wasn't serving. He eventually asked what time she finished and would she have a drink with him. 'Thanks Michael but as an employee, I can't drink here.'

'No problems, I know this great bar down the road. We can relax there,' Michael pushed for her to agree.

'Let's see what time I finish, okay?', Mia deflected, not sure if she wanted to go.

'Would you like to take your break Mia? I can cover the bar for a while,' Danny calmly said, but Michael's invitation had made him uneasy.

Mia smiled, grateful to be temporarily removed from the situation. She needed somewhere quiet to sort out her thoughts.

'Do I want to have a drink with Michael? I would prefer to spend the time with Danny. I wonder if he feels the same. Maybe if I go with Michael, it'll help him decide.'

She cruised back behind the bar, with no evidence of the dialogue that was going off in her mind.

After another hour, Danny said, 'Why don't you take off Mia? It's quiet. I can handle closing by myself.'

'Ah, okay. Thanks.' Mia was still unsure. *'Are you not interested, Danny? Oh well, let's see how this goes.'*

'Michael are you still up for that drink.'

'Absolutely,' Michael's keenness was boiling over.

'Night Danny.' Mia looked at him, hoping for a sign that he didn't want her to go.

'Night,' Danny said, not giving anything away, convinced his attraction for her was futile.

* * *

Sitting at Michael's nominated bar, Mia was trying to stay engaged in the conversation, but thoughts of Danny kept creeping in. Michael just wasn't quite hitting the right notes, even though this was the type of guy Mia should be interested in; charming, successful, polite, smart, and interested in her. But somehow, Danny had her attention.

Just as Mia was about to call it a night, the flash of a red dress caught her eye. A very solid, fit looking woman was tearing across the room like there was a fire behind her. She was heading straight for them with fury all over her face. If a look could kill, Michael would have been dead.

'You, absolute scumbag,' she screamed on approach, with no consideration that there were people around.

'Calm down Amanda,' Michael stood, trying to stop her from getting too close. He looked shaken.

'You told me you were out with some work colleagues tonight and instead you're out with some scrubber. You certainly don't waste any time, do you?'

With all her improved confidence, Mia decided she couldn't let that one go, 'Excuse me. I'm no scrubber.'

Without a blink, Mia was struck, open handed, so hard that she saw stars. *Probably should have kept my mouth shut.'*

'Oh my God, Amanda! You're completely out of control,' Michael was overwrought. 'Are you okay?', his concern turned to Mia.

'Of course, focus on your new whore, you piece of trash.' The woman spat the words out just as security came to remove her from the premises. 'Come and get the rest of your stuff. It'll be on the front lawn,' she screamed, as the door to the establishment slammed behind her.

Michael was so embarrassed. This lack of class was so far removed from the way he presented himself.

'That was unexpected', Mia said.

'I'm so sorry. Can I explain?' Michael pleaded.

Mia hadn't answered before Michael began, 'We met about two years ago and were happy for a while. Then she told me she was pregnant. I was shocked. I wasn't sure I wanted to spend my life with her, let alone be a father. But I felt I needed to take responsibility, so, we got engaged, bought a house, and moved in together. A few months later I found out, there was no baby. She admitted to making the whole thing up, to see if I'd commit to her.'

'That's appalling.' Mia was sympathetic.

Michael was thankful Mia was prepared to listen. 'I decided to give it a go anyway. The wedding invitations went out, and everything was organised. But the closer the day got, the more I felt trapped. Two weeks before the big day, I called everything off and moved out. I've told her, many times, it's over, but she won't let me go. She still calls every Friday, asking me what I'm doing for the weekend. I don't tell her too much, but now, I think she must be following me. There is no other way she could have known I was here.'

'It's probably a good thing you're out. She seems a little unhinged. What sort of person pretends to be pregnant, just to test how you feel about them? She should have considered you may have needed more time, and things may have worked out differently.'

And with that thought, Mia realised that she was a little guilty of the same with Danny. Certainly not on the same scale but she'd only said yes to having a drink with Michael to test Danny and push him into admitting he might be interested.

'As much as this has been fun Michael, I need to go,' Mia said, with just enough sarcasm to make Michael smile awkwardly.

'Can we do this again, without the face slap?', Michael asked.

'I don't think so.'

'Let me at least get you to a taxi.'

'I forgot something at the bar. I'm going back there.'

'Well can I walk you back there? I'd like to know you're safe.'

Mia agreed.

As they said goodnight at the front door of the hotel, Mia couldn't help but think, even the so called "perfect" guy isn't so perfect.

As she headed up the stairs, she considered how honest she should be with Danny, *'I think I'll lead with... I shouldn't have said yes to a drink with Michael. I only did it to see if you were interested in me.'*

'Umm, maybe that's a bit too honest. Ah well, let's see if getting slapped was worth it.'

As she came in, the last of Danny's customers were finishing their drinks. He looked up in surprise but was obviously glad to see her. She perched herself at the end of the bar smiling at him.

He locked the door when they were finally alone and sat down next to her. 'I didn't think I would see you until our next shift,' he said with a teasing smile.

'Very interesting turn of events. I won't bore you with the details', Mia jibed back. 'Actually, I'm not sure why I went. I was hoping you would have insisted that you needed me after work, for ... coffee.' Mia suggestively raised one eyebrow.

Danny was suddenly nervous. 'Honestly, I didn't like you going with him. I'm insanely attracted to you and was wondering if you'd be keen to take this past... coffee.'

'Do you mean something harder Danny?' Mia couldn't help the evocative taunt. Danny shifted slightly on the barstool, and she knew her hint had had the desired effect. 'Something like a hard... single malt whiskey,' she continued mischievously.

Danny joined in the playing, but decided to be a little clearer, 'I'm thinking more along the cocktail line, say a "Between the Sheets", or a "Tie Me to the Bedpost".'

Mia was aroused by his witty return, 'Now that is something I'd like to explore.'

He reached out and stroked her thigh. 'I'm not looking for anything serious Mia. My life is hectic.'

'Either am I Danny. Remember I'm overseas as soon as I can.'

Feeling the rise of anticipation of what the night might bring, Danny slowly leant forward and kissed Mia on the lips. 'I'll just get my bag,' he said, keen to see what the night was going to bring.

Mia called Elizabeth, 'Hi Mum. Yes, just finished work. Listen I've caught up with a friend and I'm staying at their house tonight. Don't worry I'm safe. I'll see you sometime tomorrow.'

As she hung up, Mia's conscience chattered, *'Why am I getting involved with him when it's just about sex?'*

As the undeniable lust rose, she conceded to the counter argument, *'Why deny myself when it's all I want from him too. I'll deal with any fallout later.'*

He was looking at her differently now. He knew they wanted the same thing but didn't want to rush her. 'Where would you like to start Mia? Should we go find a quiet spot and start with that whiskey.'

She moved so the front of their bodies touched, ensuring there was no more ambiguity. 'Take me home Danny and get that cocktail list ready.'

Chapter 11

Mia was awake listening to Danny's breathing as he slept beside her. They had been casually enjoying each other for over six months, playing by the original rules of engagement, with no talk of anything serious or a solid future together. And yet, she hadn't been so quick to "release" him.

Even though being exclusive had never been discussed, she was certain she was his only bed partner. His life consisted of studying, attending classes, working at the bar, or spending time with her. He was busy, and continually reassured her, there was no time for anything or anyone else.

In the silence of that moment, she started to review their arrangement. As it turned out, this hadn't been a one-night thing. Yes, in the beginning, they had both agreed to keep things uncomplicated, not knowing where it was going. And they still had their goals; he wanted to finish his nursing degree, and she wanted to travel the world.

But the old dogs of doubt had started to nip at Mia's heels. Did she mean anything to him past sexual gratification and had she submissively let him direct their involvement in a way he was most comfortable? It was a long time to invest together just because the sex was good.

And the fallout began. Her head pressed play on self-questioning, and she was now unexpectedly wanting validation she was worth something to Danny, even though she couldn't define what he meant to her.

'Stop it! These senseless thoughts are about justifying the sex without any talk of love. The focus should be on what I want, exploring the world.'

But by dawn, like a ticking clock in her head, she was still searching for reassurance of her value, and that there was some meaning behind their time together.

Danny's alarm went off an hour before he was to get going for the day. He rolled over to find Mia staring at the ceiling. 'Oh good, you're awake,' he said as he reached for her, hoping to pick up where they had left off the night before.

'What are your thoughts on marriage?' Of course, Mia didn't want a proposal from him, but after hours of questioning why they were still together, she threw a long ball, knowing Danny's response would destroy any attachment she had started to feel.

'Hell no! Where did that come from?' Danny was obviously confused. She had always portrayed she didn't care about commitment and her pretence of no emotional needs was very convincing.

'Relax Danny. I was just spit balling. Anyway, you'll be waving me off before you know it,' Mia flippantly answered. But the uncomfortable twinge she felt, made her aware she needed to address something. She just wasn't sure what.

'Wow, you scared me for a minute. I thought you were suggesting something more serious between us. I'm not ready for that. I've got to finish my study first.'

Danny was a one thing at a time, day-by-day kind of guy.

* * *

Over the next few weeks, as she put their association under a microscope, she realised she was fond of Danny, but she wasn't in love. So, if she knew her sexual appetite for him didn't equal a love match, why the need for emotional validation?

As she worked through these deliberations it occurred to her, she wasn't going to find love or any emotional connection while she kept her need for one so well hidden. She needed to drop the charade. *'But I do wonder if anyone will love me past my sexuality.'*

* * *

One day, while she was on her break, Mia watched Danny from the back of the bar. They had had a wonderful time together, but it was time to accept that it was a physical attraction that she chose to continue long after it should have ended.

'Is Mia working today?' the familiar voice broke her contemplation.

'Just up the back there,' Danny replied.

Mia pulled herself out of her introspection. She couldn't help but think how ironic it was that he turns up now. As he drew closer, Mia felt a comfort that involuntarily held her to him.

'What are you doing here Karl? How did you know where to find me?', she smiled.

'I went by your house. Hey, I met Reg. He seems nice. Anyway, I've got a plan, and I wanted to talk to you about it,' Karl got straight to the point. 'I think I've found my father in England and I'm planning to fly in a couple of months' time. Do you want to come?'

Chapter 12

1989 – Mia's New Year's resolutions

Travel

Stop pretending you're okay with no emotional connection

By February, Mia was placing the final things into her suitcase. Her finances looked healthy, and she'd arranged to stay with her mum's aunt in London, keeping her accommodation costs to a minimum. Karl had found a share flat close, so they could be in the same neighbourhood.

Elizabeth was over the moon regarding Mia's secure home-base and was also grateful that she had a travel companion. She was at ease now that Karl was just a friend and her daughter's heart wasn't on the line. She knew he'd look after her.

But Mia did have some trepidation. Leaving Elizabeth was a big deal for her. She had relied on her mum always. However, she knew it was time to rely on her own judgement, without any back up.

The travellers had decided to use Hong Kong as a stopover for two nights. Reg told stories about his layovers there and how great the shopping was, with custom made leather jackets and beautiful cashmere attire. He was a civil engineer of worldclass standard and consulted all over the Asia Pacific area. He had done a lot of work in Hong Kong, as it was then under English rule, and he knew it very well.

Mia loved having Reg in her life, and knew she would miss him as well.

In the departures lounge of the international airport, Mia kissed Reg and thanked him for his support in making their journey easier. They both started to cry.

She then turned to Elizabeth. 'Be safe, darling. Contact us anytime you want, day or night,' Elizabeth implored, knowing it was her daughter's time to grab a hold of life.

'Yes Mum, I promise I'll be in touch often and will send a postcard from every place I visit,' Mia reassured. 'Please don't worry about me. Just enjoy each other.'

Mia then stood in front of Danny. Their casual affiliation had continued after she had clearly labelled it, and she knew her travelling would ease it into its inevitable end. Now, all she was expecting was a friendly but impassive goodbye.

But in its place, was a man who clearly hadn't been honest with her or himself. His face was full of regret at how casual he had played it as he whispered, 'I will miss you, a lot.'

'Danny this was supposed to be the release part, remember?', she said quietly, completely caught off guard. There may have been no declaration of love, but there was obvious respect and tenderness as Danny reached for her hand and drew her to him.

This astonishing farewell was only interrupted by Karl tapping Mia on the shoulder saying, 'Come on Champion, it's time to go'. This was Karl's latest title for Mia, certifying "friendship only" vibes. Danny reluctantly let Mia go as she clearly shut the door on their chapter together.

* * *

Mia stared at the TV screen overhead, and the little plane image heading toward The Orient. *'We're on our way,'* she thought, thankful to be sharing it with Karl. They truly were back to being friends, having one another's backs and making each other laugh.

Their flight approached Hong Kong early in the evening. As their plane skipped through the sea of high-rises and their twinkling lights, Mia and Karl beamed with elation. It all felt very surreal.

They travelled to their hotel in a car that Reg had organised. After checking in, and as they headed to their rooms in the extravagant hotel elevator, Karl proposed how their night should proceed. 'So, our flight to London leaves in about thirty-eight hours. Reg told us that if we wanted anything custom made, we should give the tailors at least thirty-six. I think we should have a shower and head out to find this tailor he suggested, and get our orders in. Didn't he say they were open until midnight?'

'Yep. Sounds great. Knock on my door when you're ready.'

She opened the door to her hotel room, and it exceeded all expectations. It was spacious, with trendy décor. Her bed was massive, and the bathroom had a big bath that she intended using later. She opened the dark curtains that shielded the outside world and was instantly amazed as millions of lights shone onto people's lives through uncovered windows. She felt like she was in the clouds because she was so high up.

She quickly showered and dressed to suit the humid air that she'd felt getting from the car into the hotel. Karl's room was right next to hers, so it wasn't long before he was at her door, freshened up and looking ready to take on the world.

After some clear instructions from the front desk attendant and another car ride, they arrived at their suggested tailor and were soon being measured for perfectly tailored, leather clothing. Karl opted for just a jacket, but Mia went for the full suit, skirt and jacket in stone-wash, brown leather.

Before leaving, they confirmed with the store manager that their garments would be ready in time for pick up on the way to the airport. The retailers who had attended them had been very polite and the whole experience had been stress-free.

It was 10.00pm local time when they decided to call it a night. Back at the hotel, Mia slipped into a hot bath and let the bubbles' part around her body. She felt like she was floating. Her life had changed so much in twelve months, and her mind was full of pictures of things she'd seen throughout the day. She was pinching herself over the fact her dream of travelling overseas had come true.

* * *

The next day, the duo went sightseeing, covering off some of Reg's recommendations, Causeway Bay, a ferry to Hong Kong Island and onto Kowloon. The humidity was oppressive, and the weather was fickle, with large rainstorms descending without warning in between patches of the sun beating down.

In some areas, there was western influence, with McDonalds and Pizza Hut franchises distinct; but in others there was obvious signs of poverty and overpopulation. Laundry hung on balconies, tv antennas were ubiquitous and in no order. And despite the "No Spitting" signs posted everywhere, Mia and Karl witnessed this habit was accepted, whenever and wherever.

But Mia joyfully indulged in the endless shopping. Silk and lace blouses, cashmere jumpers, leather shoes. Shop after shop of fantastic quality wares at unbelievably cheap prices. They walked miles and spent plenty.

At the end of the day, and unsure of how far away they were from the hotel, they decided to try and catch a train. With multiple purchases clutched in both hands, they stood on the platform amongst what seemed like a million other rail users. As the train approached, a sudden swell in the crowd caused them to separate; and as the train stopped, Karl was swept into it, with hordes of people pressing forward, and Mia was pushed backwards, unable to follow. 'Mia,' Karl's cry seemed rattled. But then the doors shut, and the train was gone.

Mia was suddenly alone in a foreign country, and it was the first occasion she needed to use her own judgement whilst keeping the budding ripple of fear at bay.

As she stood still, the throng of people who had just left were replaced by a new lot of commuters waiting for the next train. Ironically in this instance, the regulator that Mia used on her emotions served her well, and rather than get overwhelmed, she imperturbably decided the train wasn't for her and went to hail a taxi.

* * *

Karl was waiting in the lobby as she came through the doors. 'You, okay?', he casually asked, trying to hide his concern.

'Yeah fine, but I could use a drink,' Mia replied as she led the way to the bar.

After a long day, they decided on an early dinner and retreated to their rooms. As they got to their doors, Mia asked, 'You seemed a bit worried about the train thing today? It's like you felt responsible for me.'

'I do feel a bit responsible for you, like a brother would. It doesn't freak me out so much these days.' Karl shrugged his shoulder as they looked at each other with platonic affection. Then he added, 'Besides I wouldn't want to be on the end of Elizabeth's wrath if anything happened to you.' He smiled and disappeared into his room.

When they checked out early the next morning, the front desk clerk handed them their leather purchases that had been generously dropped off by the tailor. There was a note attached that read, 'Say hello to Reg.'

As the plane lifted off, dancing amongst the buildings, Mia was grateful for the time they had spent there but she couldn't wait to be in London.

Chapter 13

They effortlessly settled into their new lives in the Notting Hill district. Joan, Elizabeth's aunt, was just like Elizabeth, openhearted and hospitable, and still as sharp as a tack for her elderly years. Within a couple of days of arriving, Mia felt like she was home.

Karl was comfortably nestled in his shared accommodation, not far from Mia. The area was very multi-cultural and had an artistry vibe. It was quite laid back compared to other parts of London that Mia and Karl would eventually experience.

Joan spent time advising them of the best attractions to see. They each bought a travel card which allowed them to journey via the London Underground to anywhere within the inner city. They both agreed it was the best way to get around.

London was always buzzing. Within the first couple of weeks, they spent time visiting the big tourist attractions. Each day, they picked a cluster of must-see sites, all within walking distance of each other, so they could enjoy the sensation of the city streets as well. They covered a lot in a short time frame... one day - Westminster Abbey, Big Ben, Buckingham Palace: the next - the Tower Bridge and the Tower of London.

They were also quick to elect a local establishment to socialise in, The Churchill Arms. The other patrons were fascinated by their Australianisms and within a few weeks, they became popular additions to the bar's young scene. After long sightseeing days, they found themselves having drinks and chatting with the other regulars, and strong acquaintances developed quickly.

After being in the neighbourhood for close to a month, Emily, one of the girls that Mia had warmed to, approached her with an offer, 'Hey, me and some friends are thinking about a short trip to the Greek Islands in a month or so. Would you like to come? It'll be so much fun.'

Mia was bursting to say yes but thought she'd at least inform Karl before committing. She looked over to where he was in a banter exchange with the football mad lads. Emily read Mia's thoughts and clarified, 'You can bring your boyfriend if you want but it won't be as much fun. Greek boys like it when you're single.'

'He's not my boyfriend.' Mia and Karl had spent most of the month explaining to people they were just great mates. 'Just hold that thought. I'll be back in a minute,' Mia said, before moving over to Karl.

Once there was a break in the lads good-humoured conversation, Mia quietly said to Karl, 'I've been asked to go on a short girl's trip to Greece. Do you mind if I go?'

'Of course not. With you not racing me all over town, I may get some time to sort out my father stuff', Karl said mockingly. Mia just rolled her eyes at him and hollered back to Emily, 'I'm in.'

A few days after, the girls visited a travel agent to discuss what island they should go to, and to book their flights. Rhodes was her strong suggestion, as it was the farthest island from mainland Greece and didn't heave with tourists.

May 1989

The four girls found themselves on an evening flight, leaving from Gatwick airport. They would land on the island in the early hours of the morning. They had no accommodation booked, but with sparkling wine under their belts, and a whole lot of enthusiasm, believed it would work out somehow.

Mia pulled out the in-flight magazine that clued-up travellers on their destination. As they scoured over the map of Rhodes, the flight attendant came up to pour their second round of drinks. She could see the girls had no plan after they landed. She commented, 'Lindos is beautiful. See here on the map. That's where I stay when I go to Rhodes. It's just under an hour taxi ride from the airport but it's so worth it. If you turn to page 54, you will see how amazing it is.'

The girls read the description about what this small village had to offer and marvelled at the photos of this Grecian paradise. It was on the east coast of the island and in the other direction from Rhodes town, but the girls felt adventurous. 'Lindos it is,' they all approved, clinking their glasses together.

In the last hour of the four-hour flight, the girls had quietened. The other three caught some sleep but Mia was thinking about Karl and how he planned to contact his father while she was away. *'I hope everything goes okay.'*

* * *

After passing through a blase customs process, they clambered into a taxi. Once again, the energy levels started to elevate and their extremely friendly driver, Minus, made the trip go quickly with his continual interaction, even if it was in broken English.

Just on sunrise, they saw a steep incline in front of them. 'Lindos.' Minus beamed as they reached the top of the hill. He pulled the car to the side of the road and brought it to a stop, motioning for the girls to get out.

They stood on the edge of an impressive precipice and looked across to the ruins of the Acropolis that towered over the village of white homes. The beach had a series of thatched umbrellas that were sheltering no one at that time of day and gentle waves lapped at the amber sand. There was a hint of the anticipated turquoise blue water as the sun's rays started to shine, but the hues continued to change every second.

Mia was so full of emotion; she felt like she could've cried. She had never seen beauty like it. She looked around to see that the other girls were just as stunned. Quietly, they soaked up the spectacle. Minus articulated in his thick Greek/English way, 'She is as beautiful as Elizabeth Taylor.' It was obvious he was very proud of his home.

Once everyone was ready to move on, he drove the taxi slowly down toward a circular vehicle terminus. Lindos is a pedestrian village, so this was as far as any vehicles can go.

After saying goodbye to Minus, the girls meandering their way through pokey walkways, with locals making eye contact and smiling as they acknowledged there were new people in town. It didn't take long before they found themselves in the main bustling area of eateries and cafes. They had plenty of breakfast places to choose from, even at 6.30am, and soon sat down to enjoy some fruit and Greek yogurt.

Their waiter was about their age, with flawless Mediterranean skin and blue eyes. His white shirt and black pants outlined his perfect form and charisma exuded out of every one of his pores.

'Isn't he one of the most perfect humans you've ever seen?', Mia asked the other girls as he walked away from the table.

'He is extremely easy on the eye and speaks very good English,' Emily coincided.

Mia was feeling fearless. As he reapproached to fill their water glasses, she asked, 'Could we please trouble you for some information? We haven't booked anywhere to stay. Is there somewhere you could suggest?'

'Yes, my friend's mother has a big villa that would sleep all of you. I believe it is currently available. It is very basic with one bathroom to share and single mattresses on the floor, but it is clean, and the nightly price is good. How long is your stay?'

Quickly gauging the other girls were keen to check it out, Mia swooped, 'Five nights. Could you tell us how to get there?'

'It is not far from here. After you finish your breakfast, I will ask if I can have a ten-minute break and take you there.'

After breakfast, they followed the waiter through the spaghetti like maze of paths to a blue wooden door that opened to a courtyard with masses of bright bougainvilleas draping overhead. An older woman dressed in traditional Greek attire came out of an arched doorway, greeting him fondly. Their conversation was in Greek, but the girls knew by the nodding of the heads, they had found their lodgings.

'Thank you very much for helping us out,' Mia swooned as the waiter went to leave.

'My pleasure. Have a pleasant stay.' And he was gone. Mia was so tongue-tied she didn't even ask his name.

* * *

The quartet spent their days enjoying this magical place. It was like a spell had been cast and everything beyond it was forgotten. They buoyantly drifted from soaking up the beach, to eating in the exquisite seafood restaurants, to dancing in the bars, to contently laying their heads down at night. It was therapeutic and restorative, with continual laughter and joy. This utopia was geared for pleasure and the locals relished in hosting.

After days of blossoming in this wonderland, the reality of a return to England loomed. They were flying out tomorrow and needed to make their final night one to remember.

While they savoured their last afternoon on the beach, and discussed their options for the night's proceedings, Mia's concentration was sidetracked when she saw the dreamy waiter from their first day, standing at the tree line that skirted the beach. He was wearing a singlet and shorts, showing off his perfect body.

Emily's voice interrupted Mia's focus on her diversion, 'Mia, what do you think?'

'Yep, I'm easy.' She had no idea what she was agreeing to.

'Great. Well, I might head for a nap then, prepare for our big night. Coming?'

'I'll be up soon.' Mia wasn't ready to leave.

Pulling her gaze from the waiter, she watched the other girls disappear off the beach. She decided to head for the water to have one final swim. *This place is so special,* she thought, as she plunged into the clear, aqua sea, allowing the serenity to fully engulf her soul.

After several minutes, she reluctantly decided to leave the water and was heading for her towel when she noticed someone lying on it. *'Oh my, it's him.'* She tried to steady herself as a shudder of elation ran through her. The waiter waved, knowing she had seen him.

He watched as she walked toward him. 'Hi Kangaroo, my name is Petros.' He held out his hand to shake hers, flashing a grin that highlighted his perfectly white, straight teeth and the small dimples in his cheeks.

'Mia', she responded, holding her demeanour and stare fixed.

'Kangaroo why are you such a long way from home?', Petros enquired, completely ignoring her real name.

'He can call me whatever he wants.'

'Visiting family in England and somehow, I ended up here on holiday. My turn now, why is your English so good?'

'It still needs some work,' Petros humbly acknowledged. 'My parents sent me on, how do you say... exchange. I lived in Canada for 6 months. It is beautiful there. Have you been there my travelling Kangaroo?'

'Yes, I would be very happy being your travelling Kangaroo.

'No, I hadn't left Australia before a couple of months ago. I hear Canada is beautiful. I hope to get there one day.' Mia put her sunglasses back on so she could inconspicuously look at him from top to toe as he sprawled himself so majestically on her towel. He was physically magnificent.

He smiled like he read her mind. 'I know you are leaving tomorrow. I am working at the restaurant tonight but will finish about 10pm. Could you meet me, and I will take you for a bike ride so you can see Lindos at nighttime? Let's meet at the taxi circle. Where Minus dropped you off.' Petros got up to go. 'I will see you there, yes?'

'Yes,' was all Mia could say.

* * *

The group's final night together was amazing. They went to the finest restaurant in the village, enjoying the best of the local cuisine. Then onto the nightclub, where word had got around it was their last night, so free drinks were served up and they danced until their feet hurt.

Just before 10.00pm, Mia pulled Emily to one side and smugly said, 'I have an appointment I can't miss.'

'What? Where are you going?' Emily was surprised.

'I have a motorbike ride booked with a very handsome waiter. Don't wait up.'

'We will want details,' Emily laughed as Mia left.

* * *

Petros was waiting under the lamp post in a tight, white T-shirt and a pair of jeans.

'He truly is a Greek Adonis.'

'You look lovely,' he complimented, as he handed her a helmet.

74

'Thank you, so do you.' Mia wasn't sure if he was used to being called "lovely", but nerves stopped her from searching her vocabulary for a substitute adjective.

She sat behind him, with her hands gripping his trim waist, moving with him as one, as they snaked their way to the top of the cliffs. He kept to a moderate speed, wanting to make the ride fun, not terrifying. He pulled over at the same spot Minus had, where they got off the bike and took off their helmets, so they could look directly at the breathtaking view.

'Petros, I have no words. I can't describe what I am seeing or feeling. Calling it beautiful seems such an understatement.'

He turned back to her and said, 'You are beautiful, Kangaroo.'

Mia thought her knees were going to give. She blushed and looked down at her feet to make sure they were still on the ground. She felt like she was dreaming.

'Say something and try to make sense.'

'You said on the beach to meet where Minus dropped us off. How did you know it was him who dropped us off?'

Petros chuckled at her avoidance of his admiration. 'It is a very small place. Everybody knows everybody. And when new people arrive, everyone knows. Now, are you sick of this view because I have more to show you?'

'I could never get sick of this view, but I am intrigued at what else you have to show me', Mia flirted.

He took her to a neighbouring village, Lardos, about ten minutes away. After parking the bike, he led her to a busy restaurant where he greeted the man at the front counter like they were good friends. Following a short exchange, Petros grabbed Mia's hand and led her upstairs to the rooftop. It was completely empty. He guided her to a table with a clear view over the township, pulling out her chair, indicating for her to sit.

The setting couldn't have been more idealistic. Romantic fairy lights dangled overhead; the sound of gentle waves lapping on the beach in the background; and the space to themselves.

A waiter appeared and Petros ordered something in Greek. Before long, they were sharing multiple small plates of food, and sipping Oozo on ice.

They talked about each other's lives, learning what they could in the few hours they had. Petros's eyes twinkled with liveliness, as he looked at her like she was a goddess. And she looked back at him with utter fascination. The dreamlike intoxication she felt would make it a night she would never forget.

After a slow ride home, they stood at the doorway to Mia's villa, and she thanked him for a wonderful night. He placed his strong hand on the side of her face and gently moved his thumb over her bottom lip. 'You truly are beautiful Kangaroo.' Mia's heart stopped. 'May I kiss you goodnight?'

'May you kiss me! Oh my god, please hurry up', Mia screamed inside her head. Outwardly, she calmly affirmed with a nod. And it was everything a good kiss should be, starting gently, then building with passion, teasing her thoughts to become more erogenous. After several minutes, his hands started to explore her body, and she could feel how much he wanted her. Her thoughts danced between giving into a hurried, sexual liaison, which she presumed was part of Petros's routine; or to leave him, like an unwrapped gift.

While she still could, she started to take the pace down a gear, back to gentle petting, until her mouth half-heartedly left his lips and she whispered, 'Good-night Petros.'

She walked into the villa to find the rest of the gang awake, chin-wagging. They all stopped, noticing the glow that Mia was radiating. 'Well?' Emily asked.

'I have just had the best night of my life,' Mia declared.

The following morning, the girls slowly packed. Mia was still floating on the high of the night before. When they moved to the courtyard, they found Petros talking with their land lady, as she swept fallen bougainvillea flowers. He stopped mid-sentence when he saw Mia, and she felt herself soar even higher on seeing him.

'I hope you all had a good time,' Petros address all of them but kept his eyes on Mia.

'Yes, thank you. We hope to come again,' Emily was the one to speak.

'You too Kangaroo. Will you come? I have more I would like to show you.' Petros winked, suggestively playing with Mia.

The older Greek lady didn't miss what he was insinuating. She picked up her broom and pretended to smack him to the courtyard entrance.

'I will see you another time Kangaroo.' Petros's final goodbye could hardly be heard over the roar of laughter.

As the light plane lifted, the girls quietly reflected on their sensational week. Mia felt a tinge of sadness as they headed away from this fantasy world. She knew it could never be her permanent reality, but it could be a temporary escape. She promised herself, one day, to return.

Chapter 14

It was late afternoon by the time Mia arrived back at Joan's place from the airport. She found Karl having a cup of tea with her great aunt, and they both seemed very glad to see her. She told them how extraordinary the trip was, leaving out the details of Petros. They didn't need to know about them.

When Karl made his move to leave, Mia followed him to the front door. He turned and said, 'Can we catch up tomorrow? Maybe grab a coffee and go to Hyde Park?'

'Sure, I'll get to you mid-morning. Everything okay?'

'Yep, all good. I'll tell you about it tomorrow'.

Mia presumed it was to do with his dad.

* * *

It took a little while to get to the subject, but as they sipped on their coffees, Karl finally revealed how it had gone with his father. Mia listened, knowing not to interrupt.

'When he opened the door, I recognised him straight away. I can't remember exactly what I said, but it was something about re-connecting. He was obviously in shock, but eventually invited me in. After some awkward small talk, I finally asked him to tell me his side of the story. According to him, he just wasn't ready to be a father. He admitted he was pigheaded and didn't change anything, even after I was born. He worked all day and always stopped at the pub for a few every night. Him and Mum started to argue, and after five years of the same, he figured Mum just got sick of it all. He came home one day, and we were gone.'

Mia could see the pain in Karl's eyes.

'Anyway, he said he thinks about me often and wondered what I was like. He warmed up once he was over the disbelief that I was there, and we've caught up every day since.'

Karl took a breather, and then continued, 'I'm glad we've met. He says he wants to stay in touch. But I feel I've done what I came here to do.'

'What do you mean?' Mia was perplexed.

'I'm going home. I have stuff I need to sort with Mum. I've been angry at her for years, and I'm still angry, but I have a better understanding of why she chose to leave. I need to see if our relationship can be better.'

Mia felt like the earth had moved from underneath her. 'You haven't even left London,' she griped, thinking he was being rash. 'There is so much to see Karl. And I need you.'

'You don't need me. Look at what you've done in the past few days. You'll always have people around that will help you and want to be with you. You've just started to do what you came to do. I've done what I came to do. It's time for me to go home and try and fix things with Mum.'

Mia surrendered. She knew all the protesting in the world wouldn't change Karl's mind once it was made up.

The conversation made her miss Elizabeth even more than she already did. There were regular phone calls between them, on Joan's house phone, and Mia wrote and received letters at least once a fortnight, that were only full of good news.

'Should I go home with Karl? What am I going to do when he's gone?'

'But...who knows if I'll ever get back. Lindos is just the tip of the iceberg. There's so much more I want to see. No, I need to stay.'

A week later she was staring at the bottom of her empty wine glass. She had called into The Churchill Arms on her way home after seeing Karl off at the airport. She was feeling lost, and a little unsure now that her safety net was gone.

The bar service seemed slow compared to normal and she could see the bar manager, Nick, was under the pump. 'Is everything okay Nick?'

'Anne hasn't shown up again. She's so unreliable. I was supposed to have knocked off by now cause it's my sister's birthday, but it looks like I'm stuck here,' Nick grumbled.

'I can give you hand. I worked a bar back in Aus for nearly a year,' Mia suggested.

Nick looked a bit sceptical but also relieved. 'Okay. Let's see how you go.'

And from that, Mia began to get casual shifts all the time. She lived so close; it was easy to call her at the last minute when someone couldn't make their shift, or if the bar was busy.

She settled into a somewhat normal life in Notting Hill, not venturing far that summer. She even enrolled in an art class. She was naturally creative, and particularly good at drawing with pastels. In these classes, she found herself choosing American Indians as her primary subject. The pictures in her mind were very clear, and the chalks allowed for a definite, feathery look to help depict their remarkable headdresses.

* * *

When the weather started to turn again, she was looking for somewhere warm to go for a couple of weeks. She was in the bar looking at brochures about Egypt, when Emily found her.

'Wow, when are you thinking about going?', Emily asked.

'Next month, October. My birthday month. I thought it would be a nice present to me from me,' Mia smirked.

'Would you like a travel companion. I've never been?'

Mia couldn't believe it. She had just been thinking it would be good to have someone with her, even though she was on a tour. 'Yes, one hundred percent, yes,' she hugged Emily.

The two girls had become good friends. Emily was a true Londoner. She had curly, mid-length hair, that was a beautiful shade of auburn. She was solid in build, with a "don't mess me about" attitude. But once you got to know her, she was much softer than she pretended; and had a wicked sense of humour and potent wit. Egypt was going to be a lot of fun.

* * *

The pair arrived in Cairo and made their way to their hotel. It was in the middle of the embassy district, where they saw unsettling things like intense looking men with machine guns, guarding the corners of every block.

They were already slightly on edge. Some of The Churchill Arms patrons, who had previously been to the Middle East, had given them some travel tips... lock your passport in the hotel safe, hide all evidence of any religious faith, make sure your wrists and ankles are covered and never carry a lot of cash on you. The girls chose to comply with all.

* * *

There was a spare day before their tour started, so they decided to hire a taxi for the afternoon and visit Saqqara. Their hotel concierge mentioned the Pyramid of Djoser was a must.

This was their first taste of ancient Egypt. As they wandered around the historical site, gaping at its wonder, two men approached them with camels. The girls assumed they were location guides. In very broken English they asked if they would like a photo taken sitting on the animals. Naively Emily handed over her camera, and the men hoisted them onto the camels' backs.

After some photos were taken and Mia thought they were done, she went to get off. One of men blocked her from dismounting. Panic began to rise in both the girls as the men mounted the camels, taking charge of their reins and quickly getting them into a gallop.

Mia could see Emily in front, whacking the Arab over the head, screaming for him to stop. But they didn't. As they continued into the desert, the girls could only see sand dunes surrounding them.

Suddenly, the camels were brought to a halt, and the girls were tossed off and onto the sand. They had no idea where they were or how far they had travelled.

'This was not in the itinerary', Emily's voice was raised with alarm.

The men dismounted, laughing, and speaking in their language. They clearly enjoyed the fright they had instilled. Then they started asking the girls for something, still in Arabic.

'What do they want?', Emily said with less alarm, realising that scaring them was part of the game and not wanting to give them the satisfaction.

Mia was trying to decipher what it was all about. One of the men started rubbing his thumb and two first fingers together.

'Money. You want money?', Mia exclaimed. The men looked puzzled. She reached into her wallet that was hidden under her clothes and tied around her waist. She pulled out a twenty pound note she had been carrying for an emergency. The men enthusiastically nodded, looking to Emily to do the same. She unwillingly followed Mia's lead and handed over cash.

The men seemed to be satisfied. They assisted the girls back onto the camels, returning them to the pyramid, where they politely helped them off and disappeared again. The terrifying ordeal was over.

As the girls sat in the hotel bar drinking a shot to calm their nerves, they were both perplexed. 'How many times a day do you think that happens? Thank goodness we only had a small amount of cash on us.' Mia was appreciative of the advice they had been given.

'I wonder what would have happened if we had no money on us?', Emily looked disturbed. 'And why didn't they just ask if we wanted a camel ride into the desert and back? I would have happily paid.'

Mia pondered for a minute, trying to rationalise the nightmare. 'It was all about the power. They got off on making us feel frightened and vulnerable. I've met men like that back home. Bad men. Hopefully we won't meet anymore.'

* * *

The girls started their tour the next day and enjoyed the rest of their time in the safety of numbers. They delighted in all things you would expect from Egypt, shopping in the Cairo bizarre, Tutankhamen's treasures in the museum, the Sphinx, the Giza pyramids, the Valley of the Kings and Queens, the Luxor temple and, finally, a felucca ride down the Nile, to Aswan.

On the last night they spoke with their tour guide about what had happened at Saqqara. He verified that it happened all the time and that the men did it to make extra money. 'It's just their way.'

Although knowing it happened regularly took some of the sting out of how they were feeling, they did remain a little traumatised by what had happened. They hoped that one day they would consider it just an interesting story to tell.

Chapter 15

February 1990

Mia had been in England twelve months and Emily suggested they mark the anniversary with a trip to Scotland. On telling the regulars of The Churchill Arms where they were heading, everyone said, 'You've got to go to Skye. It is the best highland experience in the country.' So, they decided that's where they would aim for.

They hired a car and headed north for ten days. They didn't book any accommodation, giving them freedom to stop wherever they wanted. On the way, they enjoyed Edinburgh and a place near Loch Ness called Drumnadrochit, overnighting in both. But they were keen to get to Skye to see what all the hype was about.

And it didn't disappoint. The ferry ride from the mainland to the east side of the island, flaunted dramatic mountain scenery. The girls arrived in Portree, the Isle's capital, and headed to the local bakery to indulge themselves with pastries and coffees as they looked over the area's map.

Portree seemed adorable but they spotted a smaller village on the west coast called Dunvegan and decided to head there. 'It's a little more remote and maybe not as busy,' Emily deduced.

It was a half an hour drive of rolling moorlands, filled with highland cattle and the legendary heather bushes, bloomless at that time, because of the harsh winter climate. The winding road was narrow, with hardly any oncoming traffic.

They passed Dunvegan Castle just before arriving in town, and in unison agreed they must visit there during their stay.

As they drove into the village, they found a scattering of homes, a bakery, a few offerings of accommodation and, of course, a pub. It was lunchtime, so they decided this would be a good place to make some enquiries.

They entered the bar, which was quite small compared to what they were used to in London. There was a door to the right that led to a separate games room where Mia could see a snooker table and darts board. The bar itself was only long enough to seat half a dozen people but was abundantly stocked with rare, top quality, single malt whiskeys. There were two customers sitting on barstools, chatting to the bartender, and Mia's attention turned promptly to him. 'Is he wearing a kilt?', she quietly whispered to Emily.

'I believe he is.' Emily grinned at the spectacle, as the young man behind the bar noticed them.

'What would you be having then?', he asked, inviting the girls to come closer. His accent was so thick, the girls only just managed to fathom his question.

Mia stepped up to the bar. 'Two scotches with coke thanks.'

His face turned very serious. 'You mean whiskey, wee lassie?'

'Oh yes, of course. Yes, that's what I meant.' Mia was a little embarrassed.

'Well then, there will be no coke with that. And the first ones are on me.' His face returned to beaming sassiness.

Straight whiskey at lunchtime. Mia looked at Emily for back up. 'The man obviously knows what he is doing,' Emily good-naturedly consented.

'Where are you from?', he continued, pouring their first shots.

Now standing at the side of Mia, Emily replied, 'London. Well, that's where I'm from. This one is an import from Australia.' Emily affectionately putting her arm around Mia.

'Australia! Now that is a long way to come. How long are you here for?', the barkeep was curious.

'A few days. We haven't got any accommodation sorted. Do you know where we could stay while we're here?', Mia queried.

'Ewan do you think you could pour me a drink and flirt at the same time,' one of the patrons jested.

As Ewan tended to the local's request, he addressed Mia, 'We have some rooms upstairs. One has two single beds if you girls want to share. Why don't you enjoy your free dram, and I will show you after that?'

* * *

The room was exactly what they needed. After checking in and cleaning up, the girls headed back downstairs for a second round of whiskey. It was freezing and wet out, so they decided to explore tomorrow. They were tired from their drive, so electing to stay in for the rest of the afternoon and night, seemed sensible. The fire in the bar was warm and inviting, and the layers of clothing they had needed earlier, had been left upstairs.

It seemed word had got around that two young ladies were in the pub, one being Australian, as the curious locals came to survey and share their generous hospitality with them. The remoteness of this small community hadn't seen a lot of guests from Downunder and Mia was like a rare creature from a distant land.

The whiskey shouts kept coming all afternoon, and they were both feeling a little drunk. They decided to treat themselves to the fresh fish on the pub menu, for an early dinner. They had found a table in the games room, and were enjoying their meal, when a large group of young men arrived in the bar, making quite the ruckus.

Ewan quickly ducked his head in and asked, 'You lassies, okay? The local football team have just finished training so I might be a while.'

Emily looked up, 'Thanks Ewan. It's probably a good thing we have a break from the drink. The fish is lovely.'

After their plates had been cleared, and they were taking their time going back into the bar, a few of the footballers came into the games room. One of them caught Mia's eye. 'Would you mind if we had a game of snooker?', he asked politely.

Mia answered, 'Not at all,' she gestured toward the games table. 'Do you mind if we stay and watch? People have been buying us shots of whiskey all afternoon and we need a little sobering up.'

He moved toward them. 'Well, I must continue the generosity. Let me know when you're ready and I will get the next round.' He held out his hand and introduced himself, 'Angus.'

Mia felt instantly drawn to him. He was medium height but solidly built. Even though he was still in his training gear and slightly grubby, she could see he was ruggedly appealing with pale, clear skin and thick brown hair. His light-coloured eyes were kind.

'Mi...,' she started.

'A, and Emily', he finished Mia's introductions. 'Yes, I know. The town have been talking about you since you arrived. You're Australian? I can't believe you've come to Dunvegan. Most of your lot stop at Portree, and we never get the chance to know about where you come from. I'm really interested.'

'Angus, it's your shot,' a fellow snooker player called.

Angus rolled his eyes. 'Please excuse me while I play this game. Hopefully you'll be ready for a drink by the time I'm finished, and you can tell me all about yourselves.' His eyes fixed on Mia until she nodded.

By the time they sat back in the bar, it had quietened. The odd drinker would come in but for most of the time, it was just the four of them. Mia did most of the talking as Angus and Ewan fired questions about kangaroos and koalas, beautiful beaches and the vast outback.

Before they knew it, it was midnight. Ewan was looking tired. The bar hours were usually 10am-10pm, so he had done an extra-long day. He started tidying the glasses and cleaning down the service areas as a subtle indication he was ready to leave.

Emily was also weary. 'I'm off to bed. Hopefully see you lads tomorrow.' She threw a sly wink at Mia and headed upstairs.

Mia and Angus were left looking at each other, not wanting to go anywhere. 'I'm playing football tomorrow night, just at the local park. Would you and Emily like to come and watch?', Angus attempted to lengthen the night just a little longer.

Before Mia could answer, Ewan said, 'I'm going Mia. I have the night off. I can take you and Emily to the game if you'd like.'

With a glint in her eye, Mia confirmed, 'I'll see you then.' She forced herself off her barstool, not looking away from Angus. He didn't move his gaze either. She took a deep breath and finally relinquished her fastening on him. As she headed up the stairs, she heard Angus laugh and say to Ewan, 'She's amazing.'

* * *

The girls spent the following day taking in some of the local attractions around Dunvegan, such as Eas Mòr waterfall and the lighthouse. Angus had asked for them not to go to the castle until he was free over the weekend. He wanted to be their personal tour guide.

When it was close to game time, Ewan met with them at the pub and escorted them to the field, arriving right on kick-off. It was bitterly cold, but the game was excitingly close, with Angus's team only just winning in the dying minutes.

After the game, Angus soon found them. Mia had only seen him looking scruffy the night before, so as he approached, showered and changed into his jeans and beautiful woollen jumper, her heart beat a little quicker with how attractive he was.

The warmth of the pub's fire soon called, and they found themselves in quite the crowd, being a Friday night. The girls resumed talking to everyone, but Mia and Angus continually caught each other's glance from across the room.

As the hoards thinned, Mia found herself under Angus's arm, leaning on the bar. 'I've been thinking about you all day,' he said, shyly.

She looked at him adoringly. 'Me too.'

As opposed to the previous night, Mia did a lot of the querying. Angus told her how his father had died when he was young, and that he still lived with his mum to look after her. He had a sister, who was married and had children.

Again, the four of them found themselves left in the bar. Emily gave Mia an indication they needed to leave, together. Although she really didn't want the night to end, Mia knew she would see Angus tomorrow, as it had been arranged all of them were going to the castle. After another lingering goodnight stare between them, Mia followed Emily up to their room.

They climbed into bed but neither of the girls were ready for sleep. A fair time had passed when Emily asked, 'Are you awake?'

'Yes. My mind won't stop,' Mia replied.

'Understandable. He is very dishy, but I feel I need to say something. You know men will love you wherever you go, right? Take your Greek God for example. He couldn't wait to wine and dine you and take you on a wild ride that had you high on life for weeks.'

Both the girls sniggered.

Emily continued, 'That's what a holiday romance should look like. And as soon as you left, he would have hit the repeat button and there would have been another, just like you.'

Mia smiled, not bothered by knowing Emily was right.

Emily's pragmatism restarted, 'But this looks to be a bit different. I don't think Angus has ever left this island, let only come across anyone like you. His heart seems open, undamaged, and he will probably trip into the love zone quickly. You may even feel things like that as well. But remember to be practical. The chances of him leaving the Highlands and his family are next to none. Especially with his mum on her own. And he may never meet anyone like you again. Just don't do too much damage.'

Mia chewed over what Emily had said. *This does feel different. I feel adored without sex being his agenda.'* She went to sleep knowing this was something new.

* * *

The four of them spent the weekend together. They finally got to Dunvegan castle, sitting high above sea level, and learnt it's MacLeod Clan history. The lads also took them to a dance in Portree on Saturday night, where they Highland jigged until the early hours. There were more locals to talk to, but Mia didn't move far from Angus.

Their connection intensified. He took any opportunity to pull her close and look at her with deep tenderness. It made her feel treasured; precious to him. But he never went beyond this simple affection.

On the Monday night, Angus came to the bar late. He seemed excited as he hugged Mia. 'I stayed back so I could finish a job ahead of time. In the morning, I've got a few things to do but I'm free tomorrow afternoon. Would you like to have some time together, just the two of us?'

Mia looked to Emily for any objection, who just smiled, knowing she had said all she could to forewarn of the inevitable hurt of leaving. Tomorrow would be their last full day.

The following afternoon, the sun was shining but the air crisp. Angus picked Mia up and headed to the Dunvegan gardens, near the castle. They sat close together on a bench and Angus wrapped them up in a huge, warm blanket, that cocooned their body heat. He produced some pastries from the bakery, a thermos of hot water and a small bottle of whiskey.

As they spent these surreal hours together, the physical attraction purred quietly in the background, without any hint of an impending seduction. Charisma dripped from Angus, through his tender, yet strong character, as he opened his heart and shared his rich spirit. There was nothing awkward about being together, and Mia was blissful, sipping on her moderated, hot toddy, and being alone with him. He made her feel so secure; she crept out from behind her protecting pretence and unmasked her true self. She unpacked her heart and allowed herself to fall in love, just a little.

It was dark by the time they got back to the pub. They sat in the car looking at each other in silence, not wanting to leave the world of just the two of them. Angus grabbed Mia's hand and continued to hold it in his lap. 'I will never forget you, Mia.'

'Nor me you,' she said softly.

* * *

He didn't let go of her hand for the rest of the night. They sat quietly, reflecting on how special their meeting had been. Mia initiated their goodnight this time, and Emily could see she was struggling at the thought of the goodbye.

Once everyone else had had their "nice to meet you" moments, they all disappeared, leaving Mia and Angus to say theirs.

'We'll write then. Stay in touch,' Angus clutched.

'Of course,' Mia grappled to find something else to say but found nothing.

He edged closer to her with his eyes asking permission. She spontaneously leant up to meet his mouth, where they feverishly kissed, knowing there would never be another time.

This was so different. It was the first time Mia felt her soul being touched. Angus's wholesome tenderness made her feel special, and she knew she would never be the same again.

Just before she lost herself too much, Mia slowly left Angus's lips. She lovingly reached for his hand. 'Please don't come to say goodbye again in the morning. This is too hard.'

Angus nodded, as they unravelled their connection, and she started to ascend the stairs.

He went back into where Ewan was discreetly tidying an already clean bar. Mia stopped on the steps, in two minds whether she wanted to leave it at that glorious kiss.

She heard Ewan say, 'That's it then? Are you sure? What I just caught an eyeful of should not be left there. There is a spare room upstairs if you want it?'

'I can't Ewan. I'm so entangled as it is. If I get any closer, I don't think I would be able to let her go,' Angus said sweetly.

Mia quietly kept moving, so the lads wouldn't know she'd heard.

As she laid in bed, tears welled. This release was hard. She believed if their geographical situation was different, Angus could have been a potential someone for her.

But Emily had been right. To permanently try to fit in each other's world, would break the spell. This is where it needed to end.

* * *

The girls packed up and went to the car early. As Mia went to get in, she noticed under the windscreen wiper, a preserved piece of heather and a note...

The further they got from Skye; the less tears fell. Mia was so thankful she had met Angus. Even in the short time together, he had opened something in her that could no longer be shut off. He had given her confidence that she was worth adoring, without offering herself physically. He had given her a point of reference regarding chivalry, courtesy and respect and she was closer to knowing what she wanted from her someone.

Chapter 16

True to his word, Angus did write. They exchanged letters, mainly about the happenings in each other's lives. This confirmed for Mia that not a lot happened on Skye or in Angus's daily life. She realised that as amazing as Angus was, Skye itself would never offer enough for her to stay and be happy; and this stopped any temptation she had to trip back up there.

Since the Scottish trip, Mia had noticed that Nick, The Churchill Arms manager, had been acting differently. He was clumsy and nervous around her, like a boy with a crush. He was aware that she had almost fallen for someone on their latest trip, and she wondered if this had prompted him to think he could be a potential suitor. She had never given him any reason to think so and, he certainly wasn't her type. He often came across entitled and arrogant, and now with his awkwardness, he was even further from the mark.

But he had become very agreeable and obliging to whatever Mia asked for, including time off. Over the next couple of months, Mia did two quick tours to the continent. Both of which gave her the highlights of a handful of countries over ten days. It was enough to give her a taste of each nation, so in the future, she could select those to revisit. She valued all of what she was experiencing, but she had started to miss home more and more.

June 1990

Emily suggested their next adventure should be a four-day tour to Jerusalem, where they would visit the mesmerising features of the city with a history professor as their guide.

Mia initially expressed some apprehensions, but Emily knew how to offset them. 'When we've finished there, we can catch a ferry from Haifa to Rhodes.'

She waited for the information to sink in with Mia. Emily then changed her tone to pure sarcasm, 'Hard to take that, thirty-eight hours cruising on the Mediterranean to a destination we are in love with.' Mia smiled at the thought and before she could think twice, she was nodding profusely.

* * *

After landing in Jerusalem, the girls met their guide, Nathaniel. He had grown up on a kibbutz but never confirmed his faith. He was well versed in all sects that were part of this city's complicated living set up.

In the four days, Mia and Emily were treated to all aspects of 'The Old City', Jewish, Christian, Muslim and Armenian. They saw the Wailing Wall, The Garden of Gethsemane and the Church of the Holy Sepulchre. They walked the way of the cross, and visited the Muslim and Armenian quarters, observing different faiths and ways of life. It was fascinating.

They did feel safe but could also feel the tension simmering just beneath the surface. No sudden movements, or calm would soon become chaos. Everywhere there were beautiful looking young people, male and female appearing peaceful enough, but carrying serious weaponry, like Mia and Emily would carry handbags. This was one of many differences in their worlds.

* * *

Leaving the Holy Land, and all its complexities, the travellers found themselves powering through the twinkling, cobalt sea, towards Rhodes and Lindos. It was over a year since their last visit, and Mia started deciphering how she felt about seeing Petros.

'Yes, undeniably excited about seeing him. He may not remember me. I'm sure there have been many others since I was there. Would that bother me?'

'Umm... not really.'

'Am I interested in sleeping with him this time?

'Again... not really.'

'Hang on! When did a night of simple sex become uninteresting?'

'When someone showed me there is so much more.'

The ferry docked at Rhodes port with its historical buildings impressively guarding the old town. The girls hadn't seen this last time as they had flown in and out of the airport.

As the crowd of disembarking vacationers started to thin, and the girls drew closer to the taxi rank, they spotted Nick, waving at them in his overly bright, floral shirt and exposed legs that hadn't seen sun in decades. 'What is he doing here?', Mia was irritated.

'Not sure,' Emily said, not so irritated.

He walked towards them. 'Hi girls. I thought I'd join you here. You kept saying how good Rhodes is, so I decided to see for myself. I haven't been abroad for years.'

He kept trying to warm them to his unexpected arrival. 'I've hired a car so we can explore the island over the next few days. I know last time you were stuck in Lindos. Won't it be great to get out and see the rest of it?'

'We weren't stuck in Lindos Nick, but the car is thoughtful,' Mia tried to hide her irritation.

Emily followed with. 'I'm glad you've taken a break.'

'The car is this way,' he said as he turned, assuming the girls would follow. Mia rolled her eyes at Emily, who smiled and shrugged her shoulders.

As they drove toward Lindos in the open-aired jeep, the girls began to get used to the idea that he was there. Emily talked to him about what they had seen in Jerusalem as Mia worked on containing her annoyance. It wasn't long before they were starting on the incline, leading to the crest before their destination. Mia instructed Nick that he needed to pull over at the top so he could take in the vision of the place.

As the three of them admired the panorama, the girls could tell he was impressed, even though his reaction was in his own reserved, indifferent way. Mia and Emily couldn't help but remember the first time they had seen this view and were still moved by its beauty.

When they got to the village terminus, Nick talked with some of the taxi drivers about where to park the car. It was only a short distance away, but the girls let him do it on his own.

As they stood, waiting for him to rejoin them, Minus, their taxi driver from the first time, waved to them from across the way. Emily sounded amazed, 'He remembers us.'

'Well of course he does. We're unforgettable,' Mia jested, secretly hoping Petros would also remember them.

The threesome went back to where the girls stayed last time. The same woman appeared in the courtyard, smiling at the girls in recognition. Somehow, even with broken communication, she managed to understand they needed two rooms, one for Nick and one for themselves to share, which she was able to provide.

By the time they settled in and freshened up, it was time to pick a restaurant for dinner. Mia deliberately led them towards where Petros worked, so she could inconspicuously have a look to see if he was there. Nick had no idea of Petros's existence.

As they slowly glided by, there was no sign of him. Mia felt disappointment, but knew they had a couple of days to find him, so the group kept moving and settled on another place to dine.

They ate glorious Greek cuisine and had too much wine before they went dancing in one of the bars that the girls had frequented last time.

It was late when they were walking home, and Nick was making no sense. He tried to grab Mia's hand, but she quickly pulled it away and evaded eye contact.

 When they got to their courtyard, Nick mumbled, 'Mia,' and staggered towards the girl's door.

'Go to bed Nick,' Mia quickly rebuked, and Emily led him to his door, helping him inside.

* * *

The next day, Nick had planned a long day of sightseeing around the island. Mia insisted Emily sit in the front with him. After last night she was sure that her suspicions of his new fondness for her were correct. Mia had a fun day, seeing all the things they hadn't seen the first time around, but she was a little uncomfortable. She was grateful to Emily who seemed to perceive the situation and ran interference when she thought it was needed.

On returning to their villa, the girls decided they needed an afternoon rest before dinner, and Nick decided to go and have a look at the local wares on offer. Just as the girls were nodding off, there was a knock at the door. Mia sprang up thinking it was Nick, ready to give him a snippy word or two.

Her heart jumped. It was Petros, looking as striking as she remembered. He threw his arms around her, twirling her out of the doorway and into the courtyard. 'Kangaroo, you came back. How wonderful it is to see you. I heard you had arrived. I went to the beach today to find you, but you were not there.'

Mia was trying to catch her breath. 'It's great to see you too. I went sightseeing today, around the island. How did you find me?'

'Lindos is very small. I tell you this before. Minus told me he saw you yesterday and I hoped you came back to where you stayed last time. And here you are. I am so happy to see you Kangaroo.'

'Is everything okay here?' Mia was so blindsided by Petros's appearance, she hadn't heard Nick come back in.

'Yes, I'm fine Nick,' she curtly responded, not taking her eyes off Petros as she glowed with joy. But Petros's face turned very serious. He was no longer smiling, as he turned to look at Nick. Nick could feel the barbs being shot out of Petros's eyes and disappeared into his room.

'An Englishman. You brought an Englishman with you?', Petros's question dripped with distaste.

'Not by choice Petros, I swear. It's a long story.'

Petros's face softened again. 'I am working until late tonight, but I may see you tomorrow. At the beach?', he asked.

'I would like that very much,' Mia smiled. 'See you then.'

She went to her room and found Emily sitting up in bed, smirking. 'I told you, Greek boys like you better when you're single.' She had obviously heard the dialogue outside.

Mia completely ignored the reference to Petros's attitude and instead whined, 'What am I going to do about Nick? I think he may have designs on some sort of romance with me.'

'And you're definitely not interested?', Emily tone was insistent for Mia not to be flippant with her answer.

Mia was adamant, 'Absolutely not. I don't find him even a bit attractive. There are times, I'm not sure I even like him.'

The girls were silent for a while. Then Mia quietly said, 'Em, I think it's time for me to go home. I mean Australia. Something has changed and I have this urge to start a real life back there; find a proper job and buy a house,' Mia's voice trailed off.

'Well then, we better make the time we have left a blast, if it's going to be the last of us travelling together. Don't worry about Nick. I'll sort him out. In fact, I'll pop my head in and see if he's okay. I'll tell him he can pick the restaurant tonight.' Emily was up and gone next door before Mia could thank her.

* * *

As they were all lying on the beach the next day, Mia was on the lookout for Petros. Nick had been a bit sulky since the afternoon before, but Emily was doing her best to distract him, and he seemed to be enjoying her attention.

It was getting close to midday, and Nick and Emily's fair skin had started to turn pink. When Nick finally gave in, and said he was retreating to find some lunch, Emily decided to go with him, leaving Mia alone on the beach.

It seemed, this was what Petros had been waiting for. He emerged from a group that had been playing in the water, a short distance away. Mia was sure this was on purpose, as it gave him a chance to saunter toward her, and all she could do was watch. His exposed, beefy chest was puffed out, and his tight black football shorts were wet and clinging. His olive skin was glistening with water beads, and his thigh muscles tensed and relaxed with every footstep. He reminded her of a prancing stallion showing off his magnificence.

As he got closer, his pearly white teeth flashed an enticing smile, that made her pulse race. He playfully shook his head, letting the droplets of water sprinkle her with coolness and she squealed with pleasure. He then dropped to the sand, to lay beside her.

'Kangaroo, you look exceptionally beautiful today. Shall we go for a bike ride tonight and I will show you... more.' Petros moved his hand to Mia's knee then slowly stroked her thigh.

'I wonder if Greek boys do a whole subject on seduction at school or is this just part of their DNA?'

She looked at his hopeful, beautiful face. But as alluring as he was, without a twitch she was able to say, 'I don't think so Petros.'

His face changed instantly.

'I bet you don't hear that very often.'

'But why not Kangaroo? Please tell me this has nothing to do with the Englishman?'

'It has nothing to do with the Englishman.' Mia did see the irony in that it was about a Scotsman actually. Someone who made her feel she didn't need to be a physical conquest to feel adored. But she knew she could never explain that to Petros. His world was all about physical conquest.

'I'm leaving tomorrow, and I don't think I'll be back. I need you to know, the night we had together the last time I was here, will be something I will never forget, and just being in your company made it so special.' Mia spoke sincerely, hoping to reach beyond his surface pretention.

He looked momentarily touched by her words. Then, suddenly, he was on his feet. He knew Mia was no longer buying what he was selling.

'I don't believe you Kangaroo. You will be back. And next time, don't bring the Englishman. He smiled and started to walk off. Every couple of metres he'd turn and say, 'I will see you again one day', as if he needed to hear her compliance. He continued, increasing his volume the further away he got, until he vanished off the beach. And that was the last time Mia ever saw Petros.

* * *

That night, the standard practice ensued, dinner, way too many drinks, and dancing. Mia was having a quiet moment outside the bar when she felt Nick stagger up behind her. She turned to face him as he started to bumble through what seemed to be a well-rehearsed speech. 'Mia I really, really like you.'

Mia went to interrupt but Nick held up his hand. 'No, please let me finish. Emily has explained to me, that as much as you feel the same way, you are sensibly going to ignore your feelings because you need to return home very soon. I respect that but will always regret that we didn't get to explore our full potential.'

Now standing at the back of Nick, Emily was winking and signalling for Mia to just agree.

'Thank you. It's for the best.' Mia obeyed Emily's indications. Nick then teetered back to the bar to slam another drink.

Emily looked at Mia sheepishly, who burst out laughing. 'Sensibly ignore my feelings. What crack are you on Emily?'

Emily laughed too. 'This way, his ego is still in one piece, and you didn't have to tell him you weren't sure if you even liked him. He thinks you've acknowledged but painfully chosen to forgo the potential love of a lifetime.' Emily's witty sarcasm trickled through her words, as she battered her eyelashes at Mia.

Mia had grown to love Emily like a sister. She appreciated her friendship, realising her time overseas would have been a lot different without her. It was going to be hard to leave her.

'Besides "Heartbreaker", with you out of the way, he just may notice me.' Emily revealed a truth that Mia hadn't considered.

Mia raised her eyebrows, realising how blind she'd been. She threw her arms around Emily and softly spoke in her ear, 'Go on then, go get your Romeo. It's time we went home.'

And as Emily went inside to find Nick, Mia quietly thought to herself, 'And it's time I went home.'

Jack

Chapter 17

1991 – Mia's New Year's resolutions

Get a job with career potential

Move out

Be open to emotional connection

Within a couple of months of coming home, Mia secured a retail assistant job, selling and renting household appliances. Over time, her leadership potential was recognised, and she was soon promoted to store manager.

Elizabeth and Reg also married six months after she got home. They built a brand-new home together and Mia used this change of circumstances to move out and rent a unit by herself, not far from where they were living. She had grown a lot whilst overseas and needed her own space on her return.

It didn't take her long to be back in the dating circus ring. Like before she met Danny, she was enjoying multiple suitors, with no one particularly standing out. She was open to finding someone serious but hadn't forgotten how special Angus had made her feel and wasn't prepared to settle for anything less.

August 1993

Mia was sipping her coffee in the arrival's lounge of the International Airport, as she waited for Emily. It was over three years since she had left England and Emily had decided to come to Australia for a month's holiday. The girls had decided the end of winter was the best time, knowing most visitors struggle with the hot weather.

Finally, the doors opened and there was Emily pushing a trolley stacked with her suitcase, hand luggage and bags of duty-free alcohol. Mia raced to greet her, and the two girls became one with a tight embrace. 'I can't believe I'm here,' Emily exclaimed with excited disbelief.

'Me neither. How was the flight?', Mia asked.

'It's a bloody long way, isn't it?', Emily affirmed, and both girls laughed, overjoyed to be back in each other's company.

Mia detoured through the city before heading toward the northern suburbs and her unit. Emily had just enough time to shower and unpack before Elizabeth and Reg called in briefly to meet her. 'We've just popped in quickly to say welcome. We won't stay long as we're sure you girls have lots to catch up on,' Elizabeth declared.

Soon, the pair were left to relax on the couch and enjoy a glass of red. They spent hours catching up on everything else, but Nick. When Emily finally said his name, Mia could see the pain was still raw. 'What a waste of time,' Emily started. Mia had known it hadn't worked through the frequent letters she had received from her, but there had been no details as to why.

'Things progressed a little after you left. We spent more time together, as friends, sometimes going to the movies or walks in the park. Then one night he asked me to stay behind after he closed the bar. We got really drunk and ended up sleeping together,' Emily reflected.

'After that night, going to the pictures and walks in the park stopped, but having sex happened frequently, always with too much alcohol involved. I wanted more from him but when I said anything about it, he said he struggled with the relationship idea. I just let it keep going, hoping it would change.'

'And obviously it didn't,' Mia surmised.

'No. But there's more. About half a year ago, I found out he had a girlfriend, whom he'd been seeing for a while and now she's pregnant. I'm such a fool,' Emily berated herself.

Mia hugged her friend. 'No, you're not. Nick's the fool. Did you confront him?'

Emily started to cry. 'He said he'd never thought of me as girlfriend material and knew he should have stopped sleeping with me, but he loved the sex too much.

Mia questioned, 'And did it stop?'

'Yes. But he did try it on a couple more times, pleading "just one more time". The whole thing still makes me feel sick.

'Nothing like a good dose of moron to kill attraction,' Mia said.

'Anyway, the good thing is this mess made me decide to come here. I need some Aussie magic.'

A momentary silence fell whilst Emily gathered herself. Then suddenly she pulled herself away from Mia and said, 'What about you? How's the dating department for you?'

'It's been a bit dry. I've been on a couple of dates, met a couple of guys but nothing that's rocked my world. Maybe now that my wing woman is in town, I might get lucky. I'm taking you to a bar tomorrow night, where I used to work. Hopefully the love gods will be good to us both.

* * *

By the time the girls stepped into the bar, they were looking sharp and ready to play. The Hilton bar looked the same as when Mia worked there, but an acoustic guitarist now played in the back corner, which gave it a different feel to when the music used to play through the ceiling speakers. The soft strumming of the instrument's strings, accompanied by the melodic voice of its player, had drawn a musically appreciative crowd.

The pair decided to sit at a high table where they had a good view of their entertainer. Halfway through his second set and a couple of wines in, Emily leaned over to Mia and whispered, 'There's a guy across the room that keeps staring at us. Just casually glance to your left.'

Mia waited an appropriate length of time and scanned the room in the direction Emily had indicated. Emily looked too, and the subject in question raised his hand to his forehead and gestured like he was tipping an imaginary hat. The girls smiled and shyly turned back to the musician.

'He's cute,' Emily purred.

'Is he?' Mia wanted to sound like she hadn't noticed, as Emily seemed quite taken. He was tall and lean, with dark features. He had a soft-hearted look and an easy-going smile.

As soon as the set was finished, the stranger made his move over to the girls' table. He coyly approached. 'Hi, how do you like the music?', he asked, with a real interest in their responses.

In her eloquent English accent, Emily said, 'It's very enjoyable.'

'I'm Joe.' He held out his hand to shake Emily's.

'Emily,' she responded, glowing with attraction.

Joe turned to Mia to politely introduce himself, but she might as well not have been there. His focus went back to Emily. 'Do I hear an English accent?', Joe asked, perceptively.

'Yes, I'm here on holiday, staying at Mia's. We met a few years ago when she was travelling overseas,' Emily explained.

'Can I buy you girls a drink? I'd love to hear about England.'

'Yes please. Two house reds.' Emily couldn't get the words out fast enough, as Joe disappeared to the bar.

'Who is the exotic fascination now?', Mia said, grinning at her.

Emily's face was radiant, and the pain of the past was gone. 'I'm trying to curb my enthusiasm, but he's exactly what I imagined an Australian man to be like. In fact, I'm sure if I could order one, he'd show up.' Emily's wit never failed to make Mia laugh.

The three of them enjoyed hours of music and conversation. After Joe had exhausted his questions about Emily's life, Mia asked, 'What do you do Joe?'

'I'm a shearer. Do you know the Woolshed as you head to Mount Glorious?'

Mia nodded.

'I demonstrate shearing out there for tourists who don't have the real outback on their itineraries. They get a taste of Australian country life without having to leave the city. It's a bit lame, but it's a job and it's a break from the remote, shearing shed life.'

'Is that near your place Mia?', Emily asked hopefully.

'Yes,' Mia responded to Emily. Then she asked Joe, 'When are you working next?'

Joe was keen. 'Tomorrow afternoon. Show is at 2.00pm. Would you like to come and watch?'

'We'll be there,' Emily answered, knowing Mia would be supportive.

'Great. Now that I know I'll get to see you again, I should head home. I need to look good for tomorrow.' Joe winked at Emily.

He turned to Mia. 'It was lovely to meet you, Mia.'

He then faced Emily, who immediately stood up, reached her arms around his neck, and hugged him goodnight.

He softly kissed her cheek and added, 'See you tomorrow.'

Chapter 18

The girls arrived at the sprawling twenty-two acres that was known as The Australian Woolshed. They walked down a path that led to a gate, where they found Joe impatiently waiting for Emily's arrival. His dark brown eyes sparkled with excitement on seeing her and Mia could see Emily felt the same.

Joe was checking the admission tickets for his show and Emily opted to loiter with him. Mia decided to go and find them seats where the action was to take place. She was coming around a blind corner, heading for the auditorium doorway, when she smacked face first into the chest of a life force like no other.

'Whoa girl. What's your rush?' He grabbed her shoulders and steadied her. Mia stood back, looking into eyes that were the most beautiful colour green. They were so vibrant against his short, jet-black hair, and tanned face. He was dressed like Joe, shearing pants and a Jackie Howe singlet, that showed off his muscular upper body.

'I'm so sorry. I need to find the best seat,' Mia tried to recover.

He laughed. 'All the seats are pretty good. I hope you enjoy the show.' His smile dazzled her.

Mia felt frozen to the spot. She watched him as he walked toward Joe, and on reaching him, turn back to look at her. She saw him shake his head and laugh.

* * *

Emily joined Mia just as Joe arrived on stage. He introduced himself to the audience and started to explain about the different types of sheep found in Australia and what a shearer's life is like.

When the actual shearing demonstration was about to start, Joe introduced to the stage his good friend Jack. 'Now Jack thinks he's a bit of a gun shearer, so we're going to race each other to see who is the fastest.' Two sheep were then brought to the stage, and the two men went head-to-head, shearing off every bit of fleece.

It was so close, neither of the girls could tell who won. Mia didn't care. She couldn't take her eyes of Jack. After he had finished, he searched the crowd and looked pleased when he found her watching him. When their eyes met, she felt a strong magnetism to him, like she had never felt. He was certainly good looking, but it was more than that. Something beyond explanation.

'Now ladies and gentlemen, would you like to follow us outside, where Jack will show off our amazing sheepdogs.'

Outside, Mia watched Jack, stunned at his skills and his gentle control over the dogs. It was obvious, he was a man of the land. Frequently through the show he locked eyes with her and seemed to present his program just to her.

When it was all over, the onlookers were invited to enjoy other attractions the venue offered; wool spinning, the petting zoo, or feeding kangaroos and koalas. Jack vanished, taking care of the dogs after their performances.

Joe came to the girls and suggested they go back to the main auditorium and order a billy tea and damper bread for afternoon tea, then indicated he would join them at his first opportunity. He wanted to lock down the next time he was going to see Emily.

When he arrived, Mia sensed he needed to keep working. 'Joe, this is my home phone number. Please call whenever you want to touch base with Emily.' She handed him a piece of paper.

She went to leave to allow Joe and Emily some space, but firstly enquired, 'Ah Joe, is Jack single?'

Joe smirked, 'Freshly.'

As they started to walk to the carpark, Emily was informing Mia that Joe had to work that night but that he wanted to see her in the next couple of days. He was going to call to finalise the arrangements. Mia wasn't really listening. She was lost in the image of Jack's face and the powerful attraction she felt.

Then, she looked up and saw he was coming toward them. Her heart quickened as he stopped. 'I'm Jack. You must be Emily. Joe hasn't stopped talking about you.'

Then he turned to Mia but remained silent.

'Mia, the clumsy, corner crasher!' She tried to defuse the intensity between them but as their hands touched, she felt a shot of electricity pass through her body.

Jack laughed nervously. 'Yes, well, no injuries, thank goodness. I hope you had a good afternoon. Visit again,' he called over his shoulder as he kept moving.

Emily looked at Mia and knew her friend was very taken. 'Come on. We can ask Joe more when we see him next.'

Before disappearing into the carpark, Mia couldn't help but look back. A rush of exhilaration coursed through her when she saw Jack had stopped to watch her leave. He smiled at being caught, before he headed back into work.

'How am I going to get to see him again? Surely this isn't it?'

'Settle down. If it's meant to be, it'll happen,' she told herself.

In that moment, she tried to put things into perspective, but her soul knew Jack was going to change her life forever.

Chapter 19

Joe and Emily went to dinner the next night. Mia was surprised to see them back by 10.00pm, but very pleased when Joe decided to stay for a cup of tea to finish their night off. It was an opportunity to enquire about Jack.

'Joe, you said the other day that Jack was freshly single,' she asked directly, hoping he would offer some more details.

'Yes, I did.' Joe was cautious about telling her too much, obviously being discreet. They stared at each other, wondering who would break the silence first.

Joe finally cracked. 'It was clear the other day, you two connected, but Jack is gun shy about getting serious with anyone. He likes to feel free and loves his own company. It's going to have to be something super special to get him to consider any involvement. If you want to get close to him, you're going to have to be casual but exceptional all at once.'

Mia smiled. 'Sounds like a challenge.'

'Yes, it will be,' Joe smiled back. 'I will tell you he did mention he hadn't been able to shake you since you met. That's a big admission for Jack. So, I have an idea that will at least get you back in front of him... I will accidently leave my jacket here tonight. You'll decide to drop it to me tomorrow, around 12.30pm, when it just so happens the staff will be having lunch.'

'Thanks Joe,' she said gratefully, satisfied she would get to see Jack again.

* * *

As instructed, the two girls arrived at the Woolshed right on time. Joe had positioned the "jacket drop-off" at the shed door, so there was no missing they were there. It wasn't long before Jack came around the corner where they had first collided, and he instantly smiled at the sight of Mia.

As he approached, Mia stepped out of the conversation zone slightly, wanting to give him a chance to talk, one on one.

'Hi. You're not lining up for the show again?'

Mia smiled, 'No. Joe left his jacket at my place last night. We thought we'd drop it off in case he needed it.'

'That's thoughtful but it's twenty-five degrees. I don't think he's going to need it.' Jack more than suspected this was a set up.

Small talk ensued, but all Mia could focus on was the enigmatic energy running between them. It was beyond excitement and physical attraction. She felt an indescribable connection to him.

Mia decided to be courageous. 'Emily and I, and I'm sure Joe, will be going to The Hilton Bar on Friday night. There's a great musician that plays there nowadays. Would you like to join us?'

Jack seemed torn with how to respond, so took the option that gave him time to think. 'Sorry, I have something on but maybe another time.'

Mia was disappointed but tried to hide it. 'Yes, sure. Anyway, we'd better let you boys have some lunch. It was nice to see you again Jack.' Mia stood back, giving Jack an escape route, and Joe and Emily stepped aside to let him through the door. Mia was starting to think that what she was feeling could be one sided.

* * *

Over the next few weeks, Mia kept herself busy, taking Emily to all the attractions her home surrounds had to offer. But her thoughts of Jack were continuous, even though there had been nothing from him, not even through Joe.

As Emily's visit was coming to an end, predictably they decided to spend the final Friday night at The Hilton Bar. Joe joined them, after playing the perfect holiday romancer and wanting to savour their last instances together.

As the guitarist was nearly at the end of his first set, Mia felt an unusual warmth run through her. She looked to her left and there was Jack, leaning against the wall, sipping on a drink, intensely looking at her. 'Oh my,' she unintentionally uttered.

'Ha, he came,' was Joe's admission.

Without taking her eyes off Jack, Mia asked, 'You knew he was coming?'

'He said he might, but you never know with Jack. I didn't want to get your hopes up.' Joe waved for him to join them.

Through Mia's eyes, Jack glided across the room like some ethereal being. She took a sip on her wine and dosed herself with some reality, *'Remember, he's just a man.'*

Emily welcomed Jack with a friendly hello, as Joe embraced him. 'Nice to see you Jack,' Mia said, wanting to hug him too.

'I couldn't miss saying goodbye to you Emily.' He then looked at Mia and said, 'It's really nice to see you too.'

This was the first time Mia had seen him out of his shearer's gear. He wore his dark jeans well, with a tight, black shirt that showed off his toned, firm body. He was so attractive, but it was more than that drawing her to him.

'What would everyone like to drink?', Jack enquired.

'I know what the girls are drinking. I'll come with you to the bar.' Joe could see his friend's nerves needed settling.

'He came. That's encouraging,' Emily said reassuringly, knowing how interested Mia was. 'It'll be fine. But maybe stop with the puppy dog eyes. You should probably get to know him a bit better before you offer to have his children,' Emily joked.

Mia loved Emily's bluntness. That's what she needed to get her feet back on the ground.

After the boys got back to the table, Mia and Jack had calmed enough to try for some normal conversation. Mia found out he lived up the mountain near her, but was born in Victoria, where his mum still lived. He hadn't spoken with his dad in years, but he was close to his stepdad. They had a lot in common regarding their family dynamics, with one difference; Jack had a sister, who also lived locally.

The foursome enjoyed different topics of conversations throughout the evening, but by the end of the night, Mia and Jack found themselves swirling in each other's orbit, not wanting to go home. The bartender was putting stools on tables before Jack was the first to stand, indicating he was going. He went to Emily's side to say good-bye. Then he high-fived Joe, leaving Mia until last. She stood as he came to her.

'Hey, next Saturday night, there is a folk music event on up the mountain. Would you like to come up? It's just a bunch of local hippies playing, but they are always good value,' he asked.

'Yes. Definitely.'

'Great. I'll get your number off Joe and give you a call to let you know the rest of the details.'

Jack let his eyes express how he was feeling, and she felt the captivation between them. As he left, he gently touched her shoulder, and the same warm feeling his presence induced at the start of the night, ran through her body.

Chapter 20

Joe came to the unit to say his farewell. It had been the perfect holiday romance. Fondness. No heartbreak.

But at the airport, it got harder, as the two girls said goodbye. 'I'm glad you had such a good time.' Mia fought back tears.

'It's been the best. I need to go now before I decide to stay illegally.' Emily laughed through tears.

Then she got serious, 'Mia, be careful with Jack. Don't get your heart smashed.'

'I've got this,' Mia tried to reassure her friend. 'But whilst we're handing out care packages, maybe find yourself a new place to drink. Nick needs to be in your rear-view mirror.'

The girls had one final embrace, declaring they would miss each other, before Emily disappeared through the departure doors.

But Mia didn't have this at all. Jack was in her every thought. She hankered to be with him but was also terrified of how he made her feel. *It's like he's permanently etched himself on me.*

And when he phoned with the music night details, she felt instant relief, just from the sound of his voice.

'So, the gig is at Maiala National Park picnic area. Do you know it?', Jack asked. 'It'd be great if we could meet there, because I've volunteered to help set up.'

'Yes of course. But how will I find you? I'm assuming there will be more than just a few people going.'

'I will find you Mia, promise.' She felt him smile.

She drove through the winding turns to reach the top of the mountain. She parked the car and started to walk toward where she could hear the music. It was late afternoon, just before sunset. The September temperature was just perfect for an outdoor event, and she was brimming with anticipation.

From the official park entrance, she followed a path that led to a huge, sloped grass area, where people were sitting on picnic rugs, enjoying the entertainment. She stopped to see if she could find him, but of course she felt him first, as he came up behind her.

On reaching her, he didn't refrain from showing her how happy he was she was there. His hug was encompassing, and she dissolved into him, feeling respite finally in his presence. As he pulled back, he gently played with a strand of her hair. 'I'm so glad you came. Come on, we're over here.' He grabbed her hand and led her to their own blanket, with wine and cheese aplenty. The music was easy listening, with the volume just right to still hear each other talk. There were people all around them, but they were completely oblivious to anyone except each other.

It couldn't have been any more perfect. They were under a million stars, as the music danced in the air, allowing them to get lost in each other. Jack looked penetratingly into Mia's eyes as they talked, and Mia helplessly fell under his charm.

As the night was coming to an end, Jack said, 'I don't live far from here. Would you like to drop me home and come in for one last drink?' He clearly wasn't ready to let her go.

Following Jack's instructions, she drove them down a dirt driveway to a single standing log cabin. He informed her the main residence was further along and that the landlords had been kind to him, renting him this place at short notice.

Mia could smell the timber as she entered the small but well-kept space. There was a couch and a bed, a kitchenette and a small ensuite. Simple, but homely. The bed was neatly made, and the place was spotless.

'Are you always this tidy?' Mia was surprised that a single man would be this orderly.

'Clean house, clean mind, Ian always says.'

'Ian being your... stepdad.' Mia came to the right answer after mentally searching through their conversation they had at the bar. 'That bed is made neater than mine. Any words of wisdom on that?' She locked eyes on him.

His eyes smouldered as he looked back at her. 'It should always look inviting.' This was his first suggestive reference to Mia. She could feel the sexual tension starting to bubble, but it hadn't taken centre stage so far.

'Please take a seat. The couch would be the safest. I'll get us a drink.'

'Hold the reigns. He's tempting but don't turn this into a passing infatuation.'

She moved to the couch, taking in more details of the room. There was a guitar near his bed and a poster above it of an old American Indian with the Ten Indian Commandments listed. No television or phone.

Once Jack was relaxed, seated next to her, she asked, 'No television. How do you amuse yourself?'

'I read, listen to music, and play,' he said as he motioned toward the guitar. 'I taught myself by ear. I've never had a lesson and can't read music. I also muck around with creating pieces that I store in here.' He pointed to his head.

'I hope to hear them one day. And the Indian? Is there a special connection?'

'I can't explain why but I'm drawn to them. I read about their history and find it really moves me. Why do you ask?'

'I did art classes when I lived in London. I had pictures of Indian Chiefs popping in my mind, so I just kept drawing them. I'm sure my mentor thought I was mad.'

'Well, I hope to see them one day,' Jack said, confirming for her he wanted this to continue.

His hand crept towards hers as they quietly looked at each other, feeling their connection grow. Jack sighed in resignation. 'You know, before I met you, I'd sworn off women. I'd just got out of a long, unhealthy relationship, where I felt trapped. She was older than me and expected things to always go her way. So, I just did what I was told. I lost myself and, in the end, was so unhappy. I just wanted to feel free, so I left. I swore I was going to be on my own for a long time.'

Mia squeezed his hand a little tighter.

'But there is something here with us that has caught me by surprise. You're with me all the time, even when you're not. I couldn't walk away from you if I tried.'

Mia used her finger to gently soothe the frown that had appeared on his face. Her touch appeared to heal his conflictions and in a quiet, sweet voice she said, 'You're amazing. I will never try and change you. And if ever you feel trapped, you need to tell me.'

With his doubts melting and still tightly holding her hand, he asked, 'And what do you want?'

'Don't hide!'

'When I was younger, I had no clue who I was. I didn't know how to be honest about my feelings. I always played it cool, scared to be vulnerable and always protected myself emotionally.'

She paused, mentally encouraging herself to keep going. 'I have waited a long time for someone like you. I can feel how special this is too. I want to be totally open with you, even if this turns out to be nothing more than an extraordinary friendship.'

Jack leaned in slowly and tenderly kissed her lips. Mia returned with tantalising softness. After several minutes of blissfully enjoying each other's touches, they decided to slow things down.

'Friends ha?', Jack said, beaming at her.

'Always.' Mia needed it to be the basis between them, if she was going to feel emotionally safe. 'I'm going to go now. But feel free to watch me as I do.'

She may have had it in "go slow" mode, but her sensual side was still very much alive.

Chapter 21

And so it began, a series of "firsts" for Mia. She disregarded any charade she once used and leapt in, heart first.

She went back to work, putting any career aspirations on the back burner. Her entire focus was Jack.

At first, they tried to only see each other every second or third night, conscious their connection was already consuming. But Jack would always ring on the nights they weren't together, even though it meant him going to the main residence to do so.

That first month was all about old fashioned dating. Jack would pick her up to go and see live music or a movie. But Mia enjoyed being invited to Jack's for dinner the most. He would cook simple meals and play guitar after they ate, while she quietly soaked up his incomparable company. Her desire for him swelled with every passionate kiss, but she knew Jack needed to take the lead and he was taking his time.

October 1993

Jack worked the first weekend of every month. They had planned not to see each other until Sunday night, but on the Friday night when he phoned just after dinner, he asked, 'Please come up for dinner tomorrow night. I know I'm working Sunday, but I really want to see you.'

When she arrived, Jack greeted her at the door and kissed her so passionately, Mia struggled to catch her breath. He led her inside where she found the cabin full of candles and a temporary, small table had been set for dinner in the middle of the room.

'Dinner is almost ready. Take a seat,' he said, pulling out one of the chairs.

'This all looks beautiful.'

He bent down and kissed her again. 'No Mia, you're beautiful. I've just done a little redecorating.' He smiled his delicious smile and went back to cooking, nonchalantly saying, 'I know it's your birthday next weekend. I've planned a couple of surprises through the week because you need to be celebrated for more than just one day. Tonight is the first treat.'

As they sat eating, Mia could sense through Jack's telling gaze, tonight was going to be different.

One thing that wasn't different, was Jack's habit of never finishing first when they ate together. He would always leave a mouthful if he was ahead of her, only finishing after she was done. As he put his fork down, waiting for her to finish, she decided to ask why.

Jack's eyes glowed as he answered, 'It would be so wrong to finish first. I need to make sure that you are satisfied, before I allow myself final gratification.'

The peek of sexual reference caused Mia's arousal to rapidly accelerate, and her sensuality switched to "go". She undid her blouses' top button, revealing to Jack a small preview of her black lacy bra that was enhancing her full breasts. He moved to her, as their thirst for the other, increased. She swivelled to face him as he knelt in front of her, fervently kissing her. Then he moved his mouth to her neck, where he lightly nibbled, as she softly groaned with want. He gently wet her ear with his tongue and whispered, 'I can't wait anymore. I need to have you.'

Mia was like a puppet. He pulled her up from the chair and led her to the side of his bed. He slowly undressed her, touching every inch of her naked skin as he progressed. He momentarily appreciated the lacy undergarments, running his finger across the top of her panties, before they ended up on his floor.

She was completely bare, standing in front of him, while he softly ran his hands up and down her back and titillating her mouth with his lips.

She unfastened his jean's button and zipper, and explored what she found, slowly stroking his firmness. Jack moaned with desire. 'Easy Mia, you need to stop, or this will be over too quickly. Lie on the bed so I can look at you.'

She unashamedly lay on her back, completely vulnerable to him and he stood back, ogling at her inviting body.

He gradually stripped in front of her, so she could study every part of his masculinity, before he joined her so their naked bodies could entwine.

Jack took his time, caressing her in ways she hadn't been before. He fed her appetite for him, tenderly but passionately, discovering how to please her the most. It was a marathon of lovemaking, that lasted until the small hours of the morning, satisfying each other more than once.

* * *

When she woke, Jack was gone. She looked at her watch and realised he would have been at work for at least two hours. She looked at his pillow beside her and found a note...

Dearest Mia,

I'm watching you sleep as I write this and can't believe you're in my bed. I'm finding it hard to leave you and would like to stay and continue what we enjoyed last night. But I do have to work, and it won't be long before we are back with each other again.

Being alone is no longer an option for me. I'm yours.

Jack x

Mia thought she was going to explode as her heart was overflowing with love.

She floated through the day, pottering around her unit, whilst being lost in flash-back moments of the night before. By the afternoon, she felt like a junkie that needed a hit. She only came off the edge when she heard his car unexpectedly pull into her driveway after he'd finished work.

She opened the front door before he knocked. Nothing was said as they beamed at each other. Jack assertively moved forward, backing Mia up against the hallway wall. He pressed himself against her and seductively placed his lips on hers.

'Hi,' she managed to say after he relinquished her mouth.

'Hi,' he continued affectionately kissing her face. 'I just wanted to make sure you were okay after last night.'

'Last night? What happened last night?', Mia playfully asked.

Jack laughed, 'Wow, looks like I'm going to have to try harder.' He pressed himself against her and she could feel how hard he was.

'Are you coming in?' Mia was wishing he would.

'Sorry no. I have plans with some mountain friends tonight. But I'll call later, okay?'

As much as Jack's teasing exasperating her, she loved the effect it had on heightening her eagerness. She nodded, and he coolly got back in his car and drove away.

* * *

He rang at 9.00pm. 'How are you?'

'Wide awake. You?'

'Aroused also.' Jack shrewdly brought it back to precisely how he was feeling. 'My cabin smells of you, us, last night.'

Mia smiled at his lustful inference. She stayed silent.

'I think it's only fair that your bedroom should smell of me, us, tonight.'

Mia's body throbbed. *Do I make him wait a day or two; or do I just unequivocally surrender myself?'* It only took a second to realise there wasn't a choice.

'I'll leave the front door unlocked.'

Chapter 22

Jack kept his promise of spoiling her throughout the week. There was a music date, a movie date and a dinner date, sleeping together every night.

On the Thursday night he came with a present. 'I know it's a couple of days early, but I wanted to give you this tonight.'

Mia excitedly opened the gift, a set of pastels and a pad of paper. 'I want you to draw me one of your Indian Chiefs, so I can hang it in my cabin. Then, a part of you will always be with me.'

It was the most thoughtful gift she had ever received. 'Thank you. This is the best.' Her hug was full of gratitude.

He lifted his head from snuggling in her neck so he could see her face. 'So, let's talk about the weekend plan. In the early hours of Saturday morning, we're heading south. Before dawn, we will be partaking in an activity of great physical exertion, different to the one we have been treating ourselves to all week,' he cheekily smirked. 'That will remain a surprise until we get there. After that, we will head towards the coast, where a weekend love nest awaits.' He nuzzled into her ear and whispered, 'I plan on spoiling you in every way.'

* * *

After travelling a couple of hours, Jack parked his car at the base of Mt Warning. It was 4.00am on Saturday when he handed Mia a flashlight and arranged a small backpack on his back. She had never climbed anything like this before but was so excited for the challenge.

They kept a good pace to ensure they were on the top by sunrise. The final section of their climb consisted of pulling themselves by chains to the summit, which they managed to reach, just before the first of the sun's rays crept over the horizon.

They had the sacred space to themselves. They stood together as the morning shafts touched their faces, and they marvelled at the grandeur of the view, and of the moment. Jack moved behind Mia and wrapped her up in his arms. He kissed her head and tenderly said, 'Happy Birthday Mia'.

He broke his clinch to remove his backpack and produced a bottle of expensive sparkling wine and two glasses, handing her a glass once it was filled. He seemed very pleased with himself, and she couldn't imagine him ever being rivalled in her devotion.

'I love you, Mia. I know we're only beginning to get to know each other but I feel like I have known you a lifetime already. I can't imagine being without you. I love your touch, your soul, and the way you make me feel. I'm so in love with you; my heart feels like it is going to erupt.'

'I love you too, Jack. I feel how connected we are, in every way. You have my whole heart. Please be careful with it.'

'I promise I will.'

As they bound their souls together, Mia confidently believed, *'I've found him. My soulmate. I will never feel alone again. Nothing will ever tear us apart.'*

* * *

The euphoria seemed unbreakable. Mia introduced Jack to Elizabeth and Reg not long after her birthday. Elizabeth was taken with him right away, but Reg appeared to be reserving his judgement. Mia put that down to his cautious nature.

Jack also introduced Mia to his sister, Amy. She was a bit older than Jack, but they were obviously close.

February 1994

One evening, after dinner at Jack's, they were listening to some American Indian flute music, when he asked, 'Do you believe in reincarnation?'

'I believe it's plausible. Mum introduced the concept to me when I was quite young, and I'm more comfortable thinking my spirit has had many, interesting lifetimes, rather than growing a pair of wings and sitting on a cloud.'

Jack smiled at her comment. 'I believe in past lives. No doubt. I'm sure I've been an Indian. This music takes me to a place where I can feel myself as one. I'm living off the land, no complications. I love the sense of freedom it gives me. It's like my soul remembers. It's so real.'

'Maybe we were Indians together. It would explain the clarity of my visions I get for my drawings, and how instantly connected we were.' Mia loved the idea their time together may not be limited to this lifetime.

'I believe we've been together many lifetimes, and this won't be the last,' Jack said sincerely.

* * *

A few weeks later, on his birthday, Mia presented Jack a pastel drawing of an Indian Chief. 'His image came to me right after my birthday.'

Then she added, feigning a studious tone, 'I have researched and firmly believe this is a picture of Wovoka. He claimed to have prophetic vision and was quite an important spiritual leader.'

'I will treasure it forever,' Jack pledged.

Within a few weeks, he had it professionally framed and hung it over his bed.

October 1994

Twelve months after their first declaration of love, and on Mia's 25th birthday, Jack set up a blanket in a secluded spot by a creek, near his place. It was late on a Sunday afternoon, just before sunset, when they were enjoying a bottle of wine, and he handed her a card...

My special Mia,

Saying I love you doesn't come close to how I truly feel. Life is long and wherever it takes us, I know we will always share this unique connection and true love that only books and movies can hope to mimic.

I know we will continue to grow, with our hearts beating as one.

Happy birthday.

Yours always

Jack x

He handed her a present. 'It's not much but I want you to keep it with you always.'

After removing the paper, Mia found three pieces of leather that had been plaited, with a tiger eye gemstone secured at one end and two feathers at the other. 'I made it just before I met you. The tiger eye is supposed to promote mental clarity and uncloud emotions. I know it belongs to you. So, you'll always be clear about how much I love you.'

'Our "featherstone",' Mia named it. 'Thank you. I'll wrap it around my bedpost so it's the first and last thing I see every day.'

'Who needs diamonds?'

But Mia had started to think of marriage and children, and her dreams were framed around Jack wanting the same. She just assumed it would be the natural progression for them. Her naivety didn't allow her to consider their future's picture was very different, and some things, she just wouldn't be able to control.

Chapter 23

1995 – Mia's New Year's resolutions

Meet Jack's mum and stepdad

Buy a house

Get engaged (fingers crossed)

Their love affair continued down its heavenly track for nearly another year, without any talk of what the future looked like. Mia was lost in the fairytale and took for granted it would be like this forever. Jack had made her feel so secure, as she floated in a sea of his romantic gestures. Her heart was completely his, and she felt loved for everything she was.

Until one day, it just finished.

August 1995

A couple of months before her next birthday, Jack took Mia to meet his mum, Mary, and stepdad, Ian. It was a wonderful visit in his hometown, northeast of Melbourne. Mia spent the week getting to know them and she felt she fitted, like a hand in a glove.

On their final night, Mia and Mary went to bed, leaving the men to talk. Mia's eyes were closing when she over-heard Ian say, 'She's a special one Jack. Don't leave it too long before you make her yours, officially I mean. A young woman like that needs to know she's the one.'

'Yes, she's special, and she knows what she means to me. But I'm not sure if I'll ever want marriage.'

'You best make sure she's thinking the same. Don't lose her Jack. You'll regret it.'

Mia went to sleep believing it was Jack being private.

* * *

But when they got home, she noticed, something had changed. Firstly, Jack was a bit distracted. Then, he started to spend a couple of nights a week away from her, explaining work was getting him down and he needed some space. She was hoping it was just a bump in what had been their perfect coupling.

However, his retraction became more evident, and despair started to engulf Mia. It reminded her of Karl's behaviour right before he removed himself from her, and she desperately started to cling to the dream that had been her life the last two years.

She was never one to shy away from tough conversations. After a month of this slow withdrawal, she finally cracked. He had called in after work, with no intention of staying, when she asked, 'Jack, are you okay? Things feel different between us.'

He took a deep breath. 'Mia, I need to be honest with you. You know I love you and always will. But I think this is as far as we can go. I've never wanted to get married or have children and I know you probably do.'

'Not right now, but yes, one day. Maybe in time you will too.'

'No, I won't change my mind, and it would be selfish for me to stop you having the life you want. I've been trying to sort out my feelings over the last few weeks, but I just can't.'

'Jack this is ridiculous. We have plenty of time to work this out. We're meant to be together, aren't we?'

Jack's voice started to escalate in a way she had never heard. 'No. I don't think so anymore. I'll never want that life. I'm a shearer. I love moving on when I want to. That won't change.' He started to walk away.

131

'Jack stop.'

'No Mia, you stop.' Then he yelled, 'I feel trapped.'

And with those words, Mia's heart broke and she let him run.

She was bewildered. *'How can things change so quickly? We're in love. This can't be over. He just needs some space. We've never been able to stay away from each other for long. He'll be back in a couple of days, once his head's straight.'*

But a couple of days turned into over a week. Mia hadn't heard from him and her desperation grew. When she couldn't stand it any longer, she rang him at the Woolshed. 'Jack, I need to see you. Please come over this afternoon.' He agreed.

He stood in her doorway, shoulders slouched, looking defeated. She invited him in, but he defiantly stood in the doorway.

'Jack this can't be it. We're tied together, remember? There is no breaking it, even over lifetimes. What we have won't be found with anyone else. Please tell me you still feel the same.'

Jack kept his face somewhat hard. 'We'll always be connected, but that doesn't mean we should be together. You want a normal life of marriage, children, a house to play in and to stay in one spot. I want to be free, no one relying on me. I need to be able to pick up and go whenever I want. I've been doing that all my life. I'm not going to change. I don't want to change.'

'But I want you more than marriage and children.'

Jack said firmly, 'That's just how you feel now. But one day, you will want the marriage and children more. And I have no doubt there will be someone that will give you the life I can't. Initially, this will be hard but it's for the best. It's time to let this go.'

Mia was distraught after Jack left. She paced around not knowing what to do. She felt like half of her being had been sliced away. Her intuition guided her when she was incapable of thinking, and she drove to Elizabeth and Reg's house.

She collapsed into her mother's arms, as inconsolable agony poured out of her. Elizabeth listened intently to Mia's account of their whole relationship, from their special love and their belief of lifetimes together, to his final oration on freedom and what he now thinks is best for them – not to be together.

Elizabeth was trying to give some reasoning for his actions, but she struggled to articulate anything substantial, floundering in anger over the hurt Jack had caused.

Once Mia had depleted this first wave of distress, she noticed Reg sitting quietly, his hands folded in his lap and a look of contemplation on his face. 'Reg, what do you think? Does any of this make sense to you?'

Reg decided to give his honest interpretation. 'Jack is a rolling stone. He likes his life carefree with no responsibility. It may be his age, but personally, I think it's his character and he will never be any different. I have no doubt he loves you Mia, but he loves his lifestyle more. On one hand, I applaud him for letting you go, knowing you deserve a man who will give you everything you want. And on the other, I think he's weak for thinking he will find peace in his so-called freedom.'

'You never liked him, did you?', Mia questioned.

'He's okay, but he's not your other half. I know you can't even consider this right now, but there will be someone that makes you feel like Jack does, who will be better suited.'

Reg's words gave Mia some comfort. Her world was still swirling; however, they were an anchor to grab onto.

But the process would be slow. Mia became despondent, not able to work, and her heart ached. Her once perfect world had shattered without warning. She felt displaced and lost. She didn't want to go home, as there were too many memories, and decided to stay at Elizabeth and Reg's until she was no longer spiralling with grief.

After a week, she started to feel a bit stronger. Her mind and
heart were still fragile, but she wanted to try and get some of her
life back. Late one afternoon, she went back to her unit, only to
find Wovoka leaning on the front door, and a post-it note...

Mia,
I've decided to take some shearing work out west. I
don't want Wovoka to be damaged in my travels,
and I was hoping you would look after it for me.
I'm not sure how long I'll be gone. I thought it was
I good idea to start anew.
Take care of yourself.
Jack.

Her heart broke a little more and her mind splintered. *'He's
gone. Really gone. Fuck, I need a drink.'* She opened a bottle
of wine and didn't bother to pour it into a glass. She drank half
of it in no time.

*'Maybe he hasn't left yet. I might be able to change his mind, or
at least say goodbye.'* Mia's mind was racing, her thoughts
frenzied. She got in her car and drove to his place, taking the
rest of the bottle with her.

* * *

It was empty. He was gone, along with everything he owned.
There was no sign he had ever been there. Their life together
had vanished. She looked up at the darkening sky and
remembered the first night they had on the mountain. The
music festival, looking at the stars and the way they had felt just
being together.

'Those memories need to be packed up and labelled "Done".'

She sat on the front steps and finished the bottle, the hurt
convincing her she had meant nothing. All he had wanted was a
bit of fun while it suited him. And when he needed something
new, he just slinked away.

134

By the time she got back in her car, any care for herself was gone. She knew she shouldn't drive but her normal responsible nature had been replaced with reckless abandon.

As she drove down the mountain, through the U-turn switch backs, the emotional emptiness increased, and the unhealthy hopelessness started to pester.

'I really am worthless. I gave him everything I have, but it still wasn't enough.'

She went further down the black hole. *'Where do I go from here? There's nothing left. I just need to give up. Surrender to the pain. Drive off the edge, then it will all be over.'*

And for more than a moment, she thought it was the answer.

She didn't remember the rest of the drive to her mum's. 'I don't think I can survive this,' were her first words to her mum, as a second wave of gut-wrenching damage was emancipated. Her mind and heart completely shattered.

Elizabeth laid her in the spare bed and gave her a low dose relaxant to calm her nerves. Mia slept for two days.

The bedroom became her refuge. Mia couldn't bring herself to leave it. She had lost her trust in life and needed to isolate in this space that provided a small amount of solace. She couldn't eat as her stomach was doing backflips. She was trying to find some mental stability, but whenever her mind quietened to a place of limited sanity, her hurt voice would start again, *'He couldn't have loved me, or he wouldn't have walked away. How did my life change so quickly?'* She was trying to piece her mind and heart back together but, if she was a thousand-piece jigsaw, she was still looking for the border pieces to get started.

When the darkness would swallow her up, Elizabeth pulled her out by reminding her of Reg's words, 'Jack does love you, but the dream you have for your life is too big for him. I'm sure, he will be hurting too.'

Mia felt like a zombie. She didn't recognise herself in the mirror and her mind was full of scattered views. After a week, as she lay in her semi-conscious state, she could hear a male's voice in the lounge that wasn't Reg's. When there was a knock on her bedroom door, she sat herself up, trying to ground herself back to her surroundings.

Her hopes went straight to what would ease her pain. *'Could it be Jack? Could he have come to his senses, realising he has made a terrible mistake?'*

The door opened. 'Hey Champ.' Karl looked shocked at the state of her. 'Elizabeth tells me you want off the field. You've picked up your bat and ball and don't want to play anymore.' Karl was comfortable explaining life in sports references. 'What is this madness all about? It can't be that bad. Talk to me. I'm sure we can work it out.'

Mia started to cry again. Karl's concern prompted a touch of life through her numbness. He sat himself next to her, placing his arm protectively around her.

Elizabeth, who had been hovering in the hallway, closed the door, hoping her instinct to contact Karl would be the secret to help Mia patch herself back together.

Karl patiently listened to Mia's story, letting her cry when she needed. He recognised how differently she had given herself to this relationship and could understand why the emotional gymnastics had affected her so badly.

'There is no way he could have loved me, right?', Mia asked.

'I don't know the dude, so I can't say for sure. But if you're asking what I think could be the case, I think it's as simple as he said. He doesn't want the house and the kids. I think the thought of being in the one spot for too long makes him feel suffocated. He's a shearer. That should have been your first clue that normal life isn't for him.'

Karl paused, knowing his last comment sounded like he was irritated. He decided to soften his tone. 'Now, if you'd been some wild woman, happy to tag along with him all over the country, with no responsibility, we wouldn't be having this conversation. He'd still be here, or you'd be packing.'

'But what if I could be that woman.' Mia was still clutching at the making it work.

'But you're not. You do want to build a stable life with someone. Maybe have kids; live in a nice home not far from your family. Riding around on horseback with cow shit on your boots would only be charming for so long. Let's face it Mia, you would hate to smell like shit all day.' Karl was now trying to be funny.

Mia smiled for the first-time post Jack. Hearing Karl clearly spell it out, she knew she wouldn't be happy in the life Jack wants.

'You're trying to cookie-cut yourself into a shape that best suits him. Don't do that for anyone. Someone will love you exactly how you should be loved. When the right one comes, you won't have to give up much at all.'

'When did you become an expert?', Mia was surprised at Karl's insights.

'Just read about it the other day. Didn't think I'd ever need it, but here you are dragging stuff out of me that I had filed under "not useful".' Karl was still trying to lift her heaviness as he got up to leave.

'Thanks Karl. I do feel better.'

In a moment of unguarded sentiment, he turned to her and said, 'You are worth way more than the million sunsets or whatever he's convinced himself he needs out there on his own. But you need to believe that. Stop selling yourself short. Keep your eyes on what you want. Personally, I think he'll be back. If anything, he should be the one trying to fit in with you.'

And then in typical Karl fashion when things had become too serious, he added, 'And there is no need for you to ever smell like shit.'

Chapter 24

1996 – Mia's New Year's resolutions

Get back to work

Buy a house

Stop thinking about Jack

Mia slowly completed the jigsaw. Piece by piece, she resumed her life, still not feeling whole, but functioning.

She went back to work in the New Year. Her managers were understanding of her situation and realised she was too fragile to be dealing with the public. They offered her an executive support role in head office, where she was surrounded by good people who helped her focus on her professional future.

Needing to put her energy into something other than a relationship, she decided to buy her first home. It was a small house not far from her rental, which she was happy to leave behind with all its memories. Still not up for socialising, refurbing and redecorating became her focus, helping to dumb down the small, residual ache she still had.

But Jack was still with her. His spectre was diminished but still vaguely plagued her. She tried to leave their featherstone in the packing box, but it seems the lid wasn't on tight enough, and it made its way back around her bedpost.

She had been in her house a couple of months when his first letter arrived. Mia had given her new address to the incoming tenants of her old unit, so all her post eventually found her. As she opened it, she noticed there was no return address on the envelop...

> Dear Mia,
> I hope this letter finds you well. I've been drifting from station to station, still here in Queensland, and moving as I'm needed. The days are hot and long but I have grown used to being alone again and know that this life is where I belong. I'm sorry we left things the way we did. Now that I've had space to reflect, I want to tell you how much our time together meant. It has made me a better person, and I'll always treasure it.
> I hope you've come to understand that this is just who I am, and you did nothing wrong. You'll always be special to me, and I will carry a memory of you with me forever.
> I remember you saying once that we would be friends always. I hope you meant it.
> Jack.

The letter caused Mia's new mental steadiness some imbalance. His name without "Love" preceding it, caused a shot of pain to ricochet through her body, and the rest of its content set off a dissection of what it all meant. She knew these reactions meant she still wanted a different reality to the one she was living.

But once the agitation started to subside, she reminded herself, *'He wants to be friends and I did say that's what we would be, always. I need to remember what it was like to have no expectations of him. Everything else needs to be forgotten.'*

February 1997

As time went on, she did think of him less. It had been nearly eighteen months since she had seen him, and she accepted that her intermittent curiosity was natural, but she had finally locked away any hope of him ever loving her again.

One Saturday morning, she had some mulch delivered so she could freshen up her back yard gardens. She was placing shovel loads around her plants when the familiar warmth his presence usually evoked, ran through her.

'Ignore it! There is no way he's here.'

But the feeling intensified, until she finally turned around. Jack was standing at the back corner of the house, attentively watching her, not sure how welcome he would be. It took Mia a few minutes to register he was actually there. 'Jack,' she breathlessly uttered, with shock disbelief.

'Hello Mia,' he grinned. He was unexpectedly moved to tears when her eyes met his. 'I hope you don't mind me calling in, but I was passing through and thought I'd check in.'

She had two, parallel lines of thinking running in her head. One had her wanting to be completely non-responsive, turning her back on him. The second, had her running to him, declaring how much she missed him and still loved him.

She knew neither were viable. He already noticed her reaction to his presence; but she also couldn't go to him due to the armour she now wore, protecting herself. She needed to find somewhere in between.

Jack sensed her uneasiness. He tipped his head to one side and smoothly said, 'You did it. Well, I'm assuming you own it. Part of your dream is now reality. I'm happy for you.' He unconsciously moved toward her, vaguely gesturing he wanted to hug her.

'Thanks Jack.' Mia stepped away from his advance, disregarding the girl that worshipped him and pulling out her new independence. 'I'm finding a lot of peace making it mine. Life is good. How are you?'

He felt her matured strength and stopped before he got too close, restraining what was naturally re-emerging. 'Yes, I'm good. Tired. I got a bit restless out there and decided to go home to Mum and Ian for a while. Take a break. Thought I'd come via Brisbane to see friends.' He eyeballed her, 'Are we friends?'

Mia forced a half-smile. 'I believe I did say always.'

'I'm sorry I did a runner. I wasn't sure how to be. I was happy with you Mia, and struggled to walk away, but you don't belong in shearing sheds, being dragged all over the country; and I will always end up back there. The thought of settling in one place makes me hyperventilate. But it doesn't mean I don't miss you.'

Mia had so much to say but the words wouldn't come out. She moved towards the back stairs. 'I could use a glass of water. Coming in?'

'Actually, I need to keep rolling.' He was leaving sooner than he anticipated because seeing her was harder than he expected.

She smiled at the irony of his words, recalling Reg's 'rolling stone' opinion of Jack. *'And you always will be rolling.'*

Standing in front of each other, they weren't sure how to say good-bye. Their connection was still there, but they had just established they needed to be friends. Jack couldn't help but make his way to her and hugged her tightly. Mia's indifference melted away as soon as he touched her. She felt like she was breathing clean air for the first time in a long time.

'See ya,' Jack whispered. 'I'll write soon.' He struggled to step away from her but knew he needed to leave before he said something to confuse things even more.

As he started to walk away, Mia asked, 'How did you find me?'

'I went to your old place and the new tenants told me.' Then he stopped and turned back to face her. 'I'll always find you,' he said, with a wink and a beaming smile. A shard of hope escaped from Mia's guarded heart.

* * *

After his visit, Mia kept her life going but struggled to shake his shadow, until his second letter arrived...

Dear Mia,

It was so good to see you a couple of weeks ago. Life's been busy since I arrived at Mum's. I've been helping her, and Ian, do some small renovations around the place. I've also been doing a bit of woodturning, reading, and just feeling free. Even though I seem busy, I'm enjoying the break.

I'm so glad we can be friends. I've been thinking about how special our connection is and know it will always be there. But I still can't get my head wrapped around people wanting to spend their lives together permanently. Knowing how special you are to someone but being content on your own when you can't be with them, is where I'm at. Sorry, getting carried away with my thoughts.

Anyway, I'm sitting at the local Italian restaurant, enjoying writing to you, and thinking of the last time we saw each other. It is still fresh in my mind. I'll write again soon.

Your friend always,

Jack.

'*WTF Jack?*' Mia picked through his words.

Frustrated with what she interpreted as contradictions, she decided it was all too hard.

'*It doesn't matter how much I love him; it will never be enough. I need someone who really loves me. Someone who loves me to death.*'

She should have been more careful with what she wished for.

Devon

Chapter 25

1998 – Mia's New Year's resolutions

Stop being a hermit

Stop thinking about Jack

It had been nearly nine months since Jack's letter and her decision to move on, but Mia still wasn't socialising. Her heart was still mending, but it was no longer in constant agony.

Then a parcel arrived from Jack's mum, Mary...

Dear Mia,

We hope this finds you well. I guess you're busy working and enjoying your new home. I've sent this parcel up as a little gift for you to put towards it.

Ian and I are very upset to hear you, and Jack are no longer together. We feel we have lost the chance of knowing a wonderful girl, and we would have loved you to be part of our family. We don't think Jack knows what he wants.

We do wish you all the happiness you deserve.

Please stay in touch.

Lots of Love

Mary and Ian x

'He's let his mum and Ian know it's finished. No grey area left.'

Mary's gift was two exquisite glass vases and Mia loved them. She wrote a quick thank you note back, keeping it brief, but warm, not mentioning Jack at all.

As she was sealing the envelope, the phone rang. 'Hey Mia, it's Karl. There's a pre-season soccer game at a sporting club near you this afternoon. I'm going to watch if you'd like to join me?'

'Your timing's perfect Karl. What time's kick-off?'

'3.00pm. Let's stay for a drink after.'

'Perfect. See you then.'

For the first time in ages, Mia felt ready to go out. The afternoon would give her an opportunity to be with people, without having to go total party mode. And it wasn't far from home, so she could leave if she felt overwhelmed.

She arrived at the ground and found Karl sitting in the grandstand. A couple of guys from school were with him but he had left a spot for her to sit next to him. She felt comfortable being out and spending time with Karl. She also liked soccer. With Elizabeth being English, she grew up watching games on television. She understood its rules and was comfortable commentating on it, even in front of Karl, an avid soccer fan.

On the full-time whistle, the players came marching past into the change rooms. At the end of the line came the coaches. One of them stopped on seeing Karl and made his way to him.

'Good game Devon. You must be pleased with your team's performance.'

'Thanks Karl. They're training hard but the team cohesion is still developing. I suppose today was just like a training match and they should get better.'

'Devon, do you know Mia?'

'I do. Hi Mia. Remember, we went to primary school together for a couple of years. Looks like life is treating you well.'

'Of course. Nice to see you again after a million years.' Mia recalled a twelve-year-old Devon.

'I'm sorry to cut this short but I best go and do the team de-brief. See you both in the bar?'

Karl and Mia nodded as Devon left for the after-game dissection.

Up in the bar, Karl bought Mia a drink and nestled them onto a slightly removed table from where the after-match crowd were gathering. She sensed there was something he wanted to talk about, so she limited her chatter, allowing him space to do so.

'I've met someone,' Karl announced, unusually coy.

Mia raised her eyebrow in curiosity. She was surprised, as Karl tended to date multiple girls at once, and his love life resembled that of a confirmed bachelor. For him to mention anything, she must be someone special.

'I'm not sure what's happening. I'm not myself. I feel like ringing her all the time because I miss her, and then I feel a bit giddy when I'm with her. I haven't felt like this before and I'm not sure I like it.'

'The boy is growing up,' Mia said, like a proud parent. 'Sounds like you're on the hook Karl.'

'But I'm not sure I want to be.'

'I'm not sure you can control that. You're normally on before you know it. Besides, it'll be good for you to do something different to your usual shallow liaisons. You're getting too old to be juggling multiple women. It's starting to take a toll on your complexion.' Mia ended her advice with some humorous banter. Karl would expect nothing else.

'Hey guys, am I interrupting?'

'Not at all Devon. I was just discussing some skincare tips with Karl,' Mia continued her whippy jesting.

Karl playfully snarled at her and asked, 'Another drink?'

She nodded.

As Karl went to the bar, Devon pulled up a chair. 'So, what brings you to the soccer?'

'Karl asked me to join him. I thought it was a great way to spend a Saturday afternoon.'

'You like the game then?'

'Yes, I do. My mum's English, so I've grown up watching it. Big Manchester United fan.'

'Well, this will have to be our last drink together. I'm a huge Liverpool fan.'

'Maybe you should go before the next sip then.' Mia delivered the line with a straight face. Then they both smiled.

'Remember grade seven?', Devon asked. I remember the day about fifteen of us were invited to your place for a swim. I thought you were the coolest girl I'd ever met. If I'm being completely honest, I had a major crush on you all year. It broke my heart when my mother told me we were moving.'

'Ah, that was a long time ago and I'm not so cool these days.' Mia was slightly embarrassed with Devon's confession.

'Not that long and I've never forgotten that very cool girl.'

'Is he flirting with me?'

'Hey Devon,' a weak, female voice sounded behind him.

'Oh, Tracey.' Devon got up from his seat and kissed her hello. 'Mia, this is Tracey, my girlfriend.' He then addressed Tracey, 'We had a couple of years at school together.'

Mia held out her hand offering a strong grip and vivacious 'Hi'. She received a limp handshake back and barely a mutter.

'Girlfriend. Good. He mustn't have been flirting.'

'Hope to see you again Mia. Soon,' Devon chimed, leading Tracey away.

When Karl returned, Mia asked, 'How do you know Devon?'

'I've played soccer with him over the years, but I don't know him that well. Rumour is the state soccer executives believe he has a promising future as a professional coach. Why?'

'Just curious. Not sure how to take him. I thought he was flirting with me five seconds before his girlfriend showed up. I must have read it wrong. I suppose that's what happens when you decide to be a recluse for a couple of years; you become out of touch socially.'

'I think your being a bit hard on yourself. I bet he was flirting with you. You are very flirt-worthy Miss Mia. Besides, she's just a girlfriend, not his wife.'

'Seriously Karl. You may need to tweak some of your thinking, or you're going to find yourself released off that hook before you know it.'

Chapter 26

From that day, Mia's capacity to enjoy life again, began to increase. Her recent recovery period had seen her only just functioning; existing in a flatline state. She was now ready to get back to experiencing life's stimulations.

Workwise she decided to challenge herself, starting a new job. She initially applied for a data entry role with a large motor vehicle company, but her undersold skills were quickly recognised, and she found herself working with consultants on a storage logistics project. Her work team were patient and supportive, and Mia could feel her career developing.

But she felt sceptical when it came to finding a new mate. She had been so sure that she had found her person in Jack, that she was now mystified as to what she was searching for. She felt deluded about what she had perceived love to be and convinced herself she was naive to seek the fairytale. She felt it was safer to look for someone who wanted the same things as her, and hopefully she would fall in love because of shared aspirations. Her heart was locked in fear.

* * *

As the season began, Karl kept pulling Mia to the soccer matches. She would stay after the games and had started to mingle with some of Devon's players, even accepting coffee date invitations from a few. As none of them even mildly lifted her heartrate, Mia thought of these as just opportunities to touch up her social skills.

Devon would always make a point of finding her after the game. One evening, when the two of them had been left to talk, he queried her, 'Can I ask where you're at Mia?'

'What do you mean?'

'At the start I thought you and Karl were an item. But then I hear some of my single boys talking about having coffee with you, and they all seem to be vying for your attention. So, as a concerned coach, I'm wondering if you could clear up my confusion,' Devon said, smiling.

'Ah, Karl and I get that a lot. No, we're just good friends, since leaving school. He's been very good to me. I was a bit of a mess last year, after a massive heartbreak and he's just helping me get back on my feet. As for your players, no need for concern coach. All of them are lovely, but my training wheels are still on. I'm cautious about any serious play.' Mia grinned.

'That's good to know. I've got to keep my invested interest safe,' Devon said quizzically, making Mia wonder if he was still talking about the players.

'Can I ask you a question Devon?'

'Sure.'

'I've noticed your girlfriend doesn't come to the games. She arrives just in time to take you home. Am I confused?'

'No, you're not. Tracey doesn't like soccer. I ask her to pick me up a couple of hours after the game, so I can talk with the players and such.'

'Did you just refer to me as "and such",' Mia poked fun, and Devon laughed. Then she slightly changed her tone, 'I hear you're hoping to make coaching soccer your profession. I know I may look silly but I'm pretty sure that would mean a lot of time at games. Won't that mean you would be spending a lot of time apart?', Mia asked boldly.

'You certainly don't look silly Mia.' There was a glint in Devon's eye as he looked at her. 'And it would be nice if Tracey was more involved and supportive of me.'

Mia could see a potential issue for Devon and decided to comment, 'I believe it's important to be on the same page as the person you're in love with. Otherwise, someone gets hurt.'

Then, Tracey appeared behind Devon, looking like a damaged creature waiting to be drip fed some nourishment from its owner. 'Hi Tracey,' Mia said, trying to get some animation from her. But she half smiled and remained mute.

'That's my cue to go. Thanks for the chat.' Devon ushered Tracey out of the clubhouse, saying a few brief goodbyes as they left, but Tracey's head was lowered, no engagement with anyone.

Just as Mia was getting up to go, a woman approached her. 'Mia? I thought it was you. My goodness, I haven't seen you for years.'

'Lucy, what are you doing here?' The two women greeted each other with a hug.

'I've just started dating Matthew.' Lucy pointed to one of Devon's players. 'You?'

'Not dating anyone. Just trying a new playground to meet people,' Mia said.

'I hear you. I'm over the bars and clubs in town. Do you remember after we finished our deportment course, we prowled those places for months,' Lucy recalled.

Before Mia could reminisce about that time, Matthew came to collect Lucy. 'Do you two know each other?'

'From a long time ago,' Lucy answered Matthew.

'Please come and sit with me next game. It would be great to have some female company,' Mia said, excited at the prospect of reconnecting with Lucy.

Chapter 27

Lucy added a new level of interest to going to the soccer. The two women clicked instantly, and it didn't take long before they exchanged life stories. Lucy was a theatre nurse, with a beautiful heart and a wicked sense of humour. She had long brunette hair and was very attractive. She had been married, but unfortunately it hadn't lasted.

Of course, Mia told Lucy about Jack, still fondly referring to their relationship, but stating she was gingerly looking for something and someone else.

About a month or so later, Mia, Karl, Lucy, and Matthew were having a drink after the game, when Mia asked Matthew, 'Is next week's game, Friday night?'

'Yes. It's the only one all year that isn't a Saturday,' he replied.

'Then, whose free Saturday night? How about a dinner party at my place? Karl, I think it's time I met the woman who has reformed you, and Lucy, I would love you to see the house.'

'Count us in,' Lucy and Matthew agreed.

'Let me check in with the boss. I'll get back to you tomorrow,' Karl said.

'Get back to you about what?', Devon assertively interjected, placing his drink on the table as he joined the group.

'I'm having a dinner party next Saturday night Devon. Would you and Tracey like to come?' Mia wasn't sure why she invited him, but it was out of her mouth before she really thought about it.

'That sounds like fun. Would you like us to bring anything,' Devon offered.

'No, just your own drinks everyone. I'll do the rest.' Mia was excited.

* * *

The following Saturday night, Lucy and Matthew were the first to arrive. They had poured their first drink when Karl arrived. 'Mia, this is Taylor,' Karl introduced her with pride in his voice.

'Hi Taylor.' Mia went to shake her hand.

'The famous Mia. A handshake won't do.' Taylor threw her arms around Mia like they were old friends. 'Karl has told me a lot about you. I'm glad to finally meet you.'

Mia liked her immediately. She was petite in stature but had an enormous presence and oozed class.

The last to arrive was Devon. 'Hi Devon. Where's Tracey?'

'She couldn't make it. This is for you.' Devon handed Mia a very expensive bottle of wine and snuck a quick kiss onto her cheek. 'Is everyone else here?'

'Yes, come in.' Mia's curiosity was stirred.

The evening went brilliantly. Devon took it upon himself to act like a co-host, and helped Mia serve courses, pour drinks, and clear the table. She was grateful for his help.

Just before midnight, all the guests decided to call it a night, except Devon. He offered to stay and help clean up. With the others gone, he stood with Mia in her kitchen swilling dishes, as she stacked her dishwasher, both still talking continuously, riding the high of great company and good food.

When they were done, Devon asked, 'One more glass?'

'Sure, but shouldn't you be getting home to Tracey?' Mia was snooping to find out more about how this relationship worked.

Devon poured them a glass of wine each. 'Well... let me tell you a little about Tracey and me. We've been together about two years. I asked her to move into my place after three months of dating. A little soon I know, but I don't like to waste time on anything casual. Once I fall, I like to know my mate is committed to me. Anyway, lately I have started to believe that Tracey isn't so committed, so I have asked her to move out.'

'Do you think she's cheating on you?' Mia was shocked. Even with their limited contact, Tracey did not seem the type.

'I have my suspicions. But also, what you and I talked about the other night, about a partner being supportive, it stuck with me. I'm very serious about my career, but more serious about being with the right person, on the same page, as you said. She's not who I want anymore. I need to be with someone who wants the same things as me. A good income, house, and family. Normal stuff. God, do I sound boring?'

'Not at all.' Mia felt something shift in the way she was looking at Devon. She didn't have the same magnetic pull to him as she had Jack, but suddenly, he looked attractive.

'I need to be careful with Tracey though. She's not well mentally. She's still at my place for now, and I will give her time to come to terms with us ending, but she'll be gone soon,' Devon added.

'That's kind of you Devon. Most people would want her out immediately.' Mia was in admiration of Devon's maturity, still caring for Tracey even though the relationship was over for him. What a contrast to the way Jack had handled her.

'I'm not cruel Mia. I may not love her anymore, but she still deserves respect and consideration. I did think at one stage she was going to be the mother of my children.'

'Why do you think your feelings changed?'

'I've matured. I've refined what I want in a partner. Tracey hasn't grown. In fact, she's become introverted and doesn't contribute a lot to our lives. I feel like I'm carrying her, financially and emotionally. I need an equal. Do you know what I mean?'

'Yes, I do,' was all Mia said, still not divulging her past. She wanted to keep her cards close to her chest.

'Sorry I have brought the mood down on a magical night. You're amazing Mia. Any guy would be lucky to have you by his side.' Devon started to sow the seeds of his true agenda.

'Thank you. I don't think I'm amazing, but I'm a better version of myself than what I was a few months ago.'

With that, Devon finished his wine and got up to go. Mia followed as he moved towards the front door. He turned and very naturally kissed her on the cheek again and hugged her.

'I'm glad you're back in my life. When I get this stuff sorted with Tracey, would you have dinner with me?'

'I'd like that. Here's my number if you need to talk some more.'

As Mia moved back inside, she felt confused. She hadn't considered Devon as a romantic interest, but after tonight, he was slightly outside the friend zone.

* * *

The next day, a huge boutique of flowers arrived...

Dear Mia,

Nobody is perfect, but you're so close it's scary. Thank you for a wonderful night. I'm looking forward to dinner, just the two of us.

I promise it will be soon.

Devon x

'How did he get flowers delivered on a Sunday? It would have cost him a fortune.' Mia started to be swept up in Devon's attention.

The phone rang late that afternoon. 'I'm just checking you got my flowers,' Devon asked.

'Yes, thank you. They're beautiful. Everything okay with you?'

'Yes, Tracey has just stepped out. I just wanted to touch base. I'd love to give you my number, but it's probably not appropriate you ring here yet. I hope you understand. Will you be at the game next weekend?'

'Yes, I'll be there. Have a great week.'

Mia recognised the circumstances were messy, and she felt a bit guilty that Devon's interest had already redirected to her. *'But we're just friends. And his actions are his responsibility.'*

* * *

The following Saturday, Devon found her before, during and after the game. And although he kissed her as any friend would, he decided to kiss her on all three occasions.

In the bar after the game, Mia played her role as a fond friend from his past, but Devon played his like they were already courting. He tended to her drinks and proudly introduced her to people like she was his companion. He made her feel special and his desirability stakes started to increase.

His attention intensified over the next two weeks; flowers frequently delivered to her work, always accompanied with romantic prose; and daily phone calls, that Mia presumed, were kept secret from Tracey.

She was in unknown territory. With Devon, she wasn't feeling the same enticement she was used to. But she was caught up in his straightforward adoration, and wondered, if this was how falling in love was meant to feel.

A few weeks later, after the game, Matthew suggested a small group grab some drinks and go back to his place, which wasn't far from the club.

'I've got to take care of something first. Will you still be going in another hour?', Devon enquired.

'I'm sure coach. See you when you get there.'

Devon platonically kissed Mia and said, 'I won't be long.'

Mia left her car at the club and got a ride with Matthew and Lucy. She had decided to relax by having a few drinks, as Matthew had offered his spare room if she wanted to stay.

Devon arrived at Matthew's to find a few of his players, and partners, enjoying their after-game contact. He made his way to Mia's side, happy to focus on just her. She found his manner more laidback than usual and after she had some time to study him, she whispered, 'Are you stoned?'

'A little. I use it to calm my nerves. I normally mix it with a bit of tobacco, so I never get really wasted. It's like having one or two drinks but it's better for me than alcohol.'

'I can't smell it on you.'

'I've become good at making sure no one knows. Especially my players. Please don't say anything, okay?'

Mia gestured zipping her lips together but felt unsure about this information. She hadn't been around a lot of drugs, so she spent a few minutes weighing it up. But eventually she put the sounding alarms back to silent and continued to be open to Devon's attentiveness.

Through the night, he moved closer, making sure she knew his intentions. It was more than flirtation. She was undoubtedly aware that he was not after anything casual. He was looking for a serious involvement and he was making it obvious she was his current choice.

Once everyone else had gone, Matthew and Lucy said goodnight and disappeared into Matthew's bedroom, closing the door behind them.

Mia and Devon were left, standing in the kitchen. He lent in and kissed her cheek but rather than pull away, he lingered, breathing gently on her face. Mia hesitated, *'Am I sure this is what I want?'*

Devon quietly spoke, 'Mia, I've had a crush on you since we were kids. I knew back then how special you are. I can't believe you have let me get this close. Please let me adore you.'

'Where's Tracey at?' Mia tried to keep her feet on the ground.

Devon pulled back just enough so their lips were within millimetres. 'She'll be out by morning. That's where I went after the game, to let her know it was time she left. I no longer want her in the way of what I think we could have. Please tell me you've considered you and me?'

'I have, but it feels different to anything from the past. It doesn't feel completely foreign but I'm cautious. I'm still working through some stuff.'

Devon moved his lips back to her cheek and tenderly kissed her again. Then pushed his luck a little more, moving to her neck. 'Let me love you. I will show you how good life can be.'

'Why am I hesitating? This guy knows what he wants, and he seems to want it with me. He'll treat me like I have always wanted.'

She placed her lips on his and let her body go. He pressed himself against her, lifting her onto the kitchen bench and she wrapped her legs around his waist, beginning to enjoy the feeling of him.

Her sensibility tried to slow her down, but her lust started to win. Deceleration was never Mia's strong suit and her desire to be loved, triumphed.

'Are you going to let me love you Mia?', Devon tempted, tickling her inner thigh while continuing to kiss her.

Mia consented with a nod.

'Good girl.' Devon started to take control. With Mia's legs still around him, he pulled her off the bench and carried her to the spare bedroom. He felt like a king.

Mia primed herself. *'Yes, this feels good. Relax and enjoy. My heart just needs more coaxing. Love will come in time. Now, doubts, go away. What's the worst that can happen?'*

Chapter 28

Mia woke in Devon's arms, early morning. He hadn't let go of her all night, like he feared she'd run-away. 'Good morning,' he beamed, like he had won first prize. 'Everything okay?'

'Yes, all okay,' Mia smiled to reassure him. And she was okay, but she wasn't euphoric. It didn't feel the same as Ja...

'Stop it! Stop comparing him with Jack. Jack is gone. Devon is here and he won't run away from commitment.'

'Do you mind if we get moving? I have a game I need to watch mid-morning. Let me drop you back to your car.' Devon kissed her and proceeded to get dressed.

* * *

On their way out, Matthew and Devon chattered in the hallway and Mia found Lucy in the kitchen. She soundlessly mouthed, 'Not sure.'

Lucy hugged her, whispering, 'All love affairs are different. Give it time.' Then she changed her volume and asked, 'Are you going? See you next week.' The boys had no idea of the silent exchange between them.

Devon drove Mia back to the club to pick up her car. He held her hand the whole way, assuring her his intentions were way beyond just bedding her.

'I'll call you later,' Devon stated as the car came to a halt. 'I'll need tonight to clean up after Tracey's departure but after that, we can be together whenever we want. Here's my number. Call me anytime.'

Mia took the piece of paper.

'Can I take you to dinner sometime this week? Maybe Tuesday?', Devon asked.

'Tuesday's good. Now get going. We can talk later.' Mia kissed him goodbye. It was outside a friendship kiss, but it wasn't passionate either. She was doing her best not to let Devon perceive her turmoil but the contradictions in her head were making her feel like she couldn't breathe.

She drove straight to Elizabeth and Reg. 'Cup of tea love?', Elizabeth asked, intuitively knowing Mia needed to talk.

She sat at the table with her mum, while Reg floated in the background. 'Do you remember Devon Kennedy?', Mia asked.

'From primary school days?', Elizabeth clarified.

Mia nodded.

'Oh yes, he lived with his grandparents for a while, down from us. He came to one of our pool-parties and I remember him being keen on you. Well, as keen as you can be at twelve.'

'Um, well he's a soccer coach for one of the local teams and Karl has got me going to the games.'

'So glad you're back socialising. That Karl's a good friend.'

'Yes Mum, but back to Devon. Seems his childhood keenness has been reignited. He's been showing me some serious attention over the last few weeks, and I wasn't drawn to him at first, but he's grown on me. I'm so confused about how I feel about him.'

'What you went through with Jack changed you, Mia. You're protecting yourself and your heart won't unlock on a whim. Take your time. Don't force yourself. Look for the goodness in Devon and see if he fits the picture you have for your future. The love will come if it's meant to. A solid base of respect and kindness will always lead to admiration, then love.'

'He's quite serious. Intense. He says he knows what he wants. An equal, to share his life with him.'

'Well, how refreshing. Someone who has a clear vision of what he wants. It's not a bad place to start.'

'I know. I should be feeling like I'm on a winner,' Mia paused. 'These doubts. They're just fear, right? I'm just getting used to someone new.'

'Let's have the two of you for dinner,' Reg said, deciding to break into the conversation.

Mia thought that was a good idea. Elizabeth and Reg were good judges of character, but she wanted to see how Tuesday night's dinner with just Devon went before agreeing.

She spent the rest of the day convincing herself she needed to be open to Devon and what he was offering her. By the time he rang that night, she was able to reflect on their night together with some pleasure.

'I haven't stopped thinking about you all day Mia. Last night may have happened a bit sooner than you thought it would, but I have no regrets. I hope you don't.'

'No regrets. Cautiously optimistic. I think more time together is what I need. I'm sure I'll be fine. Please be patient.'

'I can be patient. If you need to take this slow, I can do that. I just want to be with you Mia. Are you still up for dinner on Tuesday night, 6.30pm?'

'Yes, dinner sounds good.'

* * *

Devon was on time. He embraced her like they had been apart for months, tenderly stealing a quick kiss before taking her hand.

His demeanour was romantic, but not like a love-struck teenager. It was that of a determined adult who appreciated that she was sharing her time with him.

After Mia broached the subject of remembering him living with his grandparents, Devon talked about his family.

'Yes, my brother and I lived with them for two years. That's how I ended up in your neighbourhood. Dad and Mum got divorced when I was ten. At that stage, neither one of them could look after us. Dad has sorted his life out since and is married to a nice woman. They have acreage just west of the north coast. Mum on the other hand, has been married twice since and is currently single. She's my mum and I love her, but her life is constant chaos. She's a functioning alcoholic, like my older brother, and is hard work. That's why I don't drink a lot. I'm mindful of the addiction. A couple of tokes of dope suits me better.'

Mia assumed he meant a couple of tokes a week.

She knew firsthand what alcohol could do to a family and considered how dysfunctional his childhood must have been. She instantly sympathised, wanting to remedy the hurt he clearly still carried. His strength not to follow the pattern raised her respect for him, feeding her desire which was gradually awakening.

* * *

'Would you like to come in?', she asked as they arrived back at her place. Their night had been enriching, and she felt comfortable with him staying.

Devon turned off the engine. 'Stay there.' He got out of the car and came to her side, opened her door and offered his hand to help her out. Then he calmly said, 'Not tonight, Mia. We're going to play this your way. Nice and slow. Next time we sleep together, I want your doubts completely gone.'

'Classy Devon.'

Just when she felt comfortable with wanting him, he took himself off the table. He was being very clear; he needed more from her than just being at ease. He wanted her to really want him.

* * *

Later that week, they had dinner with Elizabeth and Reg. Devon was Mia's perfect escort. His conversation was engaging, and he didn't hide how serious he was about Mia. When Reg led him to the lounge room, Mia and Elizabeth had some time to themselves, clearing the dining table. 'Well?', Mia whispered, wanting her mother's opinion.

'Oh Mia, I've spent two hours with him. He seems very nice but that's not enough time to form a true opinion. I do agree with you about his intensity though. He's quite fixated on you. Just remember, this is in your time, okay?'

* * *

But Mia's hesitation had started to dissolve. As he dropped her home, she said, 'I'd like you to come in, please. Just for a drink.'

'Sure.'

They danced around each other in the kitchen, talking about the night and sipping on their wine. He commented on how nice her family was and cynically added for her to mentally prepare herself for his. He moved in sporadically, kissing her passionately, and then backing off, going back to conversation. Mia found it fun and sexy, and she genuinely found herself wanting him. And her kiss, as he was leaving, left no doubt.

'Better, but I'm still not staying,' was his small reward for her attempt to show him her uncertainties had started to wane. He continued to suggestively tease and toy with her for a while, driving her arousal sky-high, but in the end, used restraint. 'I have to go,' he smiled. 'I'll see you at the game, my Love.'

Flowers arrived the next day...

His sweetness kept melting away her reservations and he had her sexual urges stimulated with his "don't play half hearted" stance.

At the next game, he publicly claimed her before he went to the field. He found her sitting with Karl and Lucy, and kissed her openly, as a loving couple would. 'See you after the game,' he said, playfully stroking her nose, and then he went to the field.

'Ah, I think I might have missed something,' Karl quietly chuckled to himself.

'Looks like everything's on track then?' Lucy smirked and affectionately put her arm around Mia.

'Getting there,' Mia said.

After the game, Devon doted on Mia, making sure everyone knew they were an item. Mia felt worshipped.

'Let's get a bottle of wine and go back to my place,' Mia quietly suggested to Devon.

'You go; I won't be far behind you.'

When she got home, Mia freshened up, anticipating what the night could bring. She had just finished lighting some candles when her phone rang. 'Hi, I'm so sorry. I'm not going to make it. Mum is in a bit of trouble, and she needs my help.' Devon sounded a bit panicked.

'Is there anything I can do Devon?'

'Thanks, but no. I'll call you tomorrow.'

The night she had anticipated had been taken away, and her disappointment hit hard. The promised treat was confiscated at the last minute, and with the craving not being satisfied, the need for it, amplified. It made any uncertainty, completely disappear.

In the week proceeding, Devon kept up his daily phone calls and a bunch of flowers arrived, with a card, apologising again for messing up their Saturday night. But he kept himself from seeing Mia, citing that his mum needed him.

His drip-fed contact was enough to cause Mia to fantasise about how good they could be together, and his absence felt exaggerated. She started to dream about helping him build the life he wanted, and by Friday night when he called asking if she was free, she responded like a child wanting candy.

He arrived with an expensive bottle of wine, kissing her longingly and then pulling himself away. Mia seemed to choke on any words she tried to say, as her want for him started to boil over. She tried to open the wine but felt Devon come up behind her, moving his hands around her waist to pull her against him, making sure she could feel how much he wanted her. She turned around, and let her appetite for him, run uncontrollably.

'Are you sure? I'm willing to wait some more,' Devon said, with a perceptible hint of insincerity.

'No doubts. I really want this.'

'You've almost convinced me Mia, but I need to hear you ask me to stay. Beg me to stay.'

Mia wasn't sure if this was Devon playing or part of his insecurities. She decided to give him what he asked for. 'Please stay,' she seductively pleaded.

Devon laughed. 'That's exactly what I want.'

She thought she was in control, but she had no idea Devon was a mastermind of hidden coercion.

Chapter 29

As they lay in Mia's bed the next morning, it didn't take long before Devon asked about the featherstone.

'An old friend made it for me.' Mia didn't want to go into too much detail, but Devon wasn't going to let it go.

'An old friend or lover?', he asked.

'Lover and heartbreaker. The one Karl was helping me with.'

'I assume it was serious then.'

'I thought it was. But he wants to live his life free. No marriage or children.'

'And he had you wanting those things with him? What an idiot.' Devon squeezed Mia's hand.

'We just wanted different things.' Mia defended Jack as she felt a twinge in her heart. She hadn't heard from him in ages.

'Is it over?'

'Yes. Definitely. He's, my past. I'm looking at a different future now,' she said, gazing at him assuring. But there was still a stab of pain as Jack's name hung in the air.

'You know I want marriage and children, right? One day, I mean. I know we're still in the "try out" phase but it's important to me we want the same things.'

'We do Devon. But the loving relationship needs to come first. I won't have children for the sake of having them. So, the "try out" phase needs to be a winner.' She smiled, satisfied that she had set some expectations.

In the following few months, they were happy. But there were a couple of yellow lights Mia ignored.

She went out of her way to please Devon, not wanting another relationship to fail. She spent a lot of time supporting him, watching soccer games, and listening to him talk about the team. He commanded his players with authority, and they all respected him. But he could also be short-tempered when things didn't go his way. Unreasonably so, at times.

They started spending every night together, splitting their time between each other's houses, revealing personal habits, including how much weed he really smoked. He'd have a couple of tokes most nights, one when he came home from work and one just before he went to bed. At first, he only did this at his place, but eventually he asked to bring "just enough", if the night was at hers. Mia stated her concerns, but again, Devon compared it to having a couple of drinks. 'It's not a big deal Mia. I only use it to relax. It's not a problem, I promise.' Again, she silenced the alarms going off and agreed to let him partake at her place. But only on the back deck, never in the house.

One evening, Mia had a work function she needed to attend. She suggested a night apart as she wasn't sure what time she would be home. But when she arrived home, just after 9.00pm, Devon was sitting at her front door. 'Well, this is a nice surprise. How long have you been here?', Mia asked.

Devon stood and grabbed her like a child would a favourite toy. 'I don't like not being with you. I can't sleep without you. Mia, I'm so in love with you. You know that, right?'

'Yes, I do. I feel it. Do I love him? He makes me happy. Isn't this all I've ever wanted?' She was still stunned by his intensity.

'I love you too Devon. I'm glad you're here,' she stammered, as there was still a small dithering in her heart that Mia couldn't explain to herself.

The next morning, Devon was showered and ready for work, when he caught Mia off guard. 'I've been thinking, it's time we moved in together.'

'What?' Mia hadn't been expecting this. She was putting on her make up and could see the shock in her reflection.

He moved up behind her, holding her tight around her waist. 'We love each other. I'm tired of going between our houses. I want us to make a home together. Let's see if we can do this, for real. I'd be happy to move in here if you're worried about leaving your home.' He smiled, pleased at the picture he saw in the mirror.

'That's a big move Devon,' Mia said, collecting her thoughts.

'Did you mean what you said last night? That you love me?'

'Yes, of course I did Devon but...'

'Then no buts. It's the natural next step. Let's not waste any more time. Speaking of time, I'm late, got to go. We can talk some more later.' He kissed her goodbye, leaving her flustered. They had been together four months.

She looked at herself in the mirror. *If Jack had suggested this after four months, I would have jumped at it. Maybe he's right. Why waste time? Fear. That's all it is.'*

* * *

Devon rang her at work through the day. 'I'm cooking for you tonight, sweetheart. I'll pick up everything and will be at your place about 6.30pm, okay?'

He came in and instructed her to do nothing but unwind. He set the dining table, including candles, and served a beautiful meal. During dinner, they chatted about their days and shared a bottle of wine. He even insisted on cleaning up without her.

After dinner, they cuddled on the couch. 'Have you enjoyed tonight?', he asked.

'You've been amazing, thank you.'

'This could be your every night. Just say yes to living together.'

Mia's head was clouded. She was relaxed after being spoilt, but there was still something that she couldn't put her finger on. She decided to ask some questions to see if that eased the niggle. 'What would happen to your place?'

'I jointly own the house with Mum. I dare say, if I move out, she'd move in. If not, I'd rent it.'

'I want to stay solely responsible for paying my mortgage. We can have another conversation about that if we make a formal commitment to each other, okay?'

'Very sensible. But I'm not after your house. I want you.'

Then his manner changed from loving to annoyance. 'Why are you hesitating? Have you got doubts again? God, what do I have to do to make you want this?' Devon's voice was slightly elevated.

Mia felt guilty. He'd been wonderful. Everything she had wanted in a partner. Why was she holding back?

'It's okay. I'm just clarifying stuff. Yes, of course it's yes.'

His face softened. 'We're going to be great together. I'm going to make you so happy. I'll move in on Sunday.'

* * *

On the Friday, as they had breakfast, Devon said, 'I'll ring Mum today and ask her to meet me at the house tonight. Once we're face to face, I can let her know our plans and ask if she wants to move in. Would you like to meet her?'

'Sure. We'll stay there tonight?'

'Yes. Which brings me to something else I need to ask you. That thing you have wrapped around your bedpost, please have it gone by the time I move in?' Devon's tone was non-negotiable.

Mia looked at him, obviously unhappy.

'Mia, you can't seriously expect me to share your bed with an ex-lover's trinket wrapped around the bed post.'

His bluntness made her realise his request was reasonable. The featherstone had no place in their new world. She nodded, indicating she would obey his request.

'Good girl. See you tonight.'

* * *

Devon's mum, Shelley, was everything Devon had described. She was obviously trying to defy her age in both her grooming and behaviour, and she had a feverish energy that disturbed Mia. She was polite enough as Devon introduced Mia, but quickly changed her manner, announcing she had a date with a much younger man and needed to get ready.

'So please Devon, what's this all about.'

His plans to move in with Mia were saluted with a cynical sneer, but Shelley was overjoyed at the opportunity to move into the house she jointly owned with him.

Mia then excused herself saying she would start on dinner, thinking they may need some time to sort out details. Shelley's ignorance as to how loud she spoke allowed Mia to hear every word they said anyway.

'You're punching above your weight with her sonny. She's way too classy for you.'

'I love her Mum.' Devon tried to reach for her approval.

'You're too much like me Devon. You'll end up screwing it up. And when you do, your dear old mum will be here to pick up the pieces. Anyway, must dash. I have a hot stallion waiting for me. Say goodbye to the Princess.'

As soon as she heard the front door close, Mia went to find Devon. She understood even more now, the reason for some of his behaviour. She tried to impress all her love and empathy on him, as she held him tight, attempting to heal the wounds of his mother's lashing tongue. 'You're nothing like her. You're not going to screw this up. Together, we're going to show her how right this is.'

* * *

After a night that brought them closer together, Mia went home and untwirled the featherstone. *'Why can't I bring myself to put it in the bin?'*

'Small steps. I'll put it at the back of the wardrobe with Jack's letters and cards. Devon will never find it.'

Then the phone rang. It was like he knew. 'Hi Mia, it's Jack.'

It took her a minute to compose herself. 'Hi Jack. How are you?' She was so happy to hear his voice but felt guilty knowing Devon may have a problem with that.

'I'm good. I know it's been ages. I just wanted to check in. See that you're okay.'

'Yes, I'm great. You still in Victoria?'

'For now. There is some shearing in South Australia that I'm going to chase in the next couple of months but then I'm thinking I might come back to Queensland. My life needs a change up.' There was a long silence. 'I miss you, Mia.'

'Please Jack, don't. I'm in...,' Mia had troubles finding her words. 'I'm seeing someone.'

'Is it serious?'

'Yes, he's moving in.'

'I see.' Another long pause. 'Well, I wish you all the best. He's a lucky man.'

More silence, until Mia found a way to change the subject. 'How are Mary and Ian?'

'They're good. Although Ian is currently having some tests. We should have the results soon. Anyway, I won't keep you any longer. Ring me or leave a message at Mum's if ever you need. All the best.'

'Jack, wait,' she pleaded, but he'd hung up.

'Damn', she muttered, as the hint of regret leached in.

She considered wiping down the phone, irrationally thinking it would remove all traces of the call. *I'm on track. Don't let Jack jeopardise it. Eyes on Devon.'*

Chapter 30

After Devon moved in, he limited Mia's contact with Shelley. This wasn't hard, as his mother was so wrapped up in her own world, she didn't demand any quality time with her son.

However, they did have frequent visits with his father, Keith, and his wife Joyce. Keith had a quiet but firm temperament, that Devon seemed to listen to, and Joyce, was sweet, and always welcoming. Mia enjoyed their company.

During the first six months of living together, there were also many dinners with Elizabeth and Reg. A couple of times Mia privately asked if they thought Devon was right for her. They remained reserved about any opinion, saying if she was happy, they were happy. But Mia could sense Elizabeth had doubts about her choice of partner.

Their world was consumed with soccer. Devon trained his team three nights a week, and Saturdays were game time. 'I'll feel supported if you're with me at the pre-games as well as mine,' he firmly suggested. It wasn't her first choice on how she would like to spend her Saturdays, but she agreed, thinking it was a small sacrifice to assure him he could rely on her.

* * *

But during the off season, no soccer meant lots of down time, and Mia noticed his cannabis smoking had increased. There were additional tokes in the morning, even before work, and sometimes, he would wake through the night, to have more. 'I'll be better once next year's season starts. It's under control,' he would attempt to reassure. Mia took him at his word.

1999 – Mia's New Year's resolutions

Accept love can feel different to what you're used to
Trust Devon

Mia hoped Devon would keep his word. But he didn't. The increased levels of his drug habit continued. She kept her concerns to herself, feeling by confiding in anyone, it would be a betrayal of his trust.

A year ago, they had crossed paths by chance, and now, she was considering spending her life with him.

'Is this how I thought I'd feel sharing my life with someone?'

'Umm…I'm not ecstatic. But I'm happy. Life isn't always rainbows and bliss, is it? There needs to be darker times to appreciate the lighter ones.'

'The picture Devon originally painted, isn't my reality.'

'Umm…But I can't take for granted someone who loves me as much as he does. I may never find it again. I was looking for reliable and real. He certainly provides that.'

February 1999

It was like her evaluation pre-empted his next move. The night before Valentines Day was a Saturday night. They got home from the soccer and Devon said, 'I know I've been a bit distant, but I've planned a nice day for us tomorrow. We can celebrate our first Valentines Day, as a couple.'

By mid-morning Devon had packed a picnic lunch, and they headed towards the mountain nearby. They drove past the Woolshed and Mia consciously kept herself looking at Devon, clearly choosing her future, not her past.

As he turned down the road, heading up the mountain, Mia asked, 'Where are we going?'

'Maiala National Park.'

'Don't react. Look out the window so he can't see your face.'
She couldn't help but feel it was a poignant test the Universe was handing her. *'Stay away,'* Mia disciplined herself, as the memory of Jack and that musical night, tried to come front of mind.

Devon reached for her hand. 'I love you so much.'

She detected something unusual in Devon's voice that made her jump back into the present. 'I love you too, especially for loving me the way you do.'

She led him away from the spot her and Jack had shared on their first date, ensuring she was back in the now, appreciating the effort Devon had gone to. They sat on a blanket and enjoyed their first glass of sparkling wine.

'Should we eat?', she asked, noticing that he had finished his drink quickly.

'No, let's have one more,' he said, as he was already filling their glasses. 'Hold this,' he instructed as he handed her his glass. He then put the bottle back in the cooler. When he turned around, Mia noticed his eyes were misty.

'Devon, what's wrong?'

'Nothing's wrong. In fact, for the first time in my life, everything is right. I'm no longer lonely and I feel my life has creditability and that's all because of you. I can't lose you.' He reached in his pocket and produce a small box. 'Marry me? I want you to be my wife.' His eyes searched hers, hoping that by taking control of their future, she would realise this was the rightful next step.

Mia's mind went into overdrive. *'I walked myself through this the other day. Life with Devon is a good prospect. Look at his loving eyes. Nobody will ever love me more.'*

'Yes Devon,' she replied, choking back tears. He cried too as he slipped the massive solitaire diamond ring on her finger.

'It's beautiful. Thank you.' She kissed him, caught up in the realisation he was offering her all she ever wanted, a loving husband and, eventually, children.

'I have a confession. You're not the first to know. I went and asked your mum and Reg for their blessing. They were great. Elizabeth said to keep making you happy, and I promised her I would. Just like you make me. I can't believe you're going to be my wife. I feel like I've won the jackpot.'

* * *

The happy couple went to see Elizabeth and Reg before going home. They got emotional when congratulating her, knowing the journey she'd been on hadn't been easy. As soon as Elizabeth got the chance to be alone with her daughter, she asked how she was feeling.

'I'm very happy Mum. He's a wonderful option for me, and we'll have a great life together.'

Elizabeth frowned. 'You've just agreed to marry someone, Mia. You seem a bit flat.'

'I've done the whole feet off the ground thing, and I didn't like the crash landing. This time's different. It needs to be, for me to trust it.'

In that moment, Elizabeth understood her daughter loved Devon but wasn't in love. All she could do was hope Mia knew what she was doing, and that the relationship would keep growing.

Chapter 31

The celebration around their engagement continued over the next couple of weeks. The wedding date had been set for September, so an engagement party was organised quickly and was held at the soccer club. It was a night to remember, not for its joy.

Lucy spent a lot of time talking with Elizabeth and Reg, charming them both. 'Please make sure Lucy gets to dinners at our place. I would like to spend more time with this girl. She's a treasure,' Elizabeth said, holding Lucy's hand. Mia was happy they liked her as they had become very close.

Devon kept a close eye on his mother, particularly to see if she could be in the same room as his father and new wife, without any drama. It was relatively amicable, but eventually, Shelley did snarl some toxic remarks about them to her son, irritating Devon.

The soon-to-be groom made a speech, thanking everyone for coming and announcing he was marrying the love of his life. The plan was to keep the speeches to a minimum, but Shelley decided she needed some of the limelight. She made an impromptu speech, spruiking at how proud she was of Devon and that she had known from the start, that Mia was the girl for him. Devon's irritation level rose another notch.

'I just need five minutes to myself,' he said to Mia after the formalities were over. She watched him disappear outside, feeling disappointed, knowing their early pact of "no weed" was about to be broken.

When she next saw him, he was clearly stoned but wasn't relaxed. He was still agitated about his mother's insincere performance. He went to the bar and slammed two bourbon shots. Mia watched him from across the room and hoped no one else noticed.

As Devon stood at the bar, an old soccer friend approached him. 'Congratulations Devon. She's quite a girl. How did you guys hook up?'

'Karl started bringing her to my games. Do you know Karl?' Devon signalled to Karl and Taylor across the room.

'Yes, I went to high school with him and Mia. They were quite the pair.'

'Do you mean like a couple?' Devon's antagonism was growing.

'Nobody ever really knew. But there was a long period where Karl would stay at her place on the weekends. Everyone assumed he was sleeping with her. I mean look at her. Who wouldn't want a piece of that. Anyway, that's all in the past. She's yours now.'

Devon's anger raged within him, believing Mia had lied about her relationship with Karl. His head was swirling from the drugs, the alcohol and the tainting of his precious Mia.

He came up beside her and grabbed her arm. 'We need to go.'

'Ow, you're hurting me,' she said, turning so no one could see her reaction. She looked at Devon's face and could see the fury.

'Now Mia! Tell everyone I'm not well and I'll meet you out the front.'

She obeyed his demand. By the time she reached him he was pacing. 'What's going on, Devon?'

'Shut up. Not a word until we get home.'

Mia was too bewildered to be upset. She had never been spoken to like that. She followed him to the main road where they hailed a taxi and remained silent until the front door of the house was closed.

'You failed to tell me that you and Karl were lovers,' Devon yelled. 'Were you still sleeping with him when he first brought you to the soccer?'

Mia's bafflement soon turned to indignation. 'Hang on. What do you mean, I didn't tell you? I didn't think a one-night affair, a million years ago was newsworthy, or any of your business. And no. Karl and I have been nothing more than friends for over a decade. He's like a brother to me.' This was the first time Mia had raised her voice at Devon. It wasn't often she felt outrage, but his accusations had got her there.

'One night,' Devon's disbelief echoed in his tone. 'I was told you were quite the pair at school, and he would stay at your place on weekends. I'm sure it was more than one night.'

'Yes, he did stay. He was having a terrible time at home. And yes, we were close. But it wasn't until a year later and when someone we loved died, that we had sex, once.' Mia's voice was now even but her teeth were clenched. 'Devon why is this a big deal? You knew you weren't my first.' Mia couldn't understand why he had her on trial.

'Because you told me you were just friends. You lied. And he's still in your life.'

'I didn't lie; I told you we had been friends since just after school. And that's the truth. We even went overseas together, and I promise you; it was completely platonic by then. He's been a good friend to me, why shouldn't he be in my life.'

'It's all too close Mia. I'm sure he still wants you. He's just waiting for me to screw up so he can steal you away. You're so easily manipulated,' Devon's words were slurred.

'You're talking nonsense. You've had too much. You need to go to bed. We can talk in the morning.' Mia wasn't game to mention that she thought it was the marijuana making him paranoid. That was something she would tackle tomorrow.

'He's not coming to the wedding Mia. I can't have him there knowing he's had sex with you. You don't see any of my ex's traipsing behind me. I don't care how good a friend he's been,' he yelled, as he went out the back to smoke some more.

And that's where he slept. On the outdoor setting. Mia was relieved. She didn't want him anywhere near her.

In the morning, he came and sat on the end of the bed as she coolly eyed him, whilst sipping on her coffee.

'I'm sorry. I overreacted. But I thought you'd lied to me. I need to know I can trust you,' Devon started with.

'You can trust me, Devon. I'm committed to making an honest, happy life with you. But I can't be accused of things I haven't done, and you can't punish me for things I've done in the past. I can't change them. Nothing from your past would make me behave like you did last night. It was disrespectful and embarrassing. You need to sort out whatever it is that is making you insecure and paranoid, including the amount of drugs you're smoking. You promised you would get it under control and it's not. It will end up destroying us.'

'I just love you so much Mia. I can't stand the thought of any other man being with you. I just want it to be you and me.'

'And it is. But I can't erase my past. Like you can't erase yours. We are both nearly thirty. Of course, there have been other lovers. And there are reasons they haven't worked. We've chosen to be together now, flaws and all. That's the deal. We need to focus on making each other happy, and the future, together.' Mia thought she had said enough to put the matter to bed, but it was only the beginning of his irrational intimidation.

For a few weeks, Devon was on his best behaviour. Mia thought he had reduced the pot smoking, to where it was when he first moved in. The rituals of when they first started dating were back; flowers, romantic cards, dinners and wanting to make her happy. She likened the engagement party incident to a volcano that had built up so much pressure, it exploded its inner filth, to then going back to lying dormant. She gullibly hoped she would never see another eruption.

The truth of it was, he just got better at hiding how much he was smoking, and his increased use facilitated a grave distortion in his thinking, including the number of men Mia had been involved with and how at ease she was at being just a sexual conquest. His irrational theories started to eat at his mental stability.

* * *

One night he presented her with a mobile phone. 'Everyone has one. I got one too. I need to be able to reach my soon to be wife if I need to.' He kissed her affectionately, trying to make the comment sound romantic but his true reasoning was so he could keep tabs on her.

However, the phone did turn out to be useful before long. Mia was on her way to work when she was involved in a car accident. She had been stopped in a line of traffic when a vehicle came over a rise and smashed into the back of her car. It was a big impact, and she was in shock. She tried to call Devon, but he didn't answer. She left him a message. That morning, he had woken feeling sick and hadn't gone to work. She reasoned he may have gone to the doctor.

She decided to call her manager. Ray was a wonderful man. He was about ten years older than her and had always acted like a mentor, helping Mia's career grow. 'Where are you, Mia? I'll be right there.'

At the scene, with the car a right off and Mia in shock, he quickly decided, 'I'm going to take you home.'

Devon wasn't home when they got there. Ray set her up in the lounge, making her a cup of tea and finding her some pain medication. He wasn't going to leave until someone else was with her.

After hearing his car pull in, Ray greeted a surprised Devon at the front door, 'Hi. You must be Devon. I'm Ray, Mia's boss. She was in a car accident on the way to work. She's okay but a bit shaken up. She's in the lounge.'

With Mia's car not there, Devon had no idea anyone was home. He pushed past Ray, without saying a word to him.

Mia could see he was stoned and, without the opportunity to cover it up, he smelt of it too.

'Are you okay?' He went to her side.

'Yes. I'm fine. A bit sore. Ray's been great.'

Devon visibly seethed with jealousy as he looked at the successful, attractive gentleman who had been looking after her.

Uncomfortable with the lack of address from Devon, Mia said, 'Thanks so much Ray. I'll call you later to let you know when I'll be back at work.'

'Just when you're up to it. No rush. I'll organise a loan car for you, until you get a new one sorted.' Ray could feel Devon's dislike and could smell the pot. He looked back at Mia not wanting to leave her with him.

'I'm fine. I'll call later,' Mia reassured him.

'She's fine Ray. I've got her now,' Devon managed to speak.

After Ray was out the door, Devon turned to Mia and asked, 'Why did you call him?', his tone reeked of displeasure.

'I tried calling you, but you didn't answer. I needed help, and thank goodness Ray could assist,' Mia kept her tone neutral. She didn't have the energy for harsh words.

'Yes, thank goodness for Ray,' Devon said, dripping with sarcasm. 'Is there anything I can do or has Ray sorted everything out for you?', the question was almost venomous.

'Ray didn't do anything except bring me home to you, where I belong,' she said, trying to dampen his fire. 'I'm glad you're feeling better,' she added, trying to defuse the situation, also deciding not to query where he had been or why he was stoned.

The mere suggestion of belonging to him seemed to work. He softened and said, 'I wouldn't cope if anything happened to you or if something took you away from me.'

Mia remained silent. She had learnt to tread gently when he was this high and anxious, teetering on the edge of a flareup. She knew the dope heightened his fears.

* * *

After a couple of days, Mia was ready to go back to work. As she was getting dressed, Devon commented, 'That skirt's too short.'

'I've been wearing this skirt forever. You've never said anything before.'

He moved in front of her and ran his finger down her cheek. 'You really have no idea how desirable you are, do you?' He sighed. 'The way Ray was looking at you the other day, was not appropriate. I don't want anyone looking at you like that. You're going to be my wife. I'm just trying to protect you. Sometimes Mia, for someone so smart, you can be so naïve.'

His words sent her into an insecurity spiral, reminding her of the past. *Is Devon, right? Does the way I dress encourage men to look at me a certain way? I had no idea how Brian was thinking about me until that Christmas dinner. Could Ray be the same?*

She changed into a pair of suit pants.

* * *

Leading up to the wedding, there were many signs that Mia was on the wrong path. But not wanting to let Devon down and believing marrying him would solve his issues, she kept going, head down, not able to find a way out. And once the wedding invitations went out, the feeling of obligation was even bigger.

Karl also needed to be told he and Taylor hadn't made the list. She organised to call around to his place without Devon knowing. She knew he would have forbidden her from seeing him, as his thoughts on the Karl matter were still unreasonable.

'Did I do something wrong?', Karl asked.

'No.' Mia decided to be honest. 'Devon has an issue about us sleeping together.'

'What? Did we sleep together?', Karl said, trying to lighten her seriousness. Her stress was evident.

Mia began to get teary. 'I'm so sorry. I really want you there. You've been such a good friend to me.'

'I don't care about the invitation. I care about you. Do you want me to talk to Devon?'

'God no! He doesn't even know I'm here. He'd kill me if he knew.'

Karl could see that Mia was fearful. 'Now Champ, I'm no expert on marriage, but this doesn't sound like the way to start one.

'He loves me, Karl. He's just a bit protective. I'm sure he'll be more secure once we're married.'

But realistically, she knew she was betting on long odds.

* * *

Their bridal party was kept to a minimum. Mia asked Lucy to be her Matron of Honour and Devon asked his brother Richard, to be his best man. Sadly, Devon's reasoning for his choice was to keep him close and under control.

Devon also insisted on no hen's or buck's night. 'They're just opportunities for things to go wrong. Surely at your age Mia, you're past getting stupidly drunk, while a stripper parades around in front of you. I know I am.'

So, Mia organised a nice dinner with Elizabeth and Lucy; and Devon had a few drinks at the club with Reg, Keith, and Richard. 'A controlled environment, free from temptation,' Devon stated, mistrust now influencing every decision.

'It will be nice to see Karl,' Elizabeth said at the girl's dinner, where the wedding was the topic of conversation.

'Karl isn't coming Mum,' Mia said, feeling a stab of guilt.

'Why not? Is he away?', Elizabeth questioned.

Mia thought about just saying yes but she had never lied to her mum. 'Devon has an issue with Karl and I being as close as we were, once. We thought it best he wasn't there.'

'We? You mean Devon.' Elizabeth was livid. 'If it wasn't for Karl getting you out of the house, you wouldn't be marrying Devon. This is ridiculous.'

Mia wanted to scream, *'Yes, it is. Everything is ridiculous. His insecurity, his possessiveness, his jealousy, his controlling behaviour, his drug use, his temper. All ridiculous. This isn't how I'm supposed to be feeling a week out from my wedding.'*

But as usual, she reverted to reason. 'All his life, he's felt unworthy and had no one to rely on. He's got stuff from his past he's working on, and he's chosen me to help him build a better life. He loves me and I'm sure I can make this work.' Mia held back her tears. 'I've explained it to Karl. He understands.'

* * *

Elizabeth stayed quiet until she got home. She was beyond worried about Mia and shared her concerns with Reg. 'Unless Devon does some growing up, this marriage is already over.'

Reg resounded her concerns. 'Yes, I agree. The behaviour I saw tonight has me worried. At one point, Devon verbally abused the bartender because he was taking too long to make his drink, apparently. Devon's rage was almost frenzied, and the berating was uncalled for. I'm also sure he was stoned.'

The he tried to offset their distress. 'But Mia's an adult, and she needs to feel we support her decision. We just need to let her know we're here if she needs us.'

September 1999

The day of the wedding was like an out of body experience for Mia. Everyone was acting like everything was fine, but she could feel the insincerity, including her own. She went through the motions of having her hair and makeup done, getting dressed, posing for photos. She kept encouraging herself to be excited about the rest of life, but what she was really feeling was just accountability to go through with her promise to Devon and, deep down, she knew it was a mistake.

Reg was to walk her down the aisle and was travelling with her to the ceremony. As they approached to where the congregation were waiting, he ordered the driver to pull over. 'Mia, if you have any doubts, we can turn the car around. I promise, I'll take care of everything after that.'

Her heart lightened at the thought of freedom, but her responsible head soon stamped on it. 'I wouldn't embarrass him like that Reg. He's counting on me to do the right thing. Besides, I can't imagine anyone else wanting to marry me as much as Devon. I don't want another failed attempt at love. I've come this far; I need to keep going.'

Reg nodded and indicated to the driver to keep going. 'We're always here, your mum and me. If ever you feel adrift, let your worth to us be your compass.'

Chapter 32

To cope with the enormity of the event, Mia convinced herself that the wedding was just a big party. The doubt she had felt that morning was diluted throughout the day as Devon put his best foot forward. He was self-assured, devoted, and full of love. When he was like that, she did feel love for him.

But the honeymoon shattered any illusion that by marrying him, his charming side would win the battle over the beast that wreaked havoc within.

They had decided to go to Fiji for five days. What neither of them considered was how dependent on the dope he was, and what effect having no access to it would have on him. He had deceived himself into thinking it wasn't addictive, and that he'd be able to enjoy a few days with his new wife in the tropical paradise without it. But after just a day, he became irritable and couldn't sleep. His stomach started to cramp, and he had pain in his legs. He tried to tell Mia it was something he ate.

She wasn't aware of the extent of his habit. Leading up to the wedding, he had secretly been smoking every four hours. He had become a master at sneaking and concealing. The amount he was smoking had completely changed the way his brain and nervous system worked, intensifying all the things Devon's beast thrived on.

Their whole trip, Mia walked on eggshells. He would lose his temper at the drop of a hat. He wouldn't let Mia out of his sight but would go for long periods without talking to her. A time that should have been filled with love and laughter, was devoid of both. She couldn't wait to get home.

Devon's downward spiral became worse, leading to a series of incidents that caused any love Mia had for him to slowly evaporate.

He tried to control his usage, but when he did, he experienced such discomfort, he conceded to using it for pain relief. And every time he went back, the beast within became louder, distorting reality and allowing his dark side to dominate and create illusions. The addiction had possessed him completely.

Mia had spent her life trying to please. She shied away from confrontation and always tried to understand another's point of view. When a situation looked to be heading in a disagreeable direction, she would often change tack to neutralise its escalation. This strategy was normally not detrimental, but in the case of her marriage, it started to condone bad behaviour, quickly leading to a power imbalance, and Mia feeling diminished.

As the months went by, there were brief periods of connection but then something would displease Devon, and he would either detonate or sulk. He became despondent with soccer and work, saying he was sick of being surrounded by idiots, and he had so much time off work, he ran out of sick leave.

April 2000

Then one night, Jack rang. His reason was to let Mia know that Ian was seriously sick and had about a year to live.

'Who's that?', Devon hissed, sensing it was someone from her past.

She covered the mouthpiece and said, 'It's Jack. His stepdad's dying.'

'Tell him to never call again Mia. Hang up. Now!', he yelled, as his drug haze filled him with jealousy.

Jack heard Devon's irrational demand. 'Mia, are you okay?'

'Yes. I've got to go. Thanks for letting me know. Please give Ian and your mum my regards.' She wrapped up the call, but disobeyed Devon just a little by omitting to tell Jack not to call.

'Was that necessary Devon?'

'I told you before, I'm not having ex's chasing behind you. Anyway, that loser broke your heart. Why do you allow people to treat you so badly and then leave the door open to them?'

'Like I am constantly doing for you these days.'

But she said nothing as she had lost her voice out of dread over his consistent tantrums and severe words.

October 2000

Devon was out visiting his mother one night when his mobile phone rang. He'd accidentally left it at home. The contact came up as "Frank" and Mia decided to answer it, as her curiosity got the better of her.

'Hi Frank, it's Mia here. Devon's wife,' she said, sounding like she knew who she was talking to.

'Ah... Hi! Is Devon there?'

'Not right now. Can I give him a message?'

'Just tell him I can't make our usual Wednesday session, but I need half a bag. Could he drop it in the usual spot, and I'll leave him the cash.'

'No worries.' Mia stayed cool, but inside, she was furious.

She scrambled to get her shrewd mind working. 'He must be dealing. Shit. Find the stash before he gets home. It must be outside.'

She went straight to the BBQ and found several sizable bags of marijuana hidden underneath its grill. She was livid.

Devon arrived home to the bags on the dining room table and Mia eyeballing his reaction. She served it straight up. 'Frank called. He can't make your usual weekly session, but he wants you to drop some of this in the usual spot. Your cash will be waiting for you there.' Devon was blindsided, as well as in need of a hit.

Still remaining calm she continued, 'So, this is what you've been doing while I'm at work; smoking dope with mates and dealing.' Mia shook her head in disgust. 'That family addiction gene you loath so much, is alive and kicking in you. You've just replaced alcohol with drugs.'

'Mia, let me explain. It's a one-time thing. I thought I could make some extra cash before we start trying for a baby?'

She knew he was lying. 'You're kidding right? I'm not bringing a child into this. You need help Devon, and this is beyond me.'

"What do you mean? We're doing okay, aren't we?"

It was at that point Mia realised that he could see nothing wrong with their picture. She had remained so passive about how far off track, for her, they had become, he had no idea. She had been so distracted in trying to please him, she had become mute as to what was important to her and was now completely submissive to his dominance. She walked away without answering him.

* * *

She was in a deep sleep when he finally came to bed. Before she was fully awake, he had her pinned down. 'I'm sorry. I know I've screwed up, but I'll try and do better.'

'Sure,' she responded impartially, believing it was just another lie, and feeling totally downhearted about him and their marriage.

'A baby would give me a new purpose to focus on.'

'It's not the right time, Devon.'

'You mean, you're not ready. Why won't you do this for me? It would help me so much.'

'Please go to sleep. We can talk more about it later.'

'Okay, I'll let the baby thing go for now. But I'm not ready to go to sleep.' He initiated foreplay.

Mia didn't want to have sex, but she knew if she didn't, it would lead to a lengthy critiquing of her wifely duties. She was tired and she just wanted to sleep. So, she lay there and went through the motions, removing herself from being present, as her self-preservation kicked in.

When he was all done, Devon got up to go to the bathroom. When he came back in, he stood at the bottom of the bed and said, 'The condom was broken.'

A wash of panic went over her. She was immediately suspicious of the timing.

'It could be fate.' Devon smiled, looking to be covertly congratulating himself.

She was reeling at the thought that he had purposefully done this to get his way. It was only a few months earlier he had insisted she go off the pill. 'The chemicals need to be out of your body for at least six months, before we start trying,' he'd insisted. Had he pre-planned all of this?

She put on her best face and half-heartedly smiled back at him, before proceeding to the bathroom herself, hoping to eliminate any potential pregnancy.

That night, her sleep was disturbed to say the least, and her every waking second was spent praying she wasn't pregnant. As much as she still wanted children, she needed to get the rest of her life right first, and she no longer wanted this life. But getting out, seemed impossible.

December 2000

Mia was full of anxiety as she got ready for her work Christmas party. It would be the first time Devon and Ray would be in the same room since her accident. Ray had never given her reason to validate Devon's suggestion of him. It was Devon who was causing her nervousness.

She'd asked him to be drug free for the night, but halfway through the event, when he said he was going to the bathroom; Mia watched him slip outside to indulge in his favourite pastime. She decided to speak with Ray and his wife while he was absent.

On spotting where she was when he came back in, Devon charged over to them, as his green-eyed monster took control. His simmering presence immediately disturbed the conversation and Ray's wife excused herself. While it was just the three of them, Devon decided to take the opportunity to vent.

'I don't like the way you look at my wife.'

'What did you say?', Ray asked in disbelief.

'Devon!', Mia was embarrassed.

'You heard me. I can see how much you want her.' Devon's voice was raised.

'I can assure you Devon, I don't want Mia. I value her. Something you should learn to do,' Ray snapped.

'Stay away from her,' Devon demanded, in a vaguely lower volume. Ray's words had taken the wind out of his sails, slightly.

'I'm sorry Ray. Let's go Devon.' Mia was completely humiliated. She had never been so angry. She couldn't even look at Devon, let alone speak to him.

* * *

Ray rang her soon after. 'Just checking you're okay.'

'Yes thanks, in a taxi, on our way home,' Mia responded.

'Mia, you shouldn't have to dim your light to be with someone. From the time I met you, until now, your light has gone from bright, to nearly out. Devon is a bully. Bullies respond to power. Remember your power.'

Devon's monster used the taxi ride home to grow with illogical fury. As soon as they were through the front door he exploded, 'You've been sleeping with him, haven't you? That's the only reason he'd defend you like that. You, silly little slut.'

Her dignity couldn't endure anymore and her chance to roar was imminent. Holding onto Ray's words, she screamed, 'I should never have married you. You make me miserable.'

'Well while we're telling truths, I know the only reason you did was out of fear that no one would ever truly love you. Once I worked that out, it was so easy to get you to do what I wanted. God, you reeked of desperation. You let men use you for years, just to feel loved.'

Mia tried to move past him, but he grabbed her wrist and with a menacing smile, he snarled, 'I'm going to show you just how a slut should be treated.'

Mia was no longer submissive. She got herself free and grabbed his collar with both hands. With her face in his, she spat, 'I don't even like you anymore, let alone love you. This is over.'

His anger blew and he shoved her backwards with such force, she tripped and landed on her back, hard, on the tiled kitchen floor. She screamed with pain. He instantly felt remorse and went to help, 'Mia, I'm...'

'Don't touch me. Get out of this house, now!'

Devon froze for a minute, all bluster gone. But he knew there was no negotiating and soon left, heading for his house.

As he arrived, a drunk Shelley looked over the top of her whiskey glass and sneered, 'I told you, you'd screw it up.'

The next morning, Mia contacted Ray, who gave her a week off to get her world right again. She used the time to start to recalibrate. She hadn't realised how suppressed she had been until, without him there breathing down her neck, she felt parts of her stifled soul wake up.

A couple of days later, she found herself ringing Elizabeth. 'Mum I'm bleeding, badly.'

Elizabeth got Mia to the hospital emergency room. They examined her internally and ran some blood tests.

Whilst waiting for further consultation, she shared what had happened and some of her most personal thoughts. 'I blame myself, Mum. I never totally gave myself to him emotionally. I'm sure he sensed that on some level and maybe that's the reason for his irrational jealousy and insecurity. I was so sure that the admiration I felt in the beginning would lead to a deep love. And when he was so sure about me, I just thought it was meant to be. But I was so wrong, again.'

'Listen to me Mia. You were right to think that admiration leads to love. But when admiring someone becomes as challenging as Devon has made it for you, of course, things are going to break.'

'Sorry to interrupt,' said the ER doctor, as he drew back the curtain. He paused for a minute and then said, 'Mia, I'm sorry. Unfortunately, you've had a miscarriage. The blood test results have confirmed that. We will need to do a small surgical procedure to ensure that all remnants of the pregnancy are gone, and so there are no future complications.' He went on to explain the procedure, but Mia zoned out, not able to take anymore.

* * *

She arrived home to numerous missed calls from Devon. It took her a day to feel strong enough to return his call.

'Mia let's have some counselling. I'm not ready to let this go. I'll get help and get off the drugs. Please don't give up on me yet.'

Her perpetual nature to put other people's needs first, sanctioned his suggestion.

Over a two-week period, they went for a session together, then sessions separately. Mia's was a couple of days after Devon's.

As she fearfully entered the therapist's room, she wondered if his observations had led to the conclusion that it was her fault. Did she have the problem?

The therapist started, 'Are you having an affair?'

'God no! I have enough trouble with one man, why would I want two?' Mia attempted to relax with humour.

The doctor continued, 'Devon is convinced you are. He is blaming that for his behaviour, his drug use, and for why the marriage is failing. He believes your so-called promiscuity is because you have issues with feeling loved. But he did say he still wants your marriage to work.'

Mia contemplated the doctor's words. After a short reflection, she started, 'He's right. I do have issues with feeling loved. A few years ago, what I thought was my forever person, left abruptly. The ending took me by complete surprise and left me feeling empty, worthless. I carry some issues from that and suppose I was still getting over them when Devon came into my life. I knew he had some issues as well, but he slowly convinced me I could rely on his love for me, and life would be great if we were together. Then as soon as I said yes to his proposal, I felt like a switch flicked. Rather than the commitment settling him, it seemed to stir increasingly controlling behaviour; unreasonable jealousy, and childish tantrums over nothing. I slowly became silent because that was the easiest. His mouth can be mean. And recently, there was a threatening, physical incident. This is the man I trusted to love me. So, yes, I do have issues feeling loved.'

Out of concern, the doctor broke his ethical code. 'The controlling language Devon used in his session, was alarming. He spoke of you like something he wants to own and manage, not like someone he loves. He won't accept his cannabis use may lend itself to his irrational jealousy and possessiveness or, that it may trigger him to snap. He put the entire blame on you.'

The doctor's face was serious as he continued, 'I believe his behaviour will get worse. In my opinion, you need to remove yourself from him, at least while he gets some help with his drug use and before he really hurts you.'

She didn't need to hear anymore. She flashed back to life with Devon and his delusions and was ready to run to anywhere he wasn't. She started to think it may have been her sixth sense all along warning her not to fall in love, but really didn't care who was to blame. She just wanted him out of her life, permanently.

Immediately after her session, Devon messaged, asking if they could meet on common ground to discuss what the counsellor had said, and to see if there was any prospect of reconciliation. Mia agreed to meet in a public place, within the hour.

* * *

'I can't help you anymore Devon. You need to find someone else who can.' Mia kept it curt and to the point. She also decided he didn't need to know about the miscarriage.

'So, it's over.'

'Yes. I won't be home Saturday morning. Please collect your things and leave the key under the front door mat.'

Luckily, she had insisted on keeping all finances and properties separate. It was as simple as him taking his personal belongings.

She walked away feeling the weight of her unhealthy marriage lift off her shoulders. It had only been sixteen months but for most of it, there had been little joy.

On that Saturday morning, as he was leaving Mia's house, Devon found Reg leaning on his car. 'Key please Devon.'

Reg was aware of Devon's sneakiness and guessed he would have no intention of leaving it, as Mia had requested. Devon handed it to him. 'Stay away from her now or you'll have me to answer to,' Reg threatened, making sure his access to her was done.

When she got home, Mia found his wedding ring on his bedside table. She immediately took her rings off and oddly, placed all of them in the BBQ. For her, when she found those drugs, that was the start of the final curtain coming down.

* * *

That night, as Mia looked in the mirror, she recognised some similarities between her and Devon's former girlfriend, Tracey. She looked jaded, emotionally drained, introverted. On reflection she realised that what he had said about Tracey could easily have been untrue, and that she too, had been a victim of his manipulation.

She thought about the miscarriage and started to cry, as the possibility of becoming a mother seemed to be slipping through her fingers. But her tears soon dried, after considering the dreadfulness of what her life could have been, forever.

And when the dust had settled, she honestly just felt relief, not heartbreak. She had lost herself in her marriage, constantly changing her behaviour or not voicing her true opinion, just to keep the peace. Devon had caused her to tie herself in knots, as she tried to please him and make him happy. In return, all she had received was criticism and ridicule.

But she'd found some self-worth buried inside and she was out, relatively unscathed. The grey cloud she had been living under was gone and now she could breathe, promising never to surrender her individuality again.

Jack's

back?

Chapter 33

2001 – Mia's New Year's resolutions

Fuck New Year's resolutions

'Where's Mia?', Lucy asked Devon as he took to the field at the pre-season game.

'That bitch was having an affair on me. It's over!', Devon hissed, not stopping to answer questions that his statement may have induced.

Lucy left the game and drove straight to Mia's.

'I can assure you I'm not having an affair.' Mia was completely unemotional telling Lucy her side of the story. Devon's fictional excuses for their marriage breakdown didn't surprise her.

'I knew he was lying.' Lucy hugged her.

'In fact, hell may have to freeze over before I let another male near me again,' Mia stated.

The ending of this relationship didn't have Mia in scattered jigsaw pieces, but she also wasn't sure if love, marriage, and family was what she wanted anymore.

Lucy confessed, 'Honestly, I'm glad it's over. I never thought he was right for you. And while I'm confessing stuff, I'm going to end it with Matthew. The festive season was challenging. So, we'll both be single, looking for new adventures together.'

'Can we make them male free for a while please? I feel like I have had an overdose of testosterone.' Mia smiled, as Lucy nodded in agreement.

Devon had been out of her house for over a month when Keith rang. 'Mia, what happened?'

'You need to talk to your son.'

'He tells us you've being having an affair.'

'I can assure you I haven't.' She decided it was time his father knew a bit more. 'Devon needs help. It's not alcohol. It's drugs. He's convinced that marijuana is harmless, but when you research the effects it can have on some people, it can be dangerous. I've seen it turn him into a different person, and I just can't help him anymore. Maybe you can.'

'Is the marriage finished for you?'

'Absolutely! No doubt.'

'Well, we wish you all the best. I'll do what I can for Devon.'

With that conversation, Mia felt she handed the responsibility of a child back to a parent. She knew she couldn't do anymore.

But of course, there was retaliation from Devon. Mia had told his dirty secret to his father, and he felt betrayed.

His phone call was ugly. Devon screamed at Mia, calling her every horrid name possible and threatened to ruin her life. When he finally took a breath, Mia emotively said, 'Don't contact me again or I will get the police involved.' She hung up, feeling nothing.

Half an hour later, the phone rang again. She stood watching it ring, deliberating whether to answer it. It would be easy to let it ring out, but she never ran from anything. As her adrenaline coursed through her, she snatched the handset and started with, 'I told you Devon, leave me alone.'

'Steady girl. It's Jack.'

The shock went right the way through her body. After everything, why does his voice still bring her so much comfort?

'I know I shouldn't ring, but I'm all the way in South Australia and can feel you from here. I know something's wrong.'

The tears rolled down her face as she tried to compose herself.

'Mia, are you there?'

'Yes Jack,' she sobbed.

'Oh Darl, what's wrong?' All Jack wanted to do was hold her and stop her crying. He gave her some time to calm and then gently said, 'Mia, tell me.'

'My marriage is over.'

'Marriage?'

The question made Mia realise how long it had been since they had spoken openly. He didn't even know she was married.

'Yes Jack. And it was nothing like I wanted. I allowed myself to be turned into someone I didn't recognise. I feel bruised and emotionally drained. I've got nothing left.'

He didn't care about the marriage. He just wanted to make her better. 'Mia, come to me. Please. I can help you with this. I'm going to Mum's for the Easter weekend to look after her house while she's away with Ian. It's only six weeks away. Please Mia. Let me help you.'

The warmth that any contact with Jack always generated, washed over her and the thought of being in his arms brought instant pain relief. So, like a moth to a flame, she said, 'Okay.'

April 2001

Mia told one person of her plans, Karl. She dropped into his place one afternoon. There was a lot to catch up on.

She went through an edited version of her marriage breakdown. She didn't feel it necessary to describe all the sordid details, and its failure didn't seem to surprise him.

'I'm going to Victoria for the Easter weekend.' Mia changed the subject once she thought the Devon stories were done.

'With Lucy?', Karl asked.

'No.' Mia paused dramatically and looked him dead in the eye.

Karl searched his mind for a moment. His sharpness and the importance she seemed to be placing on the topic would lead him to the right answer. 'The shearer.' Karl smiled, knowing he had correctly joined the dots. He remembered Jack was from Victoria and that he'd previously predicted he'd be back one day.

'Am I mad?', she asked, sincerely wanting his opinion.

'Yes, but you always have been.' He chuckled at his harmless jibe. 'I reckon you deserve some happiness after what you've been through. If you think the shearer can provide that, go for it. But don't forget, you probably still want different things. Keep your feet on the ground.'

'I'm not sure anymore. Maybe marriage and children aren't for me. Maybe it's just about being with the right person.'

'Don't write them off just yet. Besides it will still come down to you not wanting to smell like cow shit every day.' They both laughed.

Mia changed tack. 'How's things with Taylor?'

'Very good thanks Champ. I've started to think about marriage myself,' Karl declared, and Mia's face lit up.

'Now don't get too excited. I'm just thinking about it. You can't rush into these things, so keep that little chestnut under your hat.'

'As long as you keep my trip under yours. Deal?'

'Deal.'

* * *

She had never lied to her mother, but with all the worry her marriage had caused, she rationalised the small falsehood as being kind. She told her she was going to Melbourne for a shopping weekend with Lucy. Both Reg and Elizabeth were relieved that she was enjoying life again.

Mia knew she had to get Lucy somewhat on board. She phoned her a week out. 'Lucy, I have a favour to ask. It's all a bit last minute but I've decided to go to Melbourne for the Easter break. I've told Mum that I'm going with you. Can you cover for me if it ever comes up?'

Lucy didn't want to pry too much but her curiosity got the better of her. 'Are we still male-free Mia?'

'No, and yes. I'm meeting up with an old friend. Nothing more.' She didn't want to disclose it was Jack.

'Are you safe with him?'

Mia mused at the question, *'Am I safe with Jack? I may need to pack a floatation device in case I start drowning when I see him.'*

'Perfectly safe.' She quickly refuted the thought, letting it fade.

* * *

On the plane, she started to think, *'How long has it been since I've seen him? Nearly four years. The drop-in day, where he was there five minutes, and my soul felt nourished. But I've lived another lifetime since then, and we're just friends, right?'*

But as Jack approached her, beaming with joy, she fell helplessly into his embrace, and instantly felt restored. Pure love poured out of him, so appreciative to have the chance to help her heal.

And a lot of healing was needed. Mia was unsure of everything. As they travelled north to Jack's hometown, they talked like friends would, but she could sense the connecting energy ignite between them. Jack reached for Mia's hand as a sign he could feel it too, but she involuntarily pulled it away, like a scared child.

It shocked him. 'Mia, it's me.' He looked deep into her eyes, wanting her to trust him.

'I know Jack. I'm sorry. There's still a lot to unpack.'

He slowly reached for it again. This time she let him have it. 'It's a good thing I have a lot of experience at unpacking... and packing,' he said, poking fun at his restlessness.

She smiled at the reference and quickly shifted her focus to his life. 'How's your mum and Ian?'

'Ian's very sick. It won't be long now. Mum has taken him to his hometown this weekend so he can see some of his friends.' There was a resigned sadness in Jack's voice.

* * *

When they arrived at Mary's house, Jack showed Mia to the cosy bedroom they had once shared. He quickly explained he would be sleeping in the new extension he had helped build a couple of years ago.

The house smelt of a home cooked meal. 'I put the slow cooker on before I came to the airport. Dinner is all taken care of. How about I get us some wine, and we get comfy on the couch.'

After he delivered their wine to the small tables at either end of the lounge, he knelt in front of her and started to take off her shoes. Mia tried to ignore the personal gesture and continued with her small talk. He then put himself at the other end of the couch, gesturing for her to place her socked feet in his lap, and swinging his legs to the outside of hers.

As Jack started to rub her feet, and they began to study one another's face, Mia was transported back to his cabin where they had spent many nights, slipping into meaningful conversation and understanding each other on the deepest of levels. In that moment her defences started to be compromised.

He patiently waited for her to talk about the past few years. When she finally did, he tried not to react, but as she mentioned hurtful episodes, a stabbing pain went through his heart. And when she talked about the miscarriage, her tears wouldn't stop. He cried too, shifting his position to holding her tight while she fell apart.

'I'm sorry Jack. You shouldn't have to deal with this.'

'No, I'm the one that's sorry. And I'm more than happy to help you through this.' He stroked her hair. 'How about I run you a hot bath? You can take some time to relax before dinner.'

'You don't need to do that. I can sort it out.'

'Mia, please let me take care of you,' Jack tenderly asked.

* * *

As she soaked in the ideal temperature water, she noticed how much care he had taken to make the room tranquil. He'd lit candles, had healing music playing softly and a subtle fragrance of lavender was in the air.

She was so far away from the harsh, ugly environment that she had recently been living in. Mia shook her head in disbelief. *'How did I get myself there? Ah, that's right, by defining love as someone wanting to marry me. How wrong could I have been?'*

* * *

'Feeling better Darl?' Jack hugged her as she re-joined him in the kitchen. She was in a daggy tracksuit and slippers, allowing the comfort that she had started to feel to continue.

'Yes thanks. The best I've felt in a long time. More like me.'

'I hope you're hungry. Put yourself back on the couch and I'll bring it to you. Another glass of wine?'

'Yes, please.' She snuggled under a blanket that he had placed on the lounge to keep her warm. She loved Victoria in autumn.

After dinner, Jack spoke about his work in South Australia and that he had more lined up there for the next few months.

'You seem very happy.'

'It's a big part of who I am. Shearing, I mean. It's all I know how to do. I didn't finish school, so thinking about doing something else is daunting. I'm not that smart.'

'Unfortunately, it's life's hard lessons that make you smart Jack, not finishing school.' Mia sounded unusually cynical. It caused him to frown.

He paused. He wanted his words to be consequential. 'I know I briefly mentioned to you about the bad relationship I was in before I met you, but I don't think I ever told you I'd completely committed to the whole normal life thing. We were living in suburbia, and I was working at the Woolshed. But it was like your marriage. Coercion, a lot of taking, and not much giving. In the end, I had completely lost myself and felt I was worth nothing. I was in a very dark place. It was my sister that helped me get out. When I heard the pain in your voice on the phone, I understood how you were feeling and knew I could help.'

Seeing the pain on his face, Mia reached for Jack's hand.

'When I was well enough, I went straight to my default position, ready to pack up and go. I was just getting some money together when I met you.' He looked at her adoringly.

'Did I ever make you feel like that Jack? Worthless or trapped.'

'No, but I associate the life you want with feeling trapped. Being with you was the happiest time of my life, and I still miss you. But I made a deal with myself never again to lose who I am. And that means no shackles. I don't want the same workplace for years, or a mortgage or school fees or anything else that most people's lives have. I like no ties, the ability to pack everything I own in a bag and to be able to move on when I feel I need to. Does that make sense?'

'Yes. I mean, now I understand how important it is to never lose my identity again. And I was so focused on what I thought was going to make me happy, that I forgot about the most important thing, love. Pure, true love.'

'What happened to you should never have happened. And I'm partially responsible.'

Mia tried to interrupt but Jack stopped her. 'I pushed you so far away, out of fear and selfishness. You must have felt so much uncertainty that it left you exposed to a tyrant like him.' Jack couldn't bring himself to say Devon's name. 'I'm sorry for handling things so badly. My vanishing act was that of an immature boy.'

Mia couldn't argue with the last sentence but felt the rest was unnecessary guilt. 'I was the one that danced with the devil. From the beginning there were stop signs. But I rolled the dice, arrogantly thinking I could help him. I continually excused his behaviour, all because I wanted to be a wife and mum.'

'And you will be wonderful at both, when the person who deserves you comes along.' Jack tried to be selfless but the thought of someone else with her etched pain all over his face.

'It'll be a long time, if ever, before I think about that again.'

'The thought of you not being either, makes me sad.'

Unreserved love flowed between them. 'Please don't be sad Jack. I don't want to be anymore. I need to laugh and have fun.'

'Okay. Let's tuck you into bed and we'll start on that tomorrow.'

Holding her hand, he led her to her room. Once she was in bed, he pulled the covers up and caringly brushed her hair from her face. 'Night, Mia.'

'Night, Jack.'

Chapter 34

'Good morning, Sunshine.' Jack came into Mia when he heard her stir. 'Here's your coffee.'

He sat himself at the foot of the bed, keeping a safe distance between them. 'We're going to have fun today, promise.'

And before long, Mia found herself on the back of Jack's motorbike, heading towards Bright. The wind was cool on her face, but she was warm inside, as she moved with him at every lean. She felt him chuckle several times, causing her to glow with happiness.

They bought cheese and tomato toasties from a café and headed to the park. The autumn leaves had started to fall, and the ground was a carpet of red, orange, and yellow. They sat amongst them, leaving the intensity of yesterday's conversation behind and appreciating the beauty of the day.

Jack then rode them to Mt Buffalo where they explored walking trails and enjoyed scenery from the lookout. He held her hand as she basked in nature and, just being with him.

They headed back to a local pub for lunch and then onto a famous local bakery to indulge in some delightful treats. When he was momentarily distracted, she saved a bit of cream to her right index finger, hiding it behind her back. When he turned back to face her, she invited him to come closer with her gaze. As Jack smoothly leant in to kiss her, she slowly raised her arm and placed the cream on the end of his nose. He burst out laughing, closing his eyes, and shaking his head. 'What am I going to do with you?'

'Not sure yet', Mia teased between her laughter.

Jack took the ride home slowly. She loved being wrapped around his body, holding onto him firmly. Intermittently he moved his hand off the handlebar, squeezing hers with reassurance, and she couldn't help but feel vertiginous.

* * *

The routine from the night before was repeated. Jack ran Mia a bath, she relaxed into her tracksuit, they ate dinner and found themselves back on the couch, with Jack rubbing her feet. Mia talked about her work for the first time, informing Jack she was now a senior consultant on the project team. But as she spoke, it became a reminder that she just didn't belong in his world.

After he tucked her into bed, he knelt on the floor beside her and softly suggested, 'Close your eyes.' He stayed for quite a while, touching her face like he was memorising every inch. Just as Mia was about to slip away into a deep sleep, he kissed her lips ever so gently and whispered, 'I still love you.'

She felt him stand to leave and decided to let him go. She didn't want to spoil the moment with her rendition of how she felt. She was sure he knew.

* * *

They spent the following morning in the local park. Jack set up a blanket and got fresh croissants from the bakery. Mia laid close to him as he read her the local newspaper. Their conversation was light, and full of laughter. They were savouring what time they had left together, knowing that by tomorrow night, they'd be apart.

By the time they were in their post dinner, lounge position, their vocal conversation had lessened but their hearts were reverberating in unison. Both were heavy at the thought of leaving one another, but grateful for the time together.

211

Mia broke the silence first. 'I've been a fool. I spent a long time believing you never loved me. How could I have forgotten this feeling between us?'

'I've tried not to think about it too. It's easier not to acknowledge it when we can't be together. Jack's eyes were glistening with emotion. 'But there's no denying it's still here. Not after these few days.'

She spoke with pure love, 'I understand so much more now. Just because our lives have us in different directions, doesn't mean the love needs to be denied. Yes, by recognising it at times, I feel hurt, but burying it, seems to have hurt me more.' All the defences she had holding him at bay malfunctioned.

He crawled towards her, not able to hold back, and kissed her passionately. He waited for her to encourage him before he progressed any further.

She whispered, 'No fear, no shackles, no expectations. Love me like I know you want to.'

He scooped her up and carried her to the bedroom, gently placing her on the bed. They took their time, rediscovering each other's body, not knowing if this would be the last time they'd be together. It was hours of touching, spoiling, and indulging one another, until neither of them could wait any more, and Jack made love to her with deep emotion.

Afterwards, they fell asleep holding each other, with scars healed and hurts disregarded.

* * *

She woke to him tickling her back. She rolled onto it, and he kissed her good morning. He placed his head on her chest, facing away from her and said, 'I know it seems like I'm all for this being apart business, but this morning, I'm having trouble considering it.'

Mia played with his thick, dark hair, realising how hard it was going to be, for them both, to walk away.

'Any chance you'd stay with me? Come to South Australia and be with me.'

Mia couldn't help but think how easy it would be to say yes. Forget her career, her house, her mum, and Reg. Undo the tie to her responsibilities and be free with Jack. But her rational mind always won.

'I'm just finding my feet again, Jack.'

He sighed and said, 'Forgive me for asking. Just a moment of weakness.'

He turned and kissed her, believing going back to their separate lives was the only option. He got up and headed for the shower.

She went to the kitchen to find a pen and some paper. She needed to leave a note that would tell him what she hadn't said.

* * *

As they arrived at the airport, Jack said, 'Hey, Amy hasn't got many girlfriends in Brisbane and she's seeing a new guy who's a highflyer.'

Mia wasn't sure why he was mentioning his sister.

'She also might be a good substitute when you can't reach me.'

Mia took this as an indication there would be minimum direct communication between them. He was planning on using his sister to keep an eye on her.

He smiled his delicious smile. 'I'd worry much less, if I knew my two favourite girls were in touch. I'll encourage her to contact you, okay?'

'Sure. Give her my mobile number. The house phone will be going soon.'

The final boarding call sounded, and they tried to pretend everything was fine, but it wasn't. There were no promises of when they would see each other. The only future contact spoken about was Jack's word that he would write soon. They were trusting their bond would lead them back, in whatever capacity fate had for them.

He held her and kissed her one last time. She touched his face, and he kissed her hand as their eyes welled with tears.

'I'm going to go now. But feel free to watch me as I do,' Mia repeated the line from the first night he had invited her into his world. Jack laughed through the anguish of letting her go.

Once home, he found her note on the bed they had laid in...

Dear Jack,

No one else could have done for me what you have over the last few days. You've healed me just by being you and allowing me to be close to you. I will never forget this weekend and how you've made me feel. My heart is full, and my soul is replenished. Although the past, unhealthy few years still play like a bad movie in my mind, I feel someone else is starring in it, because you have helped me disassociate from it.

Love isn't hard is it, Jack? It's kind and unconditional. You reminded me of that over these past few days. Your care, your thoughtfulness and of course, your love.

I understand now, to be happy, we need to stay true to ourselves. And more than anything Jack, I want you to be happy. Always remember, I'm never far away.

Your (lots of loving) friend,

Mia xxx

Mia's love for Jack had exploded back to the surface. But she now accepted that he needed to be free to be his happiest, and this would assure their connection would always exist.

* * *

Once home, the first thing she did was reach into the back of her wardrobe to retrieve her hidden "diamond". She wrapped the featherstone back around her bedpost so, as initially promised, it would be the first and last thing she saw every day.

But Mia's greatest challenge was going to be keeping this balancing act up; acknowledging the great love she felt for Jack, but accepting that having him as a life partner, just wasn't in the cards for them.

Chapter 35

During the following week, Mia had dinner with her mum and Reg. The lie about her trip was eating her up and she knew she had to come clean.

'How was Melbourne darling? Did you and Lucy have a good time?', Elizabeth asked.

'Mum, I haven't been completely honest. The truth is, I went to see Jack. I'm sorry I lied. I didn't want you to worry.'

Elizabeth had sensed her daughter was hiding something. Mia was a terrible liar. 'I see. How did it go?', her tone was sober.

Mia's face lit up, thinking about Jack. 'It was the medicine I needed. I feel better than I have done in ages. As good as when we were together.'

'And are you back together?', Elizabeth's concern was evident.

'No Mum. I've come to realise that can't happen. But I know it's not because he doesn't love me.'

'Well then, it sounds like the visit was good for you. I'm glad you went. But don't ever lie to us again.'

'Never. It's too hard.' Mia felt the burden of the dishonesty fade as Elizabeth's serious face softened with a small smile.

After Mia left, Elizabeth asked Reg, 'Do you think Jack is the one for her and one day they'll be together?'

'No. Jack's restless and always will be. He'll break her heart if they try to be together,' Reg's response was adamant. 'There is someone else for Mia.'

August 2001

Mia wanted to put distant between her and her life with Devon.
She sold her house and bought another just down the road.

Moving day was a week away when Mary's note arrived...

Dear Mia,
How are you love? Jack told us you made a quick visit at
Easter time. We would have loved to have seen you, but as you
know, Ian isn't very well. We are making the most of the time
we have left together, and I am slowly coming to terms with
the reality I'll soon be on my own.
We were sad to hear about your recent troubles. My mother
used to say that life can feel like a long road sometimes.
Mia, there are plenty of other fish in the sea. You will meet
someone who really deserves you. I want to say a lot more, but
will just say this... I'm glad you and Jack can be friends. Ian
and I will never forget you.
Take care of yourself.
Mary x
P.S - Please know, you're welcome to come and stay anytime.

Mia sensed Mary's hope for a happier ending for her and Jack.
She penned a short reply...

Dear Mary,
I'm so sorry to hear about Ian. This is such a difficult time for
you both. Loving someone like you and Ian do, is so precious.
I'm sure it won't stop, even after he's gone. My thoughts and
love are with you.
I have sold my house and bought a new one, just down the road.
I just needed a fresh start. My new address is on the back.
Would you mind passing it onto Jack next time you talk?
I had a wonderful time at Easter. Jack was very kind and
helped repair some of the hurt I have recently experienced. I
can't tell you how grateful I am to have him in my life, even as
just a friend. I will always love him, but being friends is the
way we will both be at our happiest.
I'll be in touch again soon.
Mia x

She re-read the last paragraph, as images of their weekend together swamped her mind. The doubt leaked in, crushing the word "friends", replacing it with "together".

'Stop it! This is how we can both be at our happiest, right?'

She posted her reply, and Ian passed the day after it arrived.

* * *

Amy also got in touch and the girls visited each other regularly. At first, Amy acted like a go-between, letting Mia know about Jack's life in South Australia and that he had decided to stay indefinitely. Mia slipped her bits of information in hope they were being passed to him.

But as time went by, the girls found other things to chat about, and Mia decided not hearing about Jack's life would be better, helping to minimise the ache of missing him.

During this time, she half-heartedly dated, but no one came close to triggering her interest. And the day she watched Karl get married, her happiness for him was slightly tainted. She felt extremely lonely and wondered if she'd already had the only love she would ever know, Jack.

September 2003

After two- and a-bit years, Jack finally rang. His news would only compound how she was feeling. 'Mia, I've met someone and thought you should know. She's an artist on the island and a real free spirit. We're a lot alike, simple lifestyle, no real ties.'

Mia swallowed down the lump in her throat. She was going to need her best acting skills. 'If she makes you happy, I'm happy. That's what I want most. I know contacting me must have been hard, thank you.' She had to stop and catch her breath.

'Mia, I...'

'I know Jack. I love you too. This is for the best. I promise, I'm fine with this. I'm genuinely happy for you. Take care.'

218

She teetered on the tightrope of emotional stability, as she thought about never being with him again.

'Of course there was going to be someone else better suited. Nothing's changed. He still loves me. Breathe.'

On her next visit to Amy's, she decided to address the elephant in the room. 'Good news about Jack. I hope this new love realises the treasure she has.' Amy just nodded and changed the subject without comment.

September 2004

She was able to maintain this state of mind until his note arrived, a year later...

Dear Mia,

I hope you're well, and your life is full of joy.

Thank you for being so wonderful and understanding me.

Your words a year ago gave me the courage to move forward with my new relationship, and I have now taken it somewhere I never thought I would. I've decided to get married. Nothing conventional (you know me). It's just going to be Ava and I saying vows to each other. Mum and Amy aren't even coming. But that's the way we want it.

You will always be special to me. Please be as happy as I am.

Your friend always,

Jack x

It was a king hit. *'Married! He doesn't believe in marriage.'* And for the first time in a long time, she questioned his love for her. *'If I'm so special, why didn't he ever want to marry me?'*

And this was the catalyst for her to spend the next year leaving no stone unturned. Weekends were all about meeting new people and convincing herself this could be the one.

But she would lose interest as quickly as it started, and churned through men, like a stockbroker on a busy day.

September 2005

Amy got engaged. She had been dating the same guy Jack had mentioned to Mia way back. He was extremely successful and came from a very wealthy family. The engagement party was to be held on a river boat cruise.

When Amy handed Mia her invitation, she started with, 'Mum's coming. She'll be so happy to see you.' Mia waited for Amy to say what she had anticipated. 'And Jack and Ava are coming.'

'Great. It'll be nice to meet her,' Mia said, attempting sincerity.

'I haven't warmed to her. Neither has Mum.' Amy offered this new information straightforwardly. 'If you can understand what he sees in her, can you explain it to us?'

* * *

The morning of the party, Mia's hair and makeup appointments were in the city. As she was walking through the city arcade, she noticed a sign "Tarot Reader". She found herself drawn into the small, bohemian shop and before long, was sitting opposite a gypsy styled woman, ready for a ten-minute reading.

The woman's tone was compelling. 'The man you have let go; he will want to be with you again. The choice will be yours and it will be a major crossroad in your life. There is another who is fated to be part of your life. Both men have been with you many lifetimes, but the man you haven't met yet, will only come if the first man is gone completely. They can't cross paths. The decisions you make in the next six to twelve months, will determine if you ever meet him in this life. Choose carefully.'

Mia left, not giving what the reader said too much credit, notching the experience up as a good time filler that kept her imagination from running wild about the night's potential encounters.

* * *

Mia stepped on board the boat as Amy and her fiancé, James, greeted her. There were a lot of people, but she managed to spot Mary and made a beeline for her. 'It's so good to see you.'

Oh Mia, you look beautiful,' Jack's mum said, as she hugged her.

'Yes, she does,' came Jack's voice unexpectedly behind Mia. 'Hi, Mum.' He kissed Mary and turned to Mia to awkwardly hug her. 'Mia this is Ava. Ava, Mia.'

'Hi Mia. I've heard a lot about you.' Ava offered her hand for Mia to shake.

'Nice to meet you, Ava.' Mia wasn't sure if it was jealousy, but she quickly judged Jack's wife. She looked about ten years older than him and had an unkept vibe about her, making her look out of place in the elegance of the other guests.

'Mary.' Ava coolly greeted Jack's mum with no hug or kiss.

'Ava.' Mary eyed her daughter-in-law as only a displeased, customary, country woman could.

'I'll go and get us some drinks Jack.' Ava escaped the discomfort.

Mia tried to keep her focus on Mary, but one of Amy's friends soon called her, leaving Mia to face Jack. 'You look well.'

'And you look as beautiful as ever. Life good?'

'Yes. Very happy.'

Mia spoke about her career progress and her new home. She hoped if she created enough chatter, their usual attraction would stay regulated. But her effort was useless. Even with her raving, they were soon looking at each other adoringly.

'I've got to go and find my drink, before I forget I'm married.'

Mia blushed. 'Probably a good idea.' She was relieved, because the building intensity in his gaze was starting to consume her, and she too was starting to forget he was married.

She looked around to find Mary observing them from across the deck of the boat. Her expression said everything she wouldn't dare say out loud. Mia moved to join her.

'I do worry about my son. I feel he may have lost his way.'

Mia reassured her. 'Jack seems fine Mary. He'll always find his way home. To you, I mean.'

Mary's look clearly said, 'You do know he's still in love with you.' But Mia gave her no space to say anything on the matter.

As the boat cruised up and down the river, Mia avoided being too close to Jack and Ava. She preoccupied herself with one of James's friends, who had taken quite a shine to her. He wasn't her type but was good enough company to keep her from falling into Jack's gaze as she felt him watch her subtly from a distance.

When the boat docked, it was obvious Ava couldn't wait to get Jack off it. Mia dared to glance in his direction for a discreet good-bye, and as their eyes locked, she knew their story wasn't over. He reluctantly mouthed, 'Bye', and Mia countered with a cheeky wink, just before the pair disappeared up the ramp.

She had no idea what it all meant but believed she would be guided correctly. She went to bed that night, staring up at their featherstone, contemplating whether there just may have been something in what the gypsy had told her.

Chapter 36

September 2006

Amy and James' wedding was an extravagant affair, with minimal guests. Mia understood when she didn't receive an invitation, and after seeing Jack at the engagement party, knowing their connection didn't stop even with his wife standing next to him, she felt quite relieved to not be going.

Now, only four months after the wedding, Mia was surprised to read of his plans to return so soon...

Dear Mia,

How are you? I wish we could have caught up when I was in Brisbane for Amy's wedding but, that time needed to be all about her. I was so proud to walk her down the aisle and, I have come to like James very much.

I'm planning on coming back to Brisbane in a month's time. This trip is all about me catching up with my friends. I'm counting down the days as it is well over-due. Is there any chance I could see you? I believe it will be around your birthday. I will call you as the time gets closer.

Love

Jack x

He phoned in the last week of September, starting with a lot of small talk, but finally getting to the point. 'So, I'm arriving in Brisbane Friday October 13th, and before you say anything, I know that's not a good day to fly.' He laughed nervously. 'I'm there a week. Can you fit me in sometime?'

Mia thought there might be safety in numbers. 'I'm having a bit of a birthday party on the Saturday night. Would you like to come?'

'Sure. Any chance I could stay the night? My plan is to land on the couch of anyone who'll have me.' Mia could feel him grin.

'Ava not coming?' Mia had already assumed she wasn't but wanted to make sure. She was mentally strong but having Jack's wife stay in her house would be too much.

'No, just me.'

'Okay, I have a spare room you can stay in,' she said, clearly outlining the rules for his stay.

October 2006

It wasn't just a bit of a party. Mia's house was full of people when Jack arrived. The attendees consisted of work colleagues, neighbours, people Mia had met over the past couple of years, Lucy and some of her nurse friends and of course, Elizabeth and Reg. Those who couldn't make it were Karl, who had recently become a father for the first time, and Amy and James who had a prior engagement. Amy hadn't commented on Jack's visit or the fact he was staying at Mia's without his wife.

Mia had hired a frozen daiquiri machine and jukebox. The place was pumping with fun.

She greeted Jack with a big hug and showed him to the spare room. He noticed Wovoka hanging on the wall and smiled. He dropped his bag and came out to join the other merrymakers.

He went straight to Elizabeth and Reg. Elizabeth was warm, wanting to show him how grateful she was for the part he had played on Mia's Easter visit. But she also appreciated that Reg's opinion was most likely correct, and as they stood talking, she secretly prayed for him not to hurt Mia again. Reg was polite but still reserved.

Lucy cornered Jack at one stage, wanting to get to know the man she had heard so much about. He did well, fending off some of her subjective questions, but respectfully moved onto other people when he had enough of her probing.

Throughout the night, Mia would check on him by catching his eye across the room. He would just give a single nod and beam a smile back at her.

When other guests started to leave, he came to her and said, 'I'm tired, Darl. I'm going to bed. See you in the morning.'

'You sure you're, okay?' Mia sensed something was off.

'Yes, fine. Great party.' He kissed her on the cheek and headed down the hallway.

It was well past midnight before the last of Mia's guests left. She tinkered quietly in the kitchen, doing a bit of cleaning up, then headed to her bedroom.

As she opened the door, she found Jack in her bed, sitting up reading. He lowered the book to reveal his naked, muscley chest and the top of his pyjama shorts. Her knees went weak.

'I see our featherstone is still around your bedpost.'

'What are you doing? What about your marriage?' Mia tried to hold her ground knowing he was her kryptonite.

'I left Ava the weekend after Amy's wedding. It's over. If I'm honest, it's been over since Amy's engagement party.' He searched her eyes to see if her love for him was still there. 'I've tried to be happy without you, but I'm not. Come here, please.' He beckoned her to lay with him.

The word *"crossroads"* rang in her ears, and her soul split in two. One part... instantly acknowledged her love for him and how much she wanted him. And here he was, in her bed, begging for her to love him. A scenario she had only allowed herself to think about in the dark moments of missing him.

The other... offered some resistance. Would it ever be any different or was this going to be another intense but temporary reunion, followed by a long time apart? And by letting him close again, she would only be reminded how unrivalled he had been.

But as she started to recall their Easter together, and how much life it reinvigorated in her, any resistance crumbled. She gave into wanting him and lay beside him with her head on his chest.

He started to play with her hair. 'I ignorantly thought I could box us up into just memories and carry on with my life. I met Ava and assumed I'd found the answer. Even though part of you was still with me, she was someone I could love who wanted the same life as me.' Jack paused, gathering his thoughts.

'But when I saw you on that boat, the love I felt for you was overwhelming, more than I've ever felt for Ava. I kept thinking, I just needed time, and if I didn't see you again, it would go away. But then at Amy's wedding, even though you weren't there, I could feel you and I ached to be with you. I've tried my best to run away from you, but this time, I'm running towards you full speed. Please tell me you still want us.'

Mia was off-balance. For so long, she'd coached herself to disregard a future with Jack, that now it was being handed to her, she was hesitant to believe in it.

'And Ava, how is she?' Mia surprised herself at how much empathy she was feeling for Jack's wife, but she knew first-hand how hard it was to cope when Jack changed direction.

'She knows there's no future for her and me. She also knows that I was going to visit you while I was here, and our history. She knew things changed when I saw you at the engagement party. I just haven't told her the extent of my feelings yet.'

Mia sat up and looked at him. Was she willing to bet on her and Jack again? Could it be everything she wanted? Something in her heart said, *'Slow down.'*

'Jack, I don't think there is any need for "full speed".' She smiled. 'Maybe more like a train pulling out from the station, nice and slow. Let's see if we've got it in us to reach full steam.'

'Perfect.' Jack kissed her on the nose, desperately wanting more, but respecting Mia's request not to rush.

'Go to sleep. You look tired and I need a shower.'

When she returned, his eyes were closed but she knew he wasn't asleep. She slipped gently into bed and rolled onto her side, with her back towards him, daring him to come closer. He moved his body against her, wrapping his arm around her waist, pulling her tight against him, and tried to obey her instruction to rest. She had chosen boy-pyjamas as a feeble attempt to keep his sexual desire contained, but by dawn, she knew his hunger could no longer be quelled and she let him passionately make love to her.

* * *

The plan for the week was he would spend the days visiting friends, including Joe, while Mia went to work. But they would be together by sunset.

The Monday was Mia's birthday, and she arrived home from work to fresh flowers with a small card that read...

It is not in the stars
to hold our destiny, But in ourselves.
Happy Birthday.
Yours always, Jack xx

She thought back to the first of her birthdays they shared, on top of Mount Warning. She should have taken the name as a clear sign about her journey with Jack. But thirteen years on, she had bought another ticket and was back on the ride.

They did have dinner with Elizabeth and Reg one night, and it went surprisingly well, but Mia could feel them both hold their breaths, thinking of the possibility that Jack had her heart, again.

When his flight home was looming, Mia decided to be brave. 'Jack how's this going to work? You and me, I mean.'

'I've got work lined up in S.A, for about six months. I'd like to finish that. Then I'll make my way back to Queensland and look for some work not too far out west. I know it's not quite the life you wanted, but I'll try to be here with you as much as I can.'

It wasn't ideal but she loved to dream that it could work.

He nuzzled into her neck and softly said in her ear, 'It's only six months. And then you'll have me forever.'

* * *

She got home from the airport and found a note on her pillow...

Dear Mia,

It's certainly a strange twist of fate which has seen our hearts beating together once again.

Our love is one which can't be explained, let alone understood, however, it can't be ignored.

I had no expectations of my visit here, only that I needed to tell you that I truly love you.

By now, I'm in the air heading south, but my heart will remain with you, and I know that we'll always be together in one way or another.

Thank you for showing me love once again, for bringing out the passion in me and the romance from my heart.

Thank you for being you, for introducing me to your friends and for re-uniting me with Elizabeth and Reg.

I miss you already, just writing these words, but I am so happy for the experience of you... all of it.

Saying I love you, doesn't come close to how I truly feel. I wish you nothing but happiness until I see your beautiful eyes staring into mine once again.

I vow to always be honest with you, whatever happens while we're apart. For me, you are more than worthy for me to change my life, and I know, it will be totally worth the wait.

Take care my special, caring, beautiful Mia.

Yours always,

Jack xxx

Chapter 37

March 2007

And for six months, the train picked up speed. Mia was back, drunk on Jack. There were daily phone calls, that only just managed to dull the pain of being apart; there were impromptu weekends, where Jack would fly in, and they would gratify each other in every way imaginable; and of course, there were dozens of letters, with Jack penning poetic words about their love, how she was his only happiness and how much he needed her.

As time went on, Mia truly believed it was going to happen for them this time. She was so happy. She had lost any thought or need to have children, to be married again or to have a normal lifestyle. All she wanted was Jack.

And then... just as the train hit full speed, Jack changed direction.

In the last week of contact, Jack had seemed a bit down on their phone calls. When Mia asked if he was okay, he said he had strained his wrist at work, trying to shear too many sheep in a day. Then he laughed insincerely, commenting that his body was packing it in.

Then, after several days of this change in mood, the phone calls stopped. As the days went by without any contact, Mia's state of frantic increased, worried that something serious had happened to him.

And just as she was about to book a flight to South Australia to find him, his epic, heartbreaker of a letter arrived...

Mia desperately held onto the fragments of her mind. She re-read the letter over and over, thinking about the years she had known him and how she should have seen this coming. But he'd done a great job convincing her they were finally solid. To sabotage their future at the final hour was the ultimate disappointment. She was exhausted. *'Enough.'*

Again, she heard the word, *"crossroads"*, faintly whispered. Something was calling the part of her that had tried to caution the night this ride had started again. Then, it had stepped aside, allowing Mia's dream of having Jack back, play out. But now, it was time for it to take charge.

He phoned the next day to try to explain his change of heart.

Mia kept her voice tempered. 'I'm disappointed.'

'I know, Darl.' For the first time, his term of endearment made her skin crawl. 'I need to do this for myself. And I owe Ava this much. I did make a commitment to her.'

'You misunderstood what I'm referring to. I'm disappointed in myself. Again, I allowed you back into my life, to turn me upside down, only to leave without considering the pieces I'll need to pick up. And what about your commitment to me?'

'That's the whole point. I'm getting help so I stop doing that to the people I love. You. Ava. I need to stop running.'

'If you think you owe Ava, you need to concentrate your efforts on her. I'm taking myself out of the race. I can't do this anymore. You always acknowledge our extraordinary connection, but it's never your priority. You've always taken it for granted and I'm done this time.'

There was deadly silence on the other end of the phone. She had always been so placid and understanding of his needs. He was in shock. He wasn't expecting her to walk away.

'I don't know what's going to happen with Ava. I just need to do this. I understand you're hurting. I'll give you a couple of days and I'll phone again.'

'No Jack. I mean it. I'm done. I'm choosing me this time. I'm walking away.' Mia paused to gather her strength. 'I sincerely hope you find whatever you're looking for, but please, don't ever contact me again.'

She hung up the phone as Jack pleaded for her to reconsider.

'I can do this. This time there can't be any room for a return, otherwise I will never get off this round-a-bout.'

She closed her eyes and visualised a connecting cord running between them. She reached for an imaginary, silver sword and sliced the linkage right in the middle, letting Jack go, once and for all.

'I wish you and Ava all the best.'

And with that thought, she felt him leave her heart.

There were no tears this time. She was truly done. She walked toward her bedroom to find one of the feathers from the featherstone had dropped to the floor. She picked it up and untwirled the main part of the ornament. She gathered all his letters and cards, and placed the lot into a large, unmarked envelop. She opened her blanket box in the spare room and buried it at the bottom of a multitude of other life mementos, with no thoughts of it ever resurfacing.

Max

Chapter 38

2009 – Mia's New Year's resolutions

Get a new job

Build a house

Never renounce my power again

In the years that followed her final contact with Jack, Mia became stronger and fiercely independent. She was determined to never again let anyone influence her decisions regarding her life's direction, wanting to only answer to herself.

She switched up her career and became a public servant for the Police Service. She entered her new work environment at the lowest level but found herself grabbing opportunities to perform in higher-grade roles, quickly settling into a senior administration position and becoming more serious about her work life.

With Elizabeth and Reg getting older, she also decided to do more to help them. She bought a block of land and engaged a builder to construct a dual living home. It was a steep learning curve, as she navigated contracts and made decisions unaccompanied. But with her self-growth over the past few years, she felt confident her life was on the right course and planned for both current homes to be sold in time, and they would all move into the shared dwelling.

At this stage, re-partnering was clearly not in her thoughts. She had no regrets cutting the cord to Jack, and she no longer missed him, but the experience had left her a different person. Unlike in the past, she felt no need to actively search for someone to be with. She now believed that if there was someone else, he would find her; but also accepted, there was a good possibility this may never happen. She was comfortable on her own.

She surrounded herself with friends, Lucy being her closest. Her effervescent personality provided Mia with light-hearted fun and kept her distracted from feeling lonely. Lucy had recently met a fire officer, Sam, but even as their relationship became serious, the girls remained tight.

Mia was content. Her life was free from chaos. She used the gym at work most days, and after a series of counselling sessions and several self-help workshops, the dints in her self-esteem had been ironed out. She was the healthiest she had ever been, physically, mentally and emotionally.

October 2009

Mia felt hypnotised as she stared at the candle flames on top of her birthday cake. Although she was comfortable with where her life was at, the thought of being forty didn't seem real.

As she blew out her candles, she was happy to share the moment with just Elizabeth and Reg. It was a milestone birthday, and their bond was deeper than ever. Besides, Lucy was also celebrating a special birthday and was hosting a fancy-dress party tomorrow night. Mia would revel then.

* * *

As she arrived at Lucy's party, Mia could see a lot of people in costume. The theme of the night was fairytale characters, and she had chosen to dress as Mulan, thinking that the coming of age, female warrior appropriately embodied her present-day life. Lucy greeted her, looking stunning, dressed as Cinderella, with Sam dressed as Prince Charming.

The party had been going for a while, when from across the room, Mia noticed a strikingly handsome man standing at the doorway. He wasn't in costume, and as he awkwardly looked around for someone he knew, she thought, *'He's not sure if he wants to be here.'*

Then, Sam charge across to him and dragged him inside. The men exchanged some words and a laugh, before heading to the bar.

The next time she spotted him, she watched on as the newcomer tussled with an overzealous single, female friend of Lucy's. Mia was intrigued as he didn't seem comfortable at all, and she decided to find out his story from Sam.

'Hey, the guy that arrived late with no costume. Do you know him well?'

'Sure do.' Sam's big, bold smile taunted Mia to ask more.

'He's a fireman, right?'

'Sure is,' Sam confirmed, still grinning.

'I knew it. Well, I'm staying right away from him. I know how much trouble you boys are,' Mia teased.

Sam laughed. 'I can assure you Max and I are both past being any trouble. He's an interesting guy. You should have a chat with him, although you may need to stand in line.'

Mia followed Sam's glance over to Max, where he was now juggling two more of Lucy's single girlfriends. He looked spooked, like a deer in headlights, stunned and unable to move.

Throughout the night, Mia watched from a distance, as a revolving door of women flirted and played with him. She noticed him reservedly shy away from any of their advances and, the drunker they got, the harder he peddled backwards.

'Hey Mia, let's go to the bar and have a quiet toast to our birthdays,' Lucy said, grabbing her by surprise.

The girls ordered some sparkling wine. 'Happy Birthday to us,' Lucy toasted, as they clinked their glasses together. Then she was suddenly distracted by someone behind Mia. 'Max, I'm glad you made it. Have you met Mia?'

'Hi Mia.'

'Nice to meet you Max.' Mia immediately noticed, although he seemed a little nervous, there was a charming composure about him. And now up close, she could see how attractive he really was. He looked slightly older than her, a little taller and in great shape. His skin was olive and there were very few lines on his face. His light brown hair was flecked with the first signs of greys, only adding to his appeal.

'I'm sorry about my other girlfriends Max. They're all a little "Fireman" struck. Grab yourself a drink and relax. You're in safe hands over here.' Lucy winked at Mia.

Mia smiled with empathy, as Max seemed to sigh with relief. 'It seems you don't get out much,' she said, half enquiring.

'It's all a bit new, being out and single.'

Mia was intrigued, but when Max didn't elaborate, she changed the subject. 'I believe you know Sam through work. How long have you known each other?'

'A while. I moved up from Tasmania in 1999 and ended up at the same station as him. He's a great guy. What do you do?'

'Public Servant for the police.'

'Public Servant. Good. You need to be a little unhinged to be an officer, putting yourself in danger all the time.'

'Like running into a burning building?', Mia jested.

Max laughed. His blue eyes sparkled as he felt more at ease. 'Good point. But I don't do a lot of fire work anymore. I'm currently part of a team that specialise in other types of situations like swift water and vertical rescues. We were deployed to Samoa last week after the tsunami hit, to look for people and clean up. I just flew back this morning.'

Mia could already sense his presence would bring a lot of calm to a chaotic situation. Ironically, she found this exciting.

'I love my job. It keeps me out of trouble,' Max said, modestly downplaying the specialist work he did.

'Sam told me you're past being any trouble.'

Max looked a little surprised that her conversation about him with Sam had got to that. 'Yep, just a middle-aged buck wanting a simple life now.'

Mia explained, 'You looked a little unsure when you first arrived, so I checked with Sam to see if I should approach. He suggested I should but when I saw the line up, I thought I'd leave you to it.'

'This is all very new to me. I've just separated, and the last time I dated; women were very different. Earlier, I had someone slip me her phone number and said I had a bed for the night if I wanted it. Scared me to death.'

Mia laughed. She found his uncertainty charming. 'I promise you; not all women are the same.'

They stayed chatting together for the rest of the night. By the end of it, Mia felt he was strangely familiar, like she had met him somewhere before but couldn't quite remember where.

It was close to midnight when Mia said, 'It was so nice to meet you but it's time for me to go. I hope to see you again.' She impulsively hugged him, and he naturally responded.

She left him to find Lucy and Sam. After saying goodnight to them, she headed for the exit, where she found Max waiting. 'Are you going with Lucy and Sam to the track on Melbourne Cup Day?', he asked.

'Not sure yet. It'll depend on work.'

'I'm going. It'd be great if you'd come.' He paused and then added, 'I'm glad I left the best 'til last tonight.' His smile was intoxicating, and Mia's heart skipped a beat as his words encouraged her interest. She hadn't felt like this for a long time.

Chapter 39

'Hi Lucy,' Mia answered her mobile.

'Hi lovely. I have Max here and he wants to know what colour you're wearing on Tuesday, so he can match his tie.'

Mia heard Max protesting in the background, 'I didn't say that.' She giggled, feeling him blush through the phone. She knew Lucy was in full matchmaker mode.

'Okay, he didn't say that, but he is keen to know if you're coming. I just wanted to double check that you are.'

Max didn't protest this time. It had been three weeks since the party and Mia was relieved that he was still enthusiastic about her joining them on Melbourne Cup Day. She had thought about him often and was excited at the thought of seeing him again.

'Yes, I'm coming. Looking forward to it.'

Continuing to stir him up, Lucy relayed, 'She's coming, Max. Is there anything else you would like me to ask her, like, where she wants to go on your first holiday together?'

'Give me the phone.' Max grabbed the phone, as Lucy laughed.

'Hi Mia. Sorry, Lucy has obviously had too much wine. I briefly mentioned over dinner that it would be great to see you again. I didn't mean for her to ring you.'

Mia was keen to relieve his discomfort. 'I'm glad she did. I haven't thought about what I'm wearing. What's your favourite colour?'

'Ah... purple.'

'Great. Let's both wear a hint of purple. Deal?'

Mia could feel him smile. 'Deal.'

* * *

As Mia arrived at the track, she saw the others waiting for her outside the main gate. She nervously fiddled with her purple fascinator as she approached them. She briefly made eye contact with Lucy and Sam, but once she saw Max, her eyes never left him. She scanned him from head to toe. Under his light grey suit, he wore a pale purple shirt, accompanied by a metallic grey tie, that by chance, matched her dress perfectly. She found him outstandingly attractive.

He stepped forward so he was the first to greet her. 'You look lovely,' he said, as he went straight to hug her.

'Thanks. You look very handsome,' she admired. 'And without discussion, your tie does match my dress. Good job.'

He was slow to let her go, and she was more than happy to have his arms around her.

'Excuse us, we're here too,' Lucy playfully interrupted.

Mia and Max laughed; and didn't stop all day. He was perfect company, making sure she had everything she needed and was never far from her side. He picked the winner of the big race, and after, guided her to the dance floor in front of the live band.

At first, he kept it frisky, grabbing her hand, twirling, and flinging her from one side of him to the other. But when the opportunity came, he placed his hand on the middle of her back, and pulled her close, making sure their bodies and feet moved as one. He led her strongly around the floor, and anyone watching, would have thought they had been dancing together a lifetime. Mia was giddy with happiness, and she felt a spark ignite inside her. But she remained sedate, knowing Max was still finding his feet in his new reality.

In the early evening, as he walked her to the lineup of taxis, he stopped and reached for her hand. The joy that had been on his face all day, was now replaced with sombreness. 'Mia, I have had the best time today. I feel like I've known you forever.'

Then he looked to the ground for a minute, gathering his words. 'I'm still sorting through some stuff after my separation. I haven't even started looking for my own place yet. I'm currently staying with a work mate.'

Mia could see the pain in Max's eyes and knew there was nothing she could say that would erase it.

'Also, my mum's sick. She hasn't got long, so right now, I'm a bit of a trainwreck.'

'Oh, I'm so sorry. Is she in Tasmania?'

'Yes. Dad died a few years ago. My siblings are with her but I'll be doing a lot of travelling in the next few months so I can be there as much as possible.' It sounded like he was almost apologising.

She reassuringly squeezed his hand. 'I don't want to complicate your life any further. I'm here if ever you want to grab a coffee and have a chat. Here's my number.'

Her hug goodbye was full of compassion, desperately wanting to soothe his soul. After he released her, he slowly leant in and sweetly kissed her on her cheek. 'I'll be in touch soon.'

A bit of doubt trickled into Mia's head, but it was quickly squashed by a strong sensation that Max was going to be important to her.

'He's a risky bet. He's going to need some time.'

'But this connection is special. I need to just breathe and believe.'

Chapter 40

February 2010

There had been regular coffee-catch ups over the three months following that race day. It had been a time of undeniable paradox, with the seriousness of what was happening in Max's life, over-shadowing the irrefutable fascination that was growing between them. But they had remained on the outskirts of it, like boxers dancing on the ropes, with the expectancy of the inevitable coming together, humming in the air.

Until... his mum's funeral day, when Max finally let Mia know, she had started to mean something to him. He had phoned from Tasmania after the service and was notably upset.

'I just needed to hear your voice,' Max sniffled.

His words moved her, but she was concerned. It was the first time she felt him emotional. 'Are you still with family?'

'Yes. Everyone's still here. But I needed to talk to you.' He took a breath and said, 'Mia, you've been my light in the recent months. I can't thank you enough.'

'You've made a difference in my life too.'

'You've been so patient with me. Your understanding has been a great support. I would really like to see you. Can we have lunch on Sunday? There's a Turkish restaurant on the river, near the wharves.'

'Wild horses couldn't keep me away.'

* * *

Mia's heart went into a drum solo when she saw him at the front of the restaurant. She could see he was different. The cloud that had been with him over the last few months was gone, and she could see he was lighter.

'It's so good to see you.' Max embraced her tightly, and Mia matched his enthusiasm.

After being seated at their table, they sat smiling at each other, so grateful to be together. As the waiter poured their wine, Max said, 'I've found a unit this morning. I move in through the week. I finally feel like I'm back managing my life rather than life managing me. It feels good.'

'You look good too.' Mia threw out her first flirtatious comment, as she tipped her glass to him. 'Congratulations.' Max blushed as his glass touched hers.

Mia knew today was different from their previous get-togethers. Up until now, she had thought of their interactions as warm, but careful and considered. Today, she sensed Max's reins had loosened slightly. It felt more like a date.

After lunch, they moved to a table outside to enjoy a beautiful Brisbane afternoon and to watch the river traffic. There seemed to be no rush or time limit.

'Mia, I've been thinking about you a lot and I can't understand why you're single. Is there something you haven't told me?', Max asked with genuine curiosity.

'You mean, like I'm really a man,' Mia joked, trying to disguise how ecstatic she was that he was thinking about her.

'Well yes, or that you're a crazy person.'

'Well, some may call me crazy, but I've managed to bury most of them.'

They both laughed. She loved that they laughed a lot. Even with the emotional seriousness of the previous months, they always seemed to find humour when they were together.

But she soon brought the moment back to thoughtful. She looked into his eyes and said, 'I think I'm single because I've never found the right person. I was in love with someone for a long time, but in the end, whilst it had its positives, it wasn't right. For me, finding that great love and feeling like I can rely on it, has been like searching for the Holy Grail. She paused and added, 'It'd be nice to find it.'

Max reached for her hand, 'Do you think we can have more than one great love in a lifetime?'

'I hope so. What about you?', she asked.

'I'm open to it, but it's hard to think about, after being married for so long.'

'How long?'

'Twenty-five years. And for most of it, it was good. But I changed after Port Arthur. I was part of the team that investigated the forensics from the scene. Some of the things I experienced at that time, changed me. I became depressed. After struggling for a couple years, we decided to move to Queensland, thinking we could start again. But we never really got back to where we were, and we eventually just drifted apart.'

'Twenty-five years! He won't be ready for anything serious. The timing is all wrong, damn it.'

Mia frowned.

'Sorry. I didn't mean to bring the mood down. Not sure why I told you all that.' And as if an angel whispered in his ear, he added, 'I do hope to find love again.'

Mia's frown disappeared.

They continued to enjoy each other until the sun went down. The conversation went back to much lighter topics, but their common hope to find love again, secured the first link of their connection.

As they left the restaurant, he took her hand, and they walked by the river. Anticipation drifted through the warm night breeze until he finally got the courage to gently kiss her lips. A kiss so good, Mia thought she was going to faint. She forgot about their surroundings, as she got lost in its exhilaration.

'Easy tiger,' Max whispered, as he felt their passion accelerate. He stepped back but remained holding her hands. His clever mind helped deliver a comparison that would clearly explain his deliberations. 'Did you know, when a fire is ferocious and out of control, you're powerless to stop it from burning out?'

He paused, making sure she was listening. 'But if you tend, say a good campfire, with regular care, the warmth will last forever.'

Mia smiled at the insight he had given her. *'Okay, slow and steady.'*

She pretended she had it under control, but Mia's heart had started to sing. He was under her skin, with his perfect balance of assuredness and humility. She could feel the potential love they could have, but knew she needed to keep such a serious revelation to herself, hoping one day he would catch up.

Chapter 41

The following Friday night, Lucy decided the four of them should have dinner at her place. Mia had planned to keep her demeanour toward Max more reserved than the previous Sunday. However, at the end of the evening, when Lucy offered for them to stay on the pull-out couch in the lounge, Mia's restraint vanished as Max looked at her eagerly.

After their hosts disappeared to bed, he dimmed the lights, along with his self-control switch it seemed. Mia stood beside where they were to sleep and watched him slowly walk toward her. As he did, he confidently took off his T-shirt to reveal a perfect torso. He disregarded it, removing his belt also.

'Could he be any sexier?'

'Remember, nice and slow. A lot more tending needed yet,' Max said, before he kissed her tenderly. Then he effortlessly swooped her up and placed her gently on their makeshift bed.

She let Max lead. He remained beside her, but she could feel his hunger increase as his kisses became more passionate. She lightly touched his back, appraising its strong structure.

He soon found his way to on top of her, and Mia wrapped her legs around his waist, locking his groin next to hers. After enjoying several minutes of grinding together, he sat up, straddling her. He slowly began to undo her blouse buttons and then pushed its material out of the way. His fingers began to trace the top of her pink lacey bra, thoughtfully running over her curves, before he took his touch through her cleavage to the top of her jean's line.

She bit her bottom lip as she began to throb with desire. He
smiled, looking pleased with himself. He bent down, needing to
resume kissing her and she gently rolled him onto his back.
Sitting astride on his hips, she took off her blouse but kept her
bra on. *'No sudden moves,'* she reminded herself. She used her
light touch to tantalise him, running her fingers across his chest,
down his torso, then lingering her strokes across his waistline.
She gently started to rock her hips, and she could feel his desire
growing under her.

He groaned with longing but wasn't ready to let himself go.
Suddenly he pulled on the handbrake, grabbing her and flipping
her onto her back. He lay beside her, kissing her breathlessly,
trying to slow his lust. 'I want you so much, but I can't rush this,'
he whispered.

Mia understood. After being with one woman for such a long
time, it must feel strange being intimate with another. 'Your
campfire Max,' she good-humouredly said, as she adoringly
looked at him. She could feel how much he wanted her but
realised his cautious nature always made him play it safe.

'You're going to be the death of me, Tiger. The way you make
me feel is terrifying,' he said, as he rolled over and reached for
his shirt, knowing it would be more comfortable for her to sleep
in than her blouse. She put it on and discreetly slipped off her
bra.

Putting her head on his chest, she noticed how perfectly she
fitted next to his body. They slowly wound themselves back
from their rapture, falling into a wistful sleep.

The next morning, he rolled over and kissed her on the cheek to
wake her. 'I've got to get going.'

She presumed he needed some thinking space, and it was best to
let him go with minimal fuss.

'I best give back your shirt then,' she teased with a smile. She knelt beside him, just far enough away he couldn't reach her, and seductively slipped off his shirt. For a split second, she proudly exposed her bare breasts to him, giving aspiration to touch them, but then prudishly, she turned her back toward him, putting her bra and blouse on.

Dressed, she turned to find Max not sure what to do next. 'Call me later,' she said, with a mischievous wink, and then disappeared to the bathroom.

He was gone by the time she got back but Lucy came in when she heard her return. 'Good morning. Sleep well?'

'Very well thanks Luce,' Mia replied with a cheeky grin. 'Best "no sex" night ever.'

Chapter 42

With every catchup, they became closer, and their sexuality, more palpable. Max's awkwardness regarding intimacy with a new woman was soon superseded by his appetite for Mia and they helplessly surrendered to their rampant passion. Once initiated, their love making was insatiable.

For months, they playfully enjoyed each other. Life was fun with Max. His sense of humour made her laugh all the time. They ate at good restaurants and went dancing often. He introduced interesting people and new experiences to Mia's life; it was a richness she hadn't experienced in the past.

He also loved to cook for her. One night at his place, as she watched him prepare a restaurant quality dinner for them, she couldn't help but consider the irony of her life. It seemed all she had to do was stop looking for her perfect mate, and he would find her. Mia was falling madly in love.

October 2010

Her birthday card from him had beautiful words.

Dear Mia,
Every time I think of you, it makes me believe in magic.
Thank you for letting me be a part of your life.
You are very special to me, and I hope we continue to discover new things and enjoy new experiences together.
Max x

'Magic is good, but no mention of love.'

She quickly dismissed the creeping insecurity by believing he needed more time to be comfortable with the possible expectations that came with the word. She continued her casual act out of fear he wasn't ready to hear how serious she was. Her long time, in-built behaviours seemed to kick in automatically.

December 2010

Her house completion just before Christmas, was a great distraction from putting too much emphasis on her desires for their relationship to progress. As part of keeping him feeling free of expectations, she hadn't introduced him to Elizabeth and Reg. But when he insisted on helping them move into their shared home, their meeting naturally manifested.

As the four of them sat to dinner on the inaugural night in the new abode, Max related to her mum and stepdad, like no one from her past, and she realised she had finally introduced them to someone they would consider a salubrious adult and her equal. He further set himself as the missing piece of her life.

Max proposed a toast, 'To finally meeting you both. Hopefully this is the first of many dinners we enjoy together. And to you Mia, congratulations on completing this beautiful home. I'm in awe at how capable and independent you are.'

'Awe. Umm, still not love but I'll take it.'

She recognised restraint was part of Max's nature. It wasn't aloofness, because she could feel his warmth.

But a frustration had started to build in her, as she balanced her certainty that he was everything she had ever wanted, and his caution not to admit just how he was feeling. She found herself in a situation where she was questioning whether her feelings of their extraordinary connection would ever be reciprocated and couldn't help but feel a sense of Deja vu.

They spent a lot of the festive season together, but Max was distracted with work. A major weather event threatened to hit Brisbane, with predicted flood levels that had never been seen. He knew his team was going to be busy.

He was due to arrive for Elizabeth's birthday dinner when Mia's phone rang. She didn't recognise the number, but something urged her to answer anyway. 'Mia, it's me. I'm sorry, I'm not going to make dinner. I'm halfway to the north coast on a job, and I think we're going to be there overnight. I borrowed someone's phone to call, so you wouldn't worry.'

Mia could hardly hear him over the thunderous rain, but she could feel the adrenalin in Max's voice. 'How did you remember my number?'

'I have no idea. I must have committed it to memory.' She could feel him smile. 'I've got to go. I'll call you as soon as I can. Say Happy Birthday to Elizabeth for me.' And he hung up.

'Everything okay?', Elizabeth asked.

'Max won't be coming. He's on a job. It sounds a bit hectic.'

'I'm sure he'll be fine. He seems so competent.' Elizabeth noticed the concern on her face and realised Mia was in love.

* * *

'Hi Tiger.' Mia was the first phone call Max made when he got back to the station. 'We had to stay out overnight because of the flooding but they helicoptered us out this morning. Our guy is in hospital with hypothermia but he's going to be fine.'

'I'm glad you're safe,' Mia said, bursting with admiration.

'You know me, always safe. So, my Inspector has told me to go home and get some sleep. Can we get together tomorrow night?'

'Sure. See you then.'

But Mia didn't see him for nearly two weeks. She received a text in the early hours of that morning...

'Sorry Mia, there's been flash flooding out west and hundreds of people are missing. I'll be gone for at least a week. I'll be in touch when I can. x'

By the time Mia saw him next, he was withdrawn. Logically, she knew he was dealing with trauma, but his retraction triggered a fear in her that she was about to be abandoned, as she had been in the past whenever her love interest had started to withdraw. She supported him through the next month, but her anxiety continued to drip quietly, like a leaking tap.

* * *

She spent weeks trying to reason with herself, but it came to a head the night they attended a state fire dinner. As she met more of Max's colleagues, it became clear how well respected he was. There was an official part of the night, when an Inspector Roberts welcomed everyone and congratulated the service men on the jobs they did. He went on to specifically mentioned the rescue Max had recently led...

'Early afternoon, 9th January, an emergency communication came in regarding a middle-aged male that was stuck in a tree after kayaking in flooded creek waters. Our four-man team arrived at an outlying property, in prevailing rain and wind. They paddled the inflatable across the flooded farmland to a piece of higher ground that banked the fast-flowing river.

They could see the man downstream, wedged between two branches, notably fatigued and frightened. After setting up on the riverbank, they established communications and quickly came up with a plan. Just as they were about to enact that, there was a huge surge in the river level, accompanied by an increase in dangerous sized debris, making it apparent a rescue with the inflatable raft was not viable. They would need a new plan and had to play a waiting game.

Light was fading. They knew there was only a small opportunity for the rescue to succeed. Communications from the Coordination Centre had ruled out any helicopter assistance but they did indicate the rain had stopped up stream, and the water levels were expected to fall quickly in the next hour.

The team moved downstream, adjacent to the stranded man. There was still a remarkable volume of water between where they were on the riverbank and where he was. But in a short period, and as predicted, the water started to recede. This exposed an area of higher ground behind the tree where he was stuck. Station Officer Max Lawrence directed him to climb down and move up stream, towards the ground.

Two of the team moved in parallel with him. A rescue line was thrown to him; with the request he secure it around his chest. As they gripped the other end, they used a tree as an anchor point to harness the weight they were about to withstand. On their instruction, the fated kayaker entered the swift moving water, that carried him in a pendulum motion, toward the riverbank. As the water forced him under, the upstream rescuers judged the release of enough line, that allowed him to travel and resurface in front of the downstream team, where he was pulled to safety. A remarkable rescue. One that will be rewarded with bravery medals later in the year.'

Max humbly bowed his head, not comfortable with the attention, but Mia's admiration for him was bursting. *I'm the one drowning here.'*

After the formal addressing was finalised, and as Max went to get Mia another drink, she felt a tap on her shoulder. She turned around to see someone she never expected to.

'Joe! What are you doing here?'

'Hi there stranger.' Joe chuckled as he hugged her. 'I traded in smelling like sheep for smoke. What are you doing here?'

'I'm here with Max Lawrence. We've been dating about a year.'

'Wow. You're keeping good company these days.'

'Yes, I'm very happy. And you? What's happening in your world, apart from your change of career?'

'Married and two kids. A very different life to that of the Woolshed days. Are you up to date on Jack?'

'No. Jack and I lost touch a few years ago. How is he?'

'He's still Jack being Jack. Always restless. He left Ava a couple of years ago and moved to a small town just south of Sydney. He's never settled.'

'Here Tiger.' Max was back with Mia's drink. 'Hi Joe. Do you guys know each other?'

'Yep. We haven't seen each other in years.'

As Max engaged in a conversation with Joe about work, Mia zoned out. The news Jack's marriage hadn't worked didn't surprise her, but it still made her sad. He still didn't have peace.

The mention of his name prompted her to think that she had been ready to settle for whatever he was comfortable in giving, not daring to push him in case it scared him into running, which he did anyway.

Now, she had started the same pattern with Max. She was hiding the depth of her feelings in their playful relationship, pretending she didn't need anything serious, just so he'd stay.

'He could run, but it's time to be honest.'

* * *

The following morning at Max's place, the conversation was a little stifled. They both wanted to share their thoughts but weren't sure where to start.

'You must be happy about the bravery award,' Mia said.

'It's good the team is getting recognition, but the last couple of months have taken a toll on me. I need to decide where my future's headed.'

Max was talking about work, but it was Mia's perfect segway.

'I've been thinking about my future too. For a while now, I've been certain you're the guy I want to spend the rest of my life with, but I haven't mentioned it, because I'm not sure how serious you are. I know we've only been together a year, but it's been a long time for me to keep a lid on how serious I am.'

Max didn't move. He just intently listened.

'I love you Max and I want this to move forward.'

'I love you too, and I don't want this to end. But I'm comfortable taking it one day at a time for now. I'm still getting my head wrapped around things and I'm not ready to commit to a future yet; and certainly, wouldn't consider marriage again.'

She wasn't sure about getting married again either, but his uncertainty about a future vision, made her recoil. Past echoes were loud in her head, and she felt like a scab had been ripped off an old sore.

'I understand. It's been a big year for you. But I know exactly what I want and can see the future with you. I think it's a good idea to have a break and maybe you should use the time to work out if you want me in yours.'

For two people who had just confessed their love for each other, it was the most antithesis to romantic it could get. Mia grabbed her things and kissed him good-bye.

* * *

'What have I done?' She cried on the drive home.

'No. He needed to know. If this is going to work, <u>we</u> should be thinking about a future together, not drifting in our pasts.'

When she got home, she grabbed a glass of water and joined Elizabeth and Reg out on the back patio.

'Mia what's wrong,' her mother quickly observed.

'I decided to tell Max how I feel and how I saw our future. He wasn't ready to hear it. He says he loves me, but he's not sure what the future looks like. It didn't go according to plan.'

'Did he say he couldn't see a future with you?', Elizabeth asked.

'No. Just that he was happy with the day-by-day thing for now. He did mention that he couldn't consider marriage again.'

'Is that important to you, getting married again?'

'It'd be nice to do it with someone I was really in love with, but what I really want is someone who's committed to making a life with me, and who I can rely on loving me forever. Why am I attracted to men who are commitment phobic?'

Reg chimed in, 'If you're comparing Max with Jack, don't! Jack couldn't commit to anything, not just you. And I don't think Max has a problem with commitment. He will still be feeling bruised after his marriage breakdown. Just because he doesn't want to get married again, doesn't mean you can't have the life you want with him. You already know marriage and commitment are not the same thing, after Devon. Give him time. Be patient. And I'm sure he'll be back. He's your guy.'

Reg had never been more certain in anything he had said to Mia.

Chapter 43

'What are you doing?', Lucy asked, after a month of Mia avoiding talking about Max. Mia felt like a walking contradiction... the day she told him she loved him; she'd distanced herself.

'It got too hard being so sure about him, while he floated along, not looking past today. I'm worth more than that.'

'I just think Max is still finding his feet,' Lucy defended.

'Maybe. But what if he spends the next ten years finding his feet? It's very possible. His mantra is slow and careful. Trying to hold back the way I feel, so he doesn't feel overwhelmed, wouldn't work for me. I'm not built to curb my enthusiasm.' Mia smiled, trying for a glint of humour through her despair.

'Well, he's been down at our place talking with Sam, a lot. Apparently, he's also seeing a counsellor at work. Seems to me he's considering picking up the pace.'

'Really?' Mia took these revelations as hope that Max was still thinking about a future with her. She reached into her pocket and pulled out a piece of folded paper. 'I was going through some of my old stuff the other night and found this. I've been carrying it around ever since, hoping it might create some magic.'

'What is it?', Lucy asked, taking it from her.

'It's a list I made when I was overseas and about to come home. I was ready to settle down and I wanted to try and manifest my perfect partner. Please remember I was early 20's.'

Lucy unfolded it and started to read...

  My Perfect Man

  - *Attractive*
  - *Successful*
  - *Makes me laugh*
  - *Capable*
  - *Reliable/Trustworthy*
  - *Loves my family and they love him*
  - *Fits in with my friends*
  - *Loves to dance*
  - *Loves to cook*
  - *Self-assured without being arrogant*
  - *Prefers calm over drama*
  - *Willing to understand me*
  - *Leaves me breathless because of how much I love him*
  - *And he loves me just as much*

When she finished and looked up, Mia said, 'You know, for years I've wondered why things never worked with Jack. But after I met Max, I realised it was because Jack was just the warmup act. He had some of those attributes, but he distracted me. He wasn't who I was really looking for. I truly believe, I'm meant to be with Max. He ticks all of them, except that last one.' Mia pointed to the bottom of the page. 'I feel like that one still has a question mark or maybe a clock beside it. I need a solid tick.'

'Well at least he's trying to sort it out. Hang in there.'

* * *

Another two weeks went past and there had been no contact. Desolation had started to seep in and Mia's beliefs of a future with Max felt like a handful of sand, slipping through her fingers.

One night, after hours of tossing and turning, she finally fell into a deep, troubled sleep...

Mia felt someone sit on the bottom corner of her bed. She opened her eyes to see who it was. As they adjusted to the light, she quickly identified his outline. 'Hello Jack.'

'Hi Mia.' Jack smiled.

'Why are you here?', Mia asked in a neutral tone.

'Because we're overdue for a chat.'

Mia recalled the last, harsh words she had spoken to him, but as if he read her mind, he said, 'That's not why I've come. We need to talk about your current circumstances. What's happening with you?'

'I've met this guy who I want to be with, but I've told him we need time out.'

'I know. Why did you do that?'

'I'm scared I'm never going to be everything he wants, and history will repeat itself.'

'You are everything he wants. He is just making sure he can deliver before he promises you anything. This is the one you've been waiting for. Don't confuse his lack of grand gestures of love as him not feeling the same as you. He loves you. He's just safeguarding a smooth flight, before he offers you the sky.'

'I love him too, Jack. I want to spend my life with him.'

'I know, but before you do, your beliefs that were born out of my over-promising and under-delivering, need to go. Along with the self-worth issues you had long before me. Get rid of it all. Like a bad crop, dig deep down to the roots. It's time to turn over the soil and plant new seeds; because this guy, knows how to love you, and when he offers you his hand, you'll be safe.'

'Can you go to his dream now and make sure he hasn't lost my number?'

Jack laughed and then said, 'So, when he calls, say yes without hesitation because he needs to feel how sure you are. And when you see him, tell him you're happy to climb his ladder, at his pace, one rung at a time because it doesn't matter how long it takes, you're his. Mia, it will only be when you're brave enough to offer yourself without fear, the commitment you have always wanted will follow.'

Jack got up off the bed but stayed looking at her. 'I'm sorry. For all of it.'

'Me too, Jack. I'm not angry anymore.'

'Friends,' Jack tipped his head to one side.

'Always,' Mia responded.

'It's time for me to go now.' His face radiated joy and for the first time ever, Mia thought he looked weightless. He looked at her one last time and vanished.

Mia's eyes flashed open, and she scanned the room looking for him. His presence had been so real that she was having trouble reconciling that it was just a dream.

She spent the morning pouring her energy into willing the phone to ring. Jack's counsel had swept away her doubt and she was now confident that everything was going to work out with Max. He just needed time, and she needed the opportunity to tell him she understood that.

Her phone rang and her heart stopped. She didn't recognise the number but prayed it was Max ringing from work.

'Mia, it's Joe. I got your number off Max.'

Mia's heart sank. 'Is Max alright, Joe?'

'Yes, Max is fine.' Joe pulled on his strength. 'It's Jack.'

Mia's mind went straight to their shared encounter from the night before.

'A couple of days ago, he was in a bad car accident. Mia, he didn't survive.'

Mia reached for the bench to keep from falling to the ground. Joe lost his composure, and she cried with him.

After several minutes, Joe said, 'The funeral is next week, down where he was living. Would you like to come with me?'

Jack's final image, from her dream, flashed into Mia's view. 'No thanks Joe. I've said my good-bye to Jack.' She knew she had no place in going. They'd made their peace.

Chapter 44

April 2011

A week later, Mia finally got the call she so desperately wanted.

'Hi Mia.'

'Hi Max.'

Both were so nervous. The pent-up emotion from weeks of separation was thick in their voices.

'Joe told me about Jack. I'm so sorry. Are you okay?'

'Yes, thanks. I'm sad but I know he's finally at peace. Something he struggled to feel all his life.'

Max couldn't wait any longer. 'I'd like to see you. Can we catch up tomorrow? Please.'

'I'd like that.'

'Say midday at the art gallery bistro?'

'See you then.'

Mia lit up. Every part of her being felt alive, and she felt sure that if she rolled the dice this time, it was going to be a good bet.

She bounced out to where Elizabeth and Reg were sitting. Neither of them had heard the conversation but they instinctively knew what had happened.

Reg looked up and simply said, 'You're on your way now.' He winked after his voice cracked with emotion.

Elizabeth just had a look like everything was finally right in the world.

The sun was warm on Mia's back as she walked over the bridge towards where they were to meet. It was a beautiful autumn day, with not a cloud in the sky, and a slight breeze that made the river's water furrow with small ripples.

As she approached the gallery end, she could see Max had deliberately positioned himself to watch her approach. She was still a fair distance from him, but she could feel the connection between them hum with electricity. He was smiling, and she could see his glow, adding to her excitement.

By the time she was standing in front of him, she was out of breath. Max took her in his arms and kissed her passionately. 'I've missed you so much,' he whispered.

'Me too.' Mia could barely respond, emotionally caught up in the anticipation of the moment.

She sat at the table and Max shuffled his chair, so he was right beside her. A timely bottle of wine arrived, and Max thanked the waiter before pouring two glasses.

'You were right to call it,' Max started. 'I was marking time, scared to move forward in case I made a mistake. But I've realised, I can't stay stuck like that. If I do, I could miss out on the best thing that has ever happened to me, having you in my life. I hope I haven't missed my chance.'

'No, you haven't. And this isn't all on you. I'm still getting rid of some of my past fears as well. But I have no doubt about my feelings for you or wanting to be together.'

Max responded, 'I'm certain too. That afternoon at the restaurant on the river, I knew then I'd met someone I could spend my life with. But I've always regulated myself from charging ahead, even when I want to. It's like when I'm on a ladder, I stop at every step, needing to feel safe before I move up to the next rung.'

Mia nodded and said, 'One rung at a time.'

'Exactly.' Max was relieved. She seemed to understand him so well. 'Not having you with me has been quite the motivator to look to the next rung.' He smiled. 'I love you Mia, no doubts. And I want us to build a life together, but I can't promise marriage. That's too far up the ladder for me yet.'

She sighed, knowing she needed to be clear on what she wanted. 'I look back on my past relationships, and they were like recipes for a perfect meal, but it turned out they lacked an ingredient or two. Some were just physical desire with no chance of going the distance; a marriage, where the love was unhealthy; and a big love, that I could never rely on. What I'm looking for is a love that has all the ingredients, not a marriage proposal.'

Max smiled at her analogy and looked deep into her soul. 'I understand what you mean about right ingredients and I'm certain our recipe has all of them.'

He held out his hand and she grabbed it confidently, lost in his clear blue eyes and beautiful, reliable face. She was sure that today was going to be the start of an incomparable phase of her life. The overanalysing voices in her head were finally silent and her soul came into complete alignment.

Chapter 45

October 2012

Mia stood outside her work the Friday before her birthday, waiting for Max to pick her up. He had been very cryptic about their weekend, only saying pack a bag for both nights, including all beach essentials. Mia assumed they were going to the coast.

As they drove towards the bay, she knew Max was hiding something. Their relationship had grown without pretence, and they knew each other's habits, behaviours and personal idiosyncrasies like nobody else. 'Where are we headed?', she decided to ask.

'We're just calling into the yacht club. I want to show you something.'

Mia was aware Max loved to sail. He had a friend who owned a boat, and he would crew for him every now and then. She brushed it off thinking it must have something to do with that.

Once arrived, he led her down to the marina past rows and rows of boats, until he finally stopped admiring an impressive, yacht. 'She's beautiful, isn't she?'

'Yes. Big.' The only thing Mia knew about boats was how to sit on one and drink sparkling wine.

'It's a thirty-four-foot Bavaria. Cuts through the water like a knife through butter.' He undid the back marine line and stepped on board. 'Come and have a look inside.'

'Do you know the owner?', Mia asked, concerned they were intruding.

'I bought it yesterday. Her name is "Happy Az".' Max had the expression of a child getting the thing he wanted most from Santa.

'No way!', Mia squealed, instantly caught up in Max's euphoria. He picked her up and twirled her onto the boat, both laughing with pure joy. 'Happy birthday', Max giggled.

He unlocked the door to the downstairs cabin, and she could smell the timber; a smell she was familiar with from a long time ago, but everything else was so new. She realised instantly how happy she was going to be spending their weekends on the water, cruising around the bay.

Max taught her how to sail. In the beginning he did most of the instructing and Mia soaked up his knowledge. But as time went on, they learnt together how to cruise as an efficacious team. They believed in each other's abilities, knew what the other was thinking and, if required, acted without communication. Sailing together was heaven.

It didn't take long before this transferred to their relationship. They knew each other's minds as well as their own, giving them the ability to tend to each other's needs telepathically. It was an intimacy beyond sexual and something neither had ever experienced.

* * *

'Move in with me?'

It wasn't long before their exceptional bond gave Max the confidence to move up his ladder. 'If you think Elizabeth and Reg will be okay on their own, please come and live with me.'

Mia didn't hesitate, and living together only made them closer. For the first time, she was sharing her life completely, in a mature, healthy, loving relationship with someone she couldn't imagine her life without. But she would soon have to say goodbye to someone she loved very much.

June 2016

They had dinner with Elizabeth and Reg most weeks, back at the house. Elizabeth was still in great health, but Reg was starting to decline. One week, during dinner, Max explained that he was taking a work team up north for swift water training and wouldn't be able to come the following week. Reg looked particularly tired, and he was quiet.

After dinner, as Mia and Elizabeth stacked the dishwasher, Reg asked Max to follow him to the lounge and would he mind pouring them both a vodka. Max didn't drink vodka, but he did as he was told. Mia was eavesdropping from the kitchen. There seemed to be a long pause until she heard Reg say, 'You'll look after our girls if anything happens to me?'

'Of course, Reg. But nothing's going to happen to you. You're just a bit tired.'

'Yeah, that's it. Cheers.'

Mia heard the glasses clink, and she tried to ignore the inner voice telling her to prepare, but she knew Max felt it too.

As she hugged Reg goodnight, she whispered softly to him, 'I don't know where my life would be if you hadn't come into it. Thank you for your guidance and belief in me.'

'My pleasure,' he choked back tears. 'You're the daughter I never had.'

They left with the feeling they may never see Reg again. He died through the night.

* * *

This was the catalyst for them moving back into Mia's home. She knew her mum couldn't be on her own and there was no question in Max's mind that it was the right thing to do.

The twelve months after Reg's death had both Mia and Max restless. Max was ready to retire, and Mia wanted less responsibility at work. Again, there had been no real discussion, but they instinctively knew a change was needed.

As they sat on the back of the boat one night, enjoying some wine and the clear night air, Max said, 'Have you ever thought about moving to the north coast?'

'I've always said that's where I would like to retire to. You?', Mia returned serve.

'I would love to live up there. I know I'm not normally in a hurry, but I think if we don't move soon, we will be priced out of the market. I've been talking to someone at work who is normally right about real estate, and he's saying the coast is about to boom.'

'What about mum?'

'She's coming with us of course. Well, let's hope she wants to. I like having her around.'

Mia knew this was Max's measured way of saying how much he loved Elizabeth. *Just when I think I couldn't love him anymore.'*

Before the end of the year, they had made their move. Max retired and sold the boat. Mia's house was sold, and she started working out of the regional coast office at a lower level. They found the perfect home for the three of them, with Elizabeth occupying one end and Max and Mia the other. The common room was the kitchen, which Max happily commandeered, looking after the two of them in a way he was most comfortable, cooking for them.

It was a swift life change, and the path had been free of any obstacles. Mia felt life couldn't get any better.

October 2019

'Where are you?', Mia asked Max. He was driving out west after a company had asked him to do a one-off fire safety consult.

'I'm about halfway there. Hey, have you heard that song by Ed Sheeran called Perfect?'

'Yes Love, it's been out for a couple of years.'

'Well, I've just listened to the words for the first time. Had me blubbering like a baby. That's my song for you Tiger.'

Mia's eyes filled with tears. He wasn't romantic very often, but when he was, they were moments of quality. 'God, I love you. Please be careful.' She wouldn't relax until he was back with her. Their souls were now welded together.

* * *

Within a few days, he was. They were sitting on their back deck, having a wine, and talking about his trip. Mia sensed there was something going on because he had the same look as when he bought the boat. But she said nothing, just happy he was home.

Finally, when there was a lull in their conversation, Max said, 'I think I'm at the top of the ladder.' His eyes twinkled.

'What do you mean?' Mia was confused.

'Tiger, I think it's time I put a ring on your finger.'

'What does that mean?' She looked at him blankly not able to comprehend what he was saying as it was so unexpected.

'Marry me?', Max half asked, certain what the answer would be. He stood and pulled a ring box from his jeans pocket.

Mia shook uncontrollably. Was this really happening? She hadn't thought about marriage for years, grateful for what they had. But this involuntary reaction proved the dream had just been pushed aside, not given up.

'Yes,' she said. Without doubt or hesitation.

As he placed the ring on her finger, in his matter-of-fact way he said, 'It's a Morganite. I spoke to a gemstone expert, and a Morganite has the power to assist in maintaining love as it continues to grow. There was a whole lot of other stuff it can do too but I just thought it was better than a diamond. Diamonds are so common and what we have is anything but.'

Mia looked down at the stunning pink stone. It was a good size, standing front and centre with a few decorative diamonds either side, that only highlighted its beauty. She was speechless, as tears rolled down her face.

'I checked with Elizabeth when I first got home, if us getting married would make her happy. She cried too but assured me she was over the moon.' Max grinned, as his eyes began to well.

'Max, you have no idea.'

'Yes, I do, because I love you just as much. You're stuck with me, forever.'

Mia shook her head in disbelief... the final, solid tick.

* * * * *

'Mia.' Max's voice gently called her back to the present, and the past quickly faded. Ten years from when they first met, and she still caught her breath when she looked at him. She glanced down at their hands fused together that were now adorned with wedding bands.

She looked back into Max's blue eyes. They were showing a peace and confidence that made her feel she could breathe; a complete, oxygen consuming breath, without uncertainty. She knew she was finally home.